An American Queer

The Amazon Trail

What Reviewers Say About Lee Lynch's Work

"Lee Lynch has not only created some of the most memorable and treasured characters in all of lesbian literature, she's given us the added pleasure of having them turn up in each other's stories. *Beggar of Love* ranks with Lee Lynch's richest and most candid portrayals of lesbian life."—Katherine V. Forrest, Lambda Literary Award-winning author of *Curious Wine* and the Kate Delafield series

"Lee Lynch reads as an old friend, and in a way she is."—Joan Nestle, Lambda Literary Award-winning author and co-founder of the Lesbian Herstory Archives

"I've been a fan of Lee Lynch since I read her novel *Rafferty Street* many years ago. Her books—especially her deeply human characters—never disappoint. *Beggar of Love* is a story not to be missed!"—Ellen Hart, Lambda Literary Award-winning author of the Jane Lawless Mystery series

"*Sweet Creek* is Lynch's first book in eight years, and one that shows the maturing of her craft. In a time when much of lesbian writing is more about formula than finding the truths of our lives, she has written a breakthrough book that is evidence of her unique gifts as a storyteller and her undeniable talent in creating characters that move us and remain with us long after the final page is turned."—*Sacred Ground: News and Views on Lesbian Writing*

Sweet Creek "…is a textured read, almost epic in scope but still wonderfully intimate. Lynch, with a dozen novels to her credit dating back to the early days of Naiad Press, has earned her stripes as a writerly elder—she was contributing stories…four decades ago. But this latest is sublimely in tune with the times."—Richard LaBonte, *Q Syndicate*

"…the sweeping scope of Lynch's abilities…The sheer quality of this work is proof-positive…that writing honestly from a place of authenticity and real experience is what separates literature from 'books.'"—*Lambda Book Report*

By the Author

AN AMERICAN QUEER

THE AMAZON TRAIL

by

Lee Lynch

2014

ISBN 13: 978-1-62639-204-5

THIS TRADE PAPERBACK ORIGINAL IS PUBLISHED BY
BOLD STROKES BOOKS, INC.
P.O. BOX 249
VALLEY FALLS, NY 12185

FIRST EDITION: OCTOBER 2014

CREDITS
EDITOR: RUTH STERNGLANTZ
PRODUCTION DESIGN: SUSAN RAMUNDO
COVER DESIGN BY GABRIELLE PENDERGRAST

Acknowledgments

Thank you, Ruth Sternglantz, my friend and editor, who conceived of *An American Queer*, then selected, ordered, edited, and basically did all the work of fashioning a book from hundreds of columns. Ruth, you are a sterling person.

My deep gratitude goes to Nell Stark and Rachel Spangler for their forewords, to Radclyffe for her bold strokes, and to Gabrielle Pendergrast for the dynamic cover.

Thank you to the innumerable editors and publishers of periodicals on and off line who I've worked with over the years.

Thank you to the women who have helped create these columns, including Elaine Mulligan Lynch, Nel Ward, Sue Hardesty, Akia Woods, and the late Marcia Santee, Barbara Grier, and Tee Corinne.

Thank you to all the librarians who make lesbian books available, in particular M.J. Lowe.

Thank you, always, to Connie Ward and Shelley Thrasher for leading me to Bold Strokes Books.

And thank you to my readers. I appreciate your continuing responses and support.

Dedication

For my beloved wife, Lainie Lynch.
And for Radclyffe, lesbian visionary.

CONTENTS

The 2000s

The 2010s

FOREWORD: THE ALL-AMERICAN QUEER
RACHEL SPANGLER

It's fitting that this anthology opens with a piece called "Province-town" because that's where I first began to think about the true importance of this collection. It was Women's Week, October 2013. I sat on the front steps on a glorious autumn day watching my five-year-old son play. He's a sort of all-American boy: fair-haired, blue-eyed, and athletic. He's never met a sport he doesn't love. He's also good at dragging his favorite adults into his game. The only thing most people would find surprising about this scenario is that my all-American boy idolizes the all-American Queer.

That day in Provincetown The Boy had enlisted Lee Lynch in a round of pitch and catch. Lee cradled the ball in her hands and tossed it in a gentle arc for The Boy to trap in his glove. Then he'd lob it back across the walkway to her. He had more strength than accuracy, and Lee spent a good bit of time chasing pitches just out of her reach. He suggested she'd have an easier time if she'd go get her glove. Lee casually said she'd never owned a ball glove. The Boy, clearly unsure how one could reach adulthood without owning something so essential to life, asked why not. Lee patiently explained when she was his age, girls weren't allowed to play baseball. It wasn't until much later in her life that she saw women play the all-American game. The Boy explained that half his teammates were girls, and both his moms coached the coed team. Lee smiled and said, "A lot has changed in my lifetime."

She was right. A lot has changed in her lifetime, and while baseball is a big deal to a little boy, it's just a small matter compared to the work Lee has been a part of. Great strides of progress have been made in women's rights and queer rights, but those changes didn't just magically occur. They weren't the result of time or evolution. The changes during Lee Lynch's lifetime occurred because Lee and others like her fought to make sure they left their worlds better places than they'd found them. For her part Lee Lynch did the essential work of chronicling queer lives: hopes, dreams, fears, and insecurities, and in doing so she gave a name, a face, a voice to multiple generations of queer Americans.

For nearly half a century, Lee Lynch has shared the stories important to our community. With columns like "No Place Like Home" (1991) she discusses the drive to stay to fight a nasty wave of conservative attacks in Oregon. She shares firsthand accounts of the nascent stages in the women's movement in "Dancing in the Streets" (1999), and she marks historical milestones like the right to marry legally in "You Will Be My Wife, Will I Be Yours?" (2009). From Stonewall to the rise of feminism, from a rash of antigay ballot initiatives to the marriage equality movement, Lee Lynch has been telling our stories. That chronicling of our history would've been public service enough for most, but Lee always goes a step further in making sure none of these events, these moments, these reflections are experienced through a clinical lens or the detached voice of a news reporter. Her writing never allows her audience to separate the overarching issues from the people who shape and are shaped by those forces.

True to her roots in second-wave feminism, she offers part of herself in every piece to prove the personal is political. Whether it's a deeply personal remembrance of a young man who died of AIDS in "Patrick" (1989), reflections of the toll hiding one's true self can have over a lifetime in "Closets I Have Known" (2002), or showing the value of queer-friendly end-of-life resources in "Queer Families and Hospice," (2005) Lynch takes even the most contentious and controversial topics and breaks them down to their most personal level. At a time when queer theorists and political pundits alike talk about queer lives in the abstract and the hypothetical, Lee Lynch humanizes LGBT Americans like few other writers have. Whether it's relationship pieces liked "Without Her" (1995), in which she talks about the loneliness of being away from her partner for two weeks, or wider generational themes like retirement in an age when social security is under attack in "Social Insecurity" (2011), Lee Lynch ties the queer experience to the human experience.

No matter the topic or time period, Lynch's writing performs an invaluable public service in reminding us who we are and showing us who we can strive to be. Even as she reflects on the great changes she's seen in her lifetime, she never fails to remind us that until every single queer person is safe from harm, fear, and injustice, institutional or otherwise, our fight must continue. Starting in "Going To The Post Office" (1988) and continuing all the way up through "Have Things Gotten Better?" (2006), she reminds us that the changes she's worked for are not to be taken for granted, and it is up to every one of us to continue the fight in whatever ways we're able. As she explains in "We Are Living History" (2010), every aspect of every queer life has the potential to make a big difference for those who come after us.

The writing in this anthology offers tangible and deeply personal proof for generations present and future that ordinary people in ordinary circumstances can transform their world in extraordinary ways. I think that's what I'll take way from this anthology most, and what I'll try to convey to The Boy: everyday queer lives have the power to be revolutionary.

FOREWORD: BY THE POWER VESTED
NELL STARK

On October 12, 2013, I married my partner of four years in an outdoor wedding on a perfect day in the Catskill Mountains. Lee Lynch was our officiant, which makes me "The Kid" she references in "Butch Stag Party," the final essay in this anthology. My wife, Jane (who writes under the pseudonym Trinity Tam), and I asked Lee to do the honors before we had a venue or a caterer or even a firm date.

We wanted Lee to marry us because she is one of the greatest queer storytellers ever to have lived, and we knew she would help us frame the exciting new story on which we were about to embark together. We wanted Lee to marry us because neither of us will ever forget her emotional reaction when the Justice of the Peace at her own wedding ceremony said, "By the power vested in me by the state of Massachusetts." After the decades she has spent articulating what it means to be lesbian (not to mention her NYC roots), it seemed only fitting that she be the one to wield the power of New York for us. But most importantly, we wanted Lee to marry us because she is family.

In "My Big Butch Gay Aunt" (2008), Lee discusses her Great-Aunt Jo and the possibility that she might have been gay. After learning that Jo had never married a man but did have a close female friend, Lee "gleefully concluded that Jo Murphy was my big butch gay aunt." She goes on to speculate about how empowering it would have been to grow up with a gay role model in the family and concludes by hoping that "[m]aybe, someday, I'll be a gay great-aunt myself and can help some kid feel part of the family."

That Kid is me. My pseudonym, Nell Stark, masks the fact that Lee and I share a last name. I am a Lynch, too, and while neither of us has access to a sweeping family tree that connects us, we happily call each other "cousin." Lee was the only other Lynch in attendance at my wedding. Jane's parents refused to come, but her brother and sister-in-law were there, and they brought their nine-month-old daughter with them. We are lucky—we get to be fantastic gay aunts already. Both my brother and my parents, however, boycotted the event on the basis of their religious beliefs. While their absence made the wedding more comfortable for everyone, it still stung. But when Jane and I stood in front of Lee with our hands clasped, eager to make our vows, all I felt was joy.

That day, Lee made a beautiful and eloquent speech. She said the words that married us and signed the paperwork that made our marriage legal. But she was also my big butch gay aunt. She stood in for my biological family and reminded me that "family" is about so much more than one's accident of birth. Love, compassion, and generosity: those are the values that define a family, and to which every family should aspire.

Queer families are not bound by genes, but by stories. And the best stories, those told by the most masterful tellers, create *empathy*— that elusive and fragile human emotion that is the cornerstone of compassion. Lee Lynch is just such a masterful storyteller, and I have apprenticed myself to her in the hopes of one day finding a voice as powerful and nuanced and unapologetically queer as hers.

Because queerness is a gift. It prompts critical self-examination and a recalibration of one's perspective on the world. It is a crucible— painful but transformative. *An American Queer* confronts that pain with honesty while also celebrating the daily triumphs of endlessly becoming.

PROVINCETOWN (1988)

I miss a lot less about the East Coast than I thought I might. New York, yes, but that's my hometown. Being within distance of a store that sells the *Times*, yes, but instead I'm surrounded by powerfully peaceful mountains which do a lot more for my well-being. Friends, definitely, but I'm such a hermit that I probably communicate better by mail anyway.

It's Provincetown that sometimes calls me back. Provincetown which comes flooding into my consciousness at odd times, a place that feels like lying in a lover's arms. Provincetown, a site of easy memories and bright yellow days, and of my young quest for myself.

Carol and I went that first time, in, perhaps, 1969. Ours was a college romance. When all the others girls got engaged, we became lovers. When they all graduated and had their weddings, we collected some cats and set up housekeeping in the ghetto. When they all flew off to Puerto Rico or theVirgin Islands for honeymoons, we, somewhat belatedly, made our first timid foray into Provincetown. Ptown, as the veterans call it. Ah, to so comfortably belong!

We rented a motel room in North Truro, the adjacent town. I almost think we would have stayed there, in hiding, if we hadn't been forced into the gay mecca to find food. Bell-bottoms. I remember that we wore our very best, probably ironed, bell-bottoms into the fray. I remember that painful mixture of staring/not-staring which was cruising for us. The pinky signals with which we told each other, "There's one!"

Provincetown itself is pretty tacky. It's a tourist town. Because gays flock there, some of the touristy things are more interesting, but there were innumerable shops which specialized in plastic squeeze purses imprinted simply: *Cape Cod, Mass.*

We loved it. Bought the sweatshirts and T-shirts and hats and postcards that we, middle-class-white-state-employee-social-service types, would have bought anywhere. But back then, even before the concept of gay culture had been hatched on any large scale, because we were gay we were able to step into another level of experience. The straight tourists, secretly search as they might for the fascination of gay life, could not enter this world. It was made of nuance, colored by need, and the directions were not on any Chamber of Commerce map.

I was familiar with the history of the place. We sat one night in terribly uncomfortable folding wooden chairs, backs to the harbor, feet on a sandy, splintery wooden floor, and watched a tedious Eugene O'Neill production in a crowded firetrap called the Provincetown Playhouse. I am so grateful that I got there before the Playhouse disappeared from the beach. Djuna Barnes once sat in front of that stage, and Edna St. Vincent Millay. And many, many others, aspiring literary gays like myself. It seemed every time I went searching a biography of a suspected gay writer, they'd spent a summer, a winter, in Provincetown.

The bookstore. I can't recall its name, but on vacations I half lived there. By my most recent trip in 1983, the shelves were packed with blatantly gay literature. Back then, again, one had to know what one was looking for. *Giovanni's Room* was always prominent. Gore Vidal's books. Carson McCullers and Mary Renault and Truman Capote. The writers one suspected, just from their work, but couldn't be certain of. Yet. We wondered about the salespeople. I was writing for *The Ladder* at the time and much later learned that the woman who sometimes sat at the bookstore cash register was a *Ladder* cover artist, as anonymous as myself.

The restaurants were a special treat. Even we had no doubt about the waiters. They were all it took to make us comfortable. Their presence, as we watched the other diners watch us, was a permission to be ourselves and a confirmation that we were just where we should be.

Were there drag shows back then? I don't remember. There certainly was not an influential gay businesspersons' group, nor were there openly gay guesthouses, or a Womancrafts store. There was Herring Cove Beach. Like a combined women's music festival and faerie gathering from the future, the beach was life-changing. Never before had I seen so many gays in one place. It didn't matter a bit if I talked to anyone or anyone to me, we were all still scared of one another and shy, still raw from the rejection of the rest of the world. They were there, an incontestable fact, in the biggest, broadest, brightest daylight they could find, and I was surrounded for once by my own.

One night Carol and I put on our very best ironed bell-bottoms and strolled the town with the nonchalance of carefree window-shoppers. Our disguise did not fool us. Hearts hammering, we were looking for the notorious Ace of Spades, the lesbian bar.

Now remember, back then the word *lesbian* had a sinister cast. The word *bar* doubled it. I'd been hearing about the Ace of Spades since age fifteen. By 1969 I'd built it in my head into a towering dungeon-like affair frequented by knife-wielding, duck-tailed, leather-jacketed, burly half-women who snarled at their slight, teased-haired femmes and laughed four-eyed, college-educated, scrawny baby butches like me off the face of the earth.

Carol and I finally ran out of shops to linger in. The Ace of Spades was up toward the end of the earth—that is, the end of town. To get to it, we turned down a long, dark, narrow alley. The bar was built out over the beach. The alley smelled of salty fog and felt as clammy as my hands. It was empty, but we could hear music pound inside the walls of the bar. It was all I could do not to tiptoe. There was nothing on earth I wanted so much as to be in that bar, to join in The Gay Life—nothing except to run like hell. We approached. Lacking the nerve to go through the door, I craned my neck to peer in one of those windows. I did not recover from the shock of what I saw for years.

Inside this towering dungeon-like affair were knife-wielding, duck-tailed, leather-jacketed burly half-women snarling at their slight, teased-haired femmes and laughing this four-eyed, college-educated, scrawny baby butch off the face of the earth. We turned tail and scurried back to the bright straight lights.

Was that really what I saw? Or did I have in that moment nothing but a glimpse of my own fears, a vision of who the world predicted, and I feared, I would become?

When I next went back, a few years later, the bar had changed hands and was called The Pied Piper. The tremors of Stonewall, the tentacles of the woman's movement, had reached Provincetown. And me. When I looked inside myself now, the lesbian I saw was not an Ace of Spades at all. She was a Pied Piper. This time, when I went down that long Provincetown alley, I opened the door and went in.

GOING TO THE POST OFFICE (1988)

Going to the post office in Southern Oregon can be radicalizing. I was innocently running up the steps last month when I noticed a little man sitting at the top of them. Between him and me were nothing but a table and a huge sign which read: No SPECIAL RIGHTS FOR HOMOSEXUALS.

Like a tidal wave, rage swallowed me. I kept moving toward him. My mind scrambled and unscrambled itself in a frantic search for words. But I have always been unable to vent my anger aloud. Pictures came: Me tipping the table over onto him. Ripping the sign down. Shattering him with kicks. Being wrestled into a police car, my ability to earn a living or even live in this county with my lover destroyed. Him self-righteous, virtuous, a Christian martyr. And all for two lines about my disorderly conduct in the local police column.

Neil Goldschmidt ran for the governorship of Oregon promising to issue an executive order banning state agencies from discriminating on the basis of sexual orientation. According to Jay Brown, editor of *Just Out* in Portland, Oregon, "a clause in the executive order clearly prohibits affirmative action or preference for homosexuals in state employment." It seemed, in other words, a harmless order.

Soon after assuming office, Governor Goldschmidt, probably well aware that the state is rife with queers and our liberal friends, did as he promised. The state is also rife with Christian fundamentalists and conservatives. And these bad guys, preferring to exterminate us if they just could, found an excuse to harass us. They want to petition away the Governor's harmless work.

The little man at the top of the post office steps (and I use the term *little* in its physical and spiritual sense) was collecting signatures to this end. He only needed 63,578 to place the measure on a general election ballot.

Later, I learned that Girlfriend had engaged the little man verbally. Though little guy was curiously unresponsive to her, another man took up the cause, and when she left, he was still haranguing the little guy. While she'd been inside, Girlfriend bore down on the postal officials, who also proved curiously unresponsive to her complaint about being accosted for offensive causes. Later still, I drafted a letter of thanks to the governor.

Then, I scrounged up the cash to pay my dues to the Gay and Lesbian Press Association and joined Galon, a tiny group in a small city nearby, and Lesbian Community Project, a larger highly political group in Portland. Next, I shall write to the postal officials. I decided to march this year in the Portland Gay Pride Parade, come hell or high water. I am writing this column, which should reach thousands more people than little man and his counterparts ever will. My anger and my commitment will burn on and on.

Why did this this particular incident get to me? After all, yesterday was the day the powers that be in DC voted yea on a huge AIDS package. Why aren't I grateful?

Because nothing has essentially changed. We are so used to living in fear and with great caution that it feels normal to us. I came out in 1960 when telling one's parents was unthinkable. When there were two gay organizations, not hundreds. When there were two periodicals and the few books were published for prurience not politics. When the only gay parades were half-tanked groups boisterously strutting onto gay beaches or the lines of singles or couples nervously straggling past a bouncer into the bars night after night. One becomes used to the undercurrent of oppression. I'm not sure I know how to function without it.

Living in a time that often feels like the not-so-old days reminds me how tenuous our victories really are. It keeps me working when I'd rather rest, rather look back at how far we've come than ahead at how far we must go. It keeps me aware that although we are edging toward the very deep changes that can be made, only we can make them. Only Girlfriend, for one, taking on the bigoted beast in public. Or me, running home to write out what checks I can and scribble my protest. Despite all the good straight women and men in the world, no one is going to do it for us. Not only that, but we can do it. We are not too sick, too weak, too deranged or too liberated. We are still too scared.

We look back to our predecessors and think, how brave they were. Yes, they were, but so are we. We forget how vulnerable we are. I didn't think of it as courage when I wore my dyke finery back then, or held my lover's hand on the street. I worried, yes, I worried all the time. Still, I grabbed every opportunity I could to be in a place where I could dress as I pleased and hold her hand. When I escaped for a moment from the feeling of fear, it was the act I undertook which absorbed me, not the nobility of my deed in the eyes of history. Yet those were and are dangerous acts.

I walk down the street nervous now. I see myself as an obvious gay, and if I'm not, sometimes the person I'm with is. Maybe I'm wearing a pink triangle, or trying to think of a way to explain the double bed I share with Girlfriend. Maybe I'm scared to say where I live, or with whom, or maybe there is a gang of kids ahead and I automatically cross the street, not even aware I've done it

In the eighties we have more places to go and can more easily be with our own. We have cultural supports which enhance our condition enormously. Our politicians and our allies have been able to enact a little legislation here and there. But how much has that changed the everyday struggle of being gay in a straight world? It still takes guts to hold hands with your lover whether on Christopher or Main Street. And if I'm not aware of the danger I'm reckless. And if I'm not aware that I have the power to change the way the world sees that act I am discounting myself.

Oh, the little man on his postal mountain was a small incident. Still, how many small incidents are happening all the time—and who does he represent? There are people out there who, unbelievably, think we are intrinsically evil. They fear us and they will protect themselves against us any way they can. Legislatively, through the likes of Jesse Helms. En masse through their ignorant petitions which have enormous power. Individually through queer bashing, tire slitting, and just plain intimidation. Most destructively, through the homophobic doubts their attacks inevitably stir up in us. And this will go on until the little men and the little women are shown that they are wrong. We are the only ones who can show them this.

Before walking up the post office steps, I may have thought the local organizations were molehills in the mountains of Oregon, like me too small to do any good. But like the little man, they have their counterparts in every other city. I am one wee lesbian writer swinging my pen like a cudgel at the moment, raging the only way I know how—to action through words. Every action spreads enlightenment. The people who fight us see us through their shadowy fears. They are not likely to step into the shadows to learn anything. We must step out.

In this month of gay pride I exhort you and I join you—in signing up for the groups and in signing the checks, in writing the books and in writing the petitions, in holding the meetings and holding the hands that hold up the banners that spread across the world and wrap us all into one people, one brave, scared, angry people who marched so strongly on Washington last fall—and cannot stop marching now.

GAY FLAG (1988)

Am I the only queer in the world never to have heard of the gay flag?

All over San Francisco they flutter in the sunny Bay breezes, large rainbow-striped banners of our presence. On foggy nights they wave like baby butches in bright overalls, femmes in neon lipstick, queens in astonishing drag. They're inspiring; I want us all to fly one, so that even the winds blatantly announce us.

I was in San Francisco for the Gay and Lesbian Press Association conference. I went to be a member of the press, an experience I'd never had previously. I came away convinced that it is one of the most sacred offices one can hold in these years of gay pride.

We are powerful, those of us who speak out with our words. We are helping to create a world that is safe for us by validating our experience in print. We are also laying down roads into the wastelands of the so-called mainstream by reporting on our lives. As if we are important. As if we deserve a place in the sun.

One of the things that I learned is that we are listened to, not only by ourselves, but by the whole wide world. The straight press pirates our stories. Once, when we made news, it went unnoticed. Now that we are daring to call it news, the media is waking up. Gay coverage is increasing everywhere, not just in San Francisco.

The first GLPA event took place at the Rawhide II on Folsom Street. I expected a leather bar with effeminate bikers looking on all these writer types with disdain. As I walked deeper and deeper into streets filled with industry and warehouses all I wanted to do was run home to the peaceful country.

I was wrong, as I always am when I stereotype myself into a panic. There were as many women as men there, no one paid us untoward attention, and the management gave me a gift I never anticipated.

An announcer interrupted our journalistic chitchat to introduce the
Rawhide II Saddle Tramps. About fifteen men and one woman came
onto the floor, in black jeans, gray Western shirts, black neckerchiefs,
and cowboy boots. Then, they began to square-dance. They were great.
I felt proud to the point of tears as I watched gays perform an American
folk art. Watched the forbidden same-sex partnering—the way many
cowboys and cowgirls probably did in real life, when no one was
looking.

Early the next morning a panel of gays from the straight press
talked about their experiences. They were editors, writers, radio
broadcasters, TV anchorpersons. The TV personality, obviously the
person most at risk, told us that when Art Lazere, the conference chair,
contacted him to appear on the panel, he'd initially refused. It was
obvious that he had been afraid and that his decision to participate had
taken tremendous courage, a courage we've all experienced, whether
coming-out before one friend or thousands of strangers.

The panelists suggested strategies for increasing gay visibility in
the media. Go to work for the straight press to change its perspective.
Build the gay press, "alternative" sources of news are important.
Mostly they spoke of the delicate task which has befallen them to
accurately present the gay community to the world, without alienating
us, or the viewers, or the advertisers, or the owners. They discussed
the pitfalls they've experienced in covering gay people: getting only
sensational news items past the editors, portraying all gay males as
potential PWAs, and not including lesbians, the terminally invisible
population, at all.

At the luncheon I sat between poet Kitty Tsui and arts editor for
the *San Francisco Sentinel* Eric Hellman, hobnobbing. Well-known
Supervisor Harry Britt spoke and, in a surprise appearance, Art Agnos,
the Mayor of San Francisco. The old tears welled up again at his
presence. I have never been in an audience as a gay person and been
addressed with respect, been courted by elected officials. It felt very,
very good. For so many centuries we've been denied access to the
press. Now others were coming to us, seeking access to our presses.

And with good reason. We are an inspired, ambitious, and
committed crew. Among others I met: Rupert Kinnard, currently Art
Director for *The Sentinel*, a warm and incredibly gifted man, with
an air of taking one into his confidence. N. A. Damian, courtly and
hesitant, with several books under his belt. Evelyn C. White, a reporter
for the *Chronicle* who also teaches at Flight of the Mind, a women

writers workshop. She's a sharp, admirably outspoken professional. Kitty Tsui's red blazer, suspenders, and bodybuilder's physique belied the shyness in her quiet manner. She's an advertising rep for *The Sentinel*, selling the gay press to business, making the press viable. Robrt Pela, with his gentle dignified manner and appealingly flashy slacks, is incoming president of GLPA and publisher of *The Phoenix Resource* out of Arizona.

These people seemed determined, savvy, but assumed no mantle of tough, heartless journalist. From Jim Thomas of the *St. Louis News-Telegraph*, to Ron Zahn of Eugene's *Lavender Network*, from Pokey Bauder of LA's *The News* to Jill Posener of *On Our Backs* in San Francisco, there seemed to be a bonding in common cause.

The farewell party was held at The Galleon, an old-fashioned bar-restaurant more reminiscent of Provincetown than Market Street. The manager bent my ear for a while, explaining that my eye did not err: the owner is from Boston and apparently wanted that white-latticed, ramshackle Cape Cod effect. He also boasted that most of their bartenders were over sixty, that the bar had a continual display of art to raise funds for AIDS, and that the musical menu ran more to piano-bar and sing-alongs than loud rock.

I was pretty socialized out by this time and mostly watched. There were certainly more men at the gathering than women; one of the workshops had been devoted to coverage of lesbians and minorities. But then, a few years ago there was barely a gay press. It all takes time. And that's what we were there for, to meet each other and to make our needs known.

A tall teased-hair blonde who may have been a drag queen, and a shorter round older person, also blond, and I think biologically female, served drinks I didn't want. I began to feel out of place, just observing, so I wended my way toward the front door, along the bar, past the TV and the diners.

Something stopped me on the way out. I felt that I could not tear myself away from that place, from those people. Outside, even though I was in San Francisco, I would be alone, different, weak. I crossed Market, weary, hurrying toward the safety of my borrowed home.

That's when I saw them. The gay flags I'd just learned to recognize. Fluttering and waving and flying from windows. Telling the mayor, the straight press, the world, in bright bold colors, that, through square dancing and politics and words, we're taking our place in the sun.

ELECTRONIC SEDUCTION (1988)

It all started at the Salvation Army. I couldn't resist the Sony tuner, the KLH speakers, and the Garrard turntable—for fifty bucks. If they hadn't tempted me enough, there was the lamentable fact that at age forty I still didn't own a stereo system. No wonder I'd never been much on orchestrating seductions.

So I toted them all home. Everything was in mint shape but the turntable. It couldn't be fixed, but then there was really no surface in my trailer large enough to accommodate it or any other turntable. Two hundred credit card dollars later, the fifty-dollar bargain seduced me into a tape player.

That was it, I said. No more electronic gadgets. Too hard on the budget and the trailer's not wired for it.

Then the computer bug bit. You won't have to retype drafts, they tempted me, all those computer-owner friends of mine. No more photocopying, I was told. By filing everything on discs you'll save space, they lured me. I really had to do something about the electrical wiring anyway. Six hundred dollars later, my little old (as in obsolete) Kaypro and her trusty printer-partner were installed. Not a luxury, simply an unfortunate but necessary bow to the electronic age.

This was not to be the lowest I would stoop, however.

I went to see my doctor for some difficulty or other. As usual, he advised me on the evils of stress.

"Do you laugh much?" he asked.

"No, but I play relaxation tapes on my tape player," I offered, neglecting to add that I often did this while I worked as I hadn't time to squander on mere relaxation.

As it happened, Girlfriend was off being famous somewhere that week. Perhaps I seemed more glum than normal. The doctor looked hard at me.

"You need to laugh more. Ever go to the movies?"

"Popcorn fumes," I said, reminding him of my debilitating allergy to corn.

"Hmm," he said, pondering, or perhaps working up to his next Terrible Suggestion. "How about a VCR?"

I sniffed and probably looked haughty. At least one can play Vivaldi on a tape deck. Even the computer had been justifiable for utilitarian reasons, but one of those VCRs so you can tape *Dynasty* on the nights you're out with the bowling team? I mean, I'm grateful that reception is terrible in our little valley. There was no way I was going to spring for a satellite dish so I could see some once-a-year special about the tragedy of having a gay child or being a gay child or being gay and wanting a child or being a nun and wanting a gay or some other family-oriented approach to the forbidden topic.

"I could prescribe it for you."

I admit the idea of a medical tax write-off appealed to me.

"You could rent movies. Comedies."

I began to see that he was serious about the therapeutic value of a VCR. I remembered the opening of *High Anxiety* and how hard I'd laughed. The dope-smoking scene in *Nine to Five*. And ah, Faye Dunaway in *Network*—whoops, stick to the comedies. Like the Pink Panther films. All of a sudden, it didn't seem like such an onerous concession to middle-class America to spend my evenings with Lily Tomlin when Girlfriend was away.

Out came the magic plastic card. I zipped home with the new VCR under one arm, and *La Cage Au Folles* under the other. Quentin would be thrilled. My TV was named for Quentin Crisp. I'd never owned a TV before him, but when I turned it on, there was Quentin Crisp in a movie about his life. This, I thought, is a good omen.

I religiously watch one comedy tape a week. I do not necessarily laugh. How can I? *Porky's II*? *Meatballs*? I did stoop to *Spaceballs* one weekend, and I have developed an odd affection for that sexist, homophobic, racist, ageist, looksist, etc. series of silly Police Academy sitcoms. Then there are the Whoopi Goldberg films which luckily are called comedies, but which I watch more because I am utterly in love with Ms. Goldberg. Watching most available cinematic comedy is hard, offensive work.

To get good comedy, or gay comedy, or movies with a gay theme, is hard work too in rural southern Oregon. In order to rent *La Cage Au Folles II*, I had to go up to the counter, ask for it, spell it, stare down the clerk, and then wait weeks until a copy was located and transported, probably in rubber gloves, to my local outlet. You can imagine what it was like going back for *La Cage III*. Last week I returned *Maurice* and the super-blond aspiring Valley Girl behind the counter greeted it with a loud sneering, "Oh, that one!"

Actually, things could be worse. The Neighbor Boys share their library with us. That's where we saw *Before Stonewall* and an impressive video of artist Paul Cadmus and his friend. Kindly straight friends taped *Gertrude Stein and a Companion* and *An Early Frost*. We're not completely without resources even if I never have seen a copy of *Desert Hearts* in public.

Besides, these deprivations keep life simple. Ultimately I prefer reading in bed to spending my life staring at computer screens full of little green words or little black-and-white television heterosexuals seducing/killing/insulting one another.

Yet they've managed my seduction. My trailer's a mini-carnival of electronic whimsies now. I spend the day with my Kaypro, the night with my Quasar, and the Sony is on call. Sometimes Girlfriend and I even curl up in front of the Quasar together. And then, in this town without so much as a Desert Heart, we can watch our stars: Garbo's kissin' *Queen Christina*, Julie Andrews's *Victor Victoria*, the great Divine, and every exquisite story Ivory and Merchant ever put on film. With a little ingenuity, my VCR brings me gay culture. What a bargain.

PATRICK (1989)

Is it fair to eulogize one gay man when so many have died without even an obituary? Patrick was no more special than those you've lost—except that every living thing on this earth is special and each of us deserves to have her/his story told. Especially the gentle, laughing ones, like Patrick.

I met Patrick on Polk Street in glorious San Francisco. I'd gone to the city for writing research and while there was determined to find a used leather flight jacket, an essential for every well-dressed gay. (But only secondhand. We don't need to make clothing of animals anymore.) Someone pointed me to Polk Street.

Who could I ask for directions to a leather shop? Well, the gay man at the bus stop, of course. He was kind, not embarrassed, and mothered me all the way to the store. As we rode, we talked. Amazingly enough he had a stepbrother in the little town where I lived. Also amazingly his stepbrother turned out to be one of the Neighbor Boys, dear friends of mine.

Pleased by the coincidence, I made a point of seeing him again at the Neighbor Boys' home. I liked Patrick enormously. Thin, with deep-set sad eyes and dark hair, he was no showstopper, just a regular gay guy making it the best he could. He'd been brought up in Northern California, had a rough childhood, and ended up in the medical field, which fascinated him.

Little did we know how much more medical knowledge he would come to have, and for what tragic reasons.

We corresponded now and then, little notes, and I always got news of Patrick through the Neighbor Boys. It was a grim day when the news was of Patrick's diagnosis with HIV disease.

I didn't see him for a while. He was, of course, consumed by the increasingly complex and demanding daily rituals of his virus. Then one day I flew into San Francisco on a layover from New York. My plane was astonishingly early and I decided to try to catch an early flight home. The airline grumbled but assigned me a seat. I meandered over to the line and there, as if prearranged, stood Patrick.

His back was to me. He was fussing about the flight, his first ever, with a stranger. She was fussing back at him. When they ran out of fears to catalogue I said, "Patrick?"

His greeting was warm, but not surprised. He was on his way to a week in the country with his brother, something he'd feared he could never do again. He was scared of flying but had chosen to do so because he was too ill for the interminable bus ride and did not drive, did not own a car, had no one who could drive him. He'd been praying for help in getting through this ordeal of flying. The airline, in the universe's uncanny way with Patrick and me, had assigned us seats together. They managed, it turned out, to lose my luggage for days, but they'd inadvertently given Patrick someone to hold his hand when he was afraid.

I've never been one to attend church. Formal religion is not for me. But I was having an emotionally painful time last year, and as it happened another friend of mine, a metaphysical minister, had not long before gotten his own church. I went every Sunday for comfort, for strength, for the comradeship that this small and heavily gay congregation offered me. It happened to be the church the Neighbor Boys attended, and the church Patrick came to when he was in town.

The great airline of the universe had given Patrick and me seats in the same vessel again.

He came to be very special to that flock, and even when he wasn't there, Reverend David or his assistant would announce Patrick's condition from the pulpit. I learned to pray partly by praying for Patrick.

By this time Patrick was unable to afford his apartment in Oakland. I heard that he'd moved to a house where he lived with other people. When I talked to him it was a houseful of lesbians he'd joined, and he'd become quite central to that household.

Patrick came to Oregon one last time, late last spring, when the earth was heating up, when the flowers were bursting more spectacularly than they had in years, when rain was deluging us after drought. Almost immediately he was hospitalized, for a dangerously high and constant fever.

Of all the physicians in town, only two, partners, were willing to treat Patrick.

When I went to visit, the nurses, I thought, looked at me curiously. Patrick was in a room by himself (though he had no money) and I saw no other patients in rooms near him. I brought him a bear in a leather vest. Had the bear shopped at the same leather store? We laughed, but Patrick was taking pain medication and couldn't stay awake long.

He recovered enough for me to see him once more. I had a gathering at my apartment on a hot, hot June day. The guests, unbidden, brought their chairs into the large backyard and we made a circle which grew and grew. We just talked and laughed. Lover sang for us. We ate. Patrick sat in our midst, looking languid and pleased that he could be there with this country crowd, under a shady tree, in a circle of so many of us who had come to love this visitor in our lives.

It's December now. Four days before Christmas. The message on my machine, from an old lover, said that Patrick died. Patrick would not sit under my old shade tree again or sit in Reverend David's church. I wouldn't ride on a bus with Patrick again or fly on a plane next to him.

It had gotten harder for him recently. He'd been taken off AZT because of its side effects and was injecting something new into his stomach. He was back in Oakland where he had a home health nurse and he wouldn't be up for Christmas. The Neighbor Boys are on their way to him instead, driving south over the icy fogbound mountains.

Did I say Patrick wasn't special? He was, just as everyone we love is special. Patrick moved through this life gracefully, opening his spirit as he traveled. Many of us were caught in the glow of his passage. And on this first night of winter, the longest night of the year, he's both entered the restful dark, and become a light I never expected in my life.

OUR PROM (1989)

Like any high-school kid in a back alleyway of small-town America, I stood one day at the height of spring in a garage doorway out of the rain, dreaming of the prom. I couldn't help but think of the horticultural alchemist I'd interviewed the day before, a person who transforms living foliage to permanent decoration, who dares to change the nature of living things.

Something like this is stirring in my community, here among the undulating mountaintops. So many dreamers live here, drawn by the spirituality of ancient hills, the persistent greening of these sun-parched, fire-charred, hunted, and clear-cut holy lands. Some of the dreamers seek isolation, separation from all but their own kind: Radical Faeries, or Lesbian Separatists, and their tastes abide. But there's a coming together here in southern Oregon, an eager flocking of folk of middle ground after the catalyst of last year's ostensibly failed gay-rights battle.

For the first time in many years, or ever for some of us, women and men are crossing the barrier of sexual differentiation and are approaching one another to work on common goals and to confront common fears. The vehicle for this unification is our prom and the adventure of creating it.

There is no experience on earth, for me, quite like being among drag queens and daring femmes. They somehow incorporate the outrageousness and the courage, the brashness and the grace, the complex sexuality as well as the unique sociability of gay life. However, drag is not exactly common among the women of this lesbian community who are primarily land based, or feminist, or closeted. Finding a drag butch for the prom revue seemed to be a lost cause.

As a Prom Personnel Consultant (read that double-*P C*), I searched every talent pool I could identify. Some women were butchy but couldn't perform. Others were performers who had no hope of butching it up even with coaching from our Prom Coordinator, the Texas Femme (who's enough all by herself to put any woman into high-butch gear). Another group was politically disinclined to a) dress like men, or b) perform for a mixed audience.

Then from, of all places, a hardy local women's land collective, appeared a tall, extremely handsome woman too young for, but possessing, that old gay style which cannot be taught. I happened upon her during an evening of readers' theater and noted that she could act. I'd never met the woman before and wondered that such a personification of gay style could live, as she does, in a political community. So I gathered my courage and sidled up to her, feeling like the proverbial pervert. Hey, kid, I'm a talent scout. Want to do a transvestite act? She said yes immediately. Another stereotype shot.

Of course there are kinks, so to speak, in this prom adventure. Like the murmur of discontent on both sides when word got out that titles like *royal persons* or some such neutral label would be bestowed that evening. Some of the queens wanted their own category, perhaps worried a dyke femme would walk off with the honors; some of the dyke femmes don't particularly want to compete with the queens. And then how is the other personage chosen? A male in leather versus a butch in a tux? A jeans and flannel-shirt lesbian versus a butch man in Western drag? What a great opportunity to examine our cultural biases as well as to practice some conflict-resolution skills among ourselves before we're pitched in another battle for our rights.

Dressing up seems to be the greatest obsession of all the prom preparations. I had no idea what anyone wore to a prom. The most I ever dress up is turtleneck and corduroy jacket or tie and jeans. L.L. Bean casual, I believe it's called. The Neighbor Boys offered their box of Cinderella frocks to all the femmes, but the Sunshine Lady, whom I have the honor of escorting, announced the purchase of a real prom dress from a classy secondhand boutique. I was thrown into a tizzy.

What else could I do? I sought out my fashion consultant, Shelly the Butch, formerly of West Hollywood, and then found an ad in the paper for an exclusive shop in town which rents tuxedos. Do I dare approach them for drag apparel? I timorously queried Shelley. She'd done it lots of times, for tuxes and tails and other items of dyke elegance, but not here, not in small-town America. Yet when we stormed the het citadel, the clerks didn't bat an eye. Shelly and I stood there among the teenaged boys, poring over catalogues, not a one of us except Shelly knowing what we were doing, and ordered our glad rags. These are, after all, the days of equal rights for women, though I admit to a certain relief when female clerks were called upon to do the measuring.

Now at off hours I prowl Volume Shoe stores and the like, searching for boys' patent leathers, and the Sunshine Lady teams up with Shelly's friend to renew makeup skills. I have to remember to order the corsage, white for her light blue, and the boutonniere, light blue for my white dinner jacket, navy slacks, cummerbund, and bow tie. A bow tie and a wing collar! I'm faint with excitement. Shelly has already organized our double date. She'll chauffeur us in pre-petro-scarcity Lady Blue, her almost-limo cruiser. The Sunshine Lady and I plan a trial run at the Lavender Rhythm Ritual up north next weekend; we've never danced anywhere but in our kitchens before.

I overhear conversations which capture the diversity of prom experience: Are you going in leather or Texas? Or, I can't stand it when guys with beards wear dresses. Or, I need to find me some more women performers. There's no problem getting the men onstage. Or, Will the DJ play some waltzes? Or, seriously worried, I don't know how to dance in high heels/ I wish I could go, but I work for the school system/ I don't have a date/ I don't want to dance with men there/ I don't want to dance with women there/ I'm wearing jeans, I don't care/ The women will cream their pants when they see her doing this drag act.

Gay dance floors are darned scarce in this neck of the woods. Places where gay women and men dance together even more scarce. Almost never does a local event draw gays from the midstate deserts, the coast, and the northern cities. Suddenly, the community has bonded. The prom project is enhanced by this collusion of the sexes. This is his/ herstorical: it's cultural alchemy.

LEADING LADIES (1989)

I suppose there was dancing in the world before I fell in love with Miss B., my high-school gym teacher. Foggily, I remember jumping around a preteen girlfriend's living room doing those strange contortions called the Lindy. Miss B. taught us nothing so trendy; with her it was waltzing and Fred Astaire soft-shoe-ing to "Stepping Out With My Baby" and the bossa nova.

"Get off your toes!" she'd cry, as if to keep me earthbound.

"You're leading again! You're supposed to be the girl!" she'd yell, as if to urge me into a cautious closet.

"One, two, three, one, two, three. That's it!" she'd praise when she was sure I was learning the ropes.

The day of the Cuban missile crisis, a straight friend and I were the only students in the gym when some unwittingly romantic soul put the bossa nova record on. Of course we danced, but I danced for Miss B. Surely she'd notice what she was missing? I was wrong: John Kennedy's steps and missteps commanded her attention that day.

During those same years I was frequenting the Greenwich Village bars, learning to discreetly bump and grind. Or perhaps that's a contradiction in terms. In any case, it was against the law for same-sex partners to dance together, and the bar owners were extremely paranoid about this. We were relegated to hidden back rooms and patrolled, if that's what you call surveillance on a postage-stamp sized dance floor, for unseemly affection. Though there was quite a bit of Little Anthony and the Imperials and the Shirelles, the steps hardly mattered. If you danced in a gay bar, you did dirty dancing or it didn't count.

Sadly, I bid that dancing adieu for the most part when I went off to college. There I found modern dance and the Beatles, folk dancing and mixers. I was not impressed. I do remember swaying to Lenny

Welch's "Since I Fell For You," naked with my lover, sequestered in a dormitory room, drinking from a Chianti bottle in its jacket of straw. Later in my academic career the Mamas and the Papas revived the current Martha and the Vandella's "Dancing in the Street," but my revolution was still to come.

The post-college years were a pretty dismal time for dancing too. I lived in Bridgeport, Connecticut, and it was 1967. If we wanted to dance, Carol and I had to go into New York, pay exorbitant hotel costs, or travel home with a trainload of Yankee fans returning from a big boozy game. There was no gay social group and no bar for "nice" lesbians (yes, that's what college had turned me into).

By the early seventies, though, we lesbians began to kick up our heels. Women's dances were held everywhere. The Firehouse in the Village put on the best. An alternative to the ever-beckoning bars, it was the creation of one of the first gay-lib groups. At least one night a week was women only. Later, a lover told me that's where she'd come out, having gone to the Firehouse for just that purpose. A big, loud dance floor all to ourselves? That's what freedom was all about: praise Kennedy for stopping the missiles! On breaks we moved to the fire escapes which hung over the New York streets and called down to the ubiquitously gay pedestrians in this darkened warehouse district. In our revolutionary fervor, we did dance in the streets.

It was only a matter of time before gay women would want not just the right to bear dancing shoes, but to make our own music. The New Haven Women's Liberation Rock Band was created to do just that. I was privileged to be a groupie, living by that time in New Haven, and I gloried in the opportunity to carry equipment, or provide support during rough recording sessions. Not to mention dancing. It was one of the few rock-and-roll bands to use a French horn, and to this day I want to tear up the floor when I hear the instrument.

Group dancing was the trend then, a far cry from the bump and grind. I wrote a scene into my first novel, *Toothpick House*, describing such mass gyrations at a women's event in the Yale Law School. Main character Annie Heaphy and her crowd watch with astonishment. In real life I was with Annie's crowd and, like Annie, was swept into the ritual, the incredibly intoxicating tide of women claiming our freedom. When our music played, we danced in onesomes, threesomes, foursomes, hundredsomes. We did snake dances and war whoops and clapped till our hands were raw and stomped till Yale's floors must forever bear our mark.

I, however, had a counterrevolutionary tendency to want to dance in a couple with the woman I loved. Romance was frowned upon in those early years of the 1970s, and by the time the disco era hit I was ready for a change. My lover and I would join the gay men and dance till closing to Gloria Gaynor and Sylvester. Wonderful as foreplay, it was also a great way to diet, shedding calories with each beat; a great way to exercise, sweating and building those leg muscles before the jogging craze took over; and a great way to stop drinking since Perrier was much more compatible with marathon dancing than chemicals which caused wobbling.

Now disco is gone, as is street dancing, closet swaying, and group dancing. When I find a bar where I can let loose, or a dance sponsored by a gay group, I often must really reach to match the rhythms in that hard-edged music which seems to enjoy such popularity. I'm out of step, having come out into the era of free-form, informal, abandoned dance. Though my will to keep on dancing is strong, and one can bump and grind to just about anything, I'm finding that something is missing in the choreography of my life.

I don't want to dirty dance to every song; I don't want to learn what the baby dykes are doing. I want Miss B. back, with her classic steps, her one, two, threes, her prodding and prompting. But, Miss B., this time around let's get one thing relatively straight. It's time to let all the young dykes dip and sway across gymnasiums floors, up on our toes, far from earthbound. I'll be the girl, but the kind that knows the ropes. It's time to teach me to lead!

Lammy Fashion (1990)

Many columns ago I described the major dilemma of dressing a butch for a job interview. The problem was solved when my Birkenstocks met the male manager's earring and I was hired. Today I am faced with an even greater difficulty: what to wear to the Lambda Literary Awards.

Here it is laid out simply:

1. Lesbians are traditionally rebellious in garb. I am, in that sense, very traditional.

2. Writers are traditionally without the wherewithal to dress fancy. I'm pretty traditional in that way too.

3. The Lammys are being held at Caesars Palace in Las Vegas—at a black-tie banquet.

4. What does a traditional dyke writer wear to a black-tie shindig in Vegas?

Of course I'll wear the black tie, but somehow I don't think that's what they mean.

The last gay dress code I recall was at the Sea Colony in Greenwich Village in 1963 where I had to get past a bouncer. What do gay bouncers look like in 1990? And would s/he bounce a cross-dressing author from the gay lit gala of the year? What if the author is a nominee?

I consulted Lover. "It depends," she said, "on whether you're willing to wear women's clothes."

"Ick."

What Look do I want? Men's off-the-Goodwill-rack dress slacks tend to have bulgy pockets in back, making one look like a well-fed middle-aged matron in her hubby's old clothes. Suit jackets definitely give me all the style of an early sixties diesel-dyke bouncer. On the other hand, it takes moola to scare up custom-made garb with a woman's fit and non-femme lines.

As for women's wear, it's either polyester pantsuit city, or the teenage gangster look with ultra-broad shoulders and anklet-narrow pegged pants. The latter only works with a spiked hairdo.

My family had a rescue poodle once. Lambert had no pretensions. He got his fur cut only because he had to. Now and then an ambitious groomer would give him the works: a tassel on his tail, a teased pompadour, a stripe down his back like a landing strip for fleas. Poor Lambert would skulk in corners for days, a hangdog look on his barbered face. He was embarrassed.

Just like I would be if I wore spiked hair and shoulder pads.

This nagging voice in my head says, "Be yourself. Jeans and a cord jacket. Maybe some elbow patches so you look like a writer."

"In June, in *Nevada*?" points out Lover.

Back to square one.

There's a problem beyond this superficial predicament of dress. I'm having trouble integrating my dyke storyteller role with black-tie banquets. Of fitting the me who lugs wood for the fire in the morning to warm my writing space, to the me among the white tablecloths and glittery silverware, not to mention glittery people.

Of fitting the dykes in my books—blue-collar butches and career-waitress femmes, civil servants and schoolteachers, old dykes, disabled dykes, truck driver dykes—to glitter at all. Not that I disapprove of the Lammys. I think they're the greatest thing for publicity and gay book sales since Radclyffe Hall's obscenity trial.

The concept of honoring our writers and presses is incredibly important. My confusion about the event itself comes from a class conflict rather than one intrinsic to gay life. I'm honored to be a part of the hoopla and proud of our aggressively self-aggrandizing literary establishment.

The paradox for me is the one I play out in my writing. It's the experience of everyday ordinary dykelife which moves me to write. And I must try to make that experience interesting for today's sophisticated reader, who is used to glamour, suspense, exotica.

I read and enjoy gay male lit, so much of which is about glib good-looking professional characters. I read the new lesbian lit with its rich passing women who always make graceful passionate love to one another. I understand the appeal. It's hard to communicate the simple way in which my characters take flight in their mundane lives, to describe the magic of everyday. Dusty and Elly in *Dusty's Queen of Hearts Diner* would have to work for hours to make the silverware in their diner glitter. And my 4'9" Swashbuckler, Frenchy Tonneau, would look exactly like a fifties bouncer in any evening clothes.

Unlike Frenchy, though, or Dusty, I want to participate in our new honor-bestowing, somewhat elegant culture. (Elly the femme, of course, would give her eyeteeth to be there and would know just what to wear.) I'm stuck in my old gay bar and political gay origins. Pointy black boots and hip-pocket combs, flannel shirts and jeans, ain't going to make it in the new age. Obviously this lesbian needs some new resources. Fashion shows perhaps? Newspaper columns on the well-dressed dyke? Off with the softball uniforms and on with the patent leather loafers! The T-shirt rack at the local wimmyn's bookstore doesn't cut it anymore.

Yet that brings me right back to what being a dyke is all about. A way to be ourselves, to free ourselves from the trussed-up state society puts us in. Sure, black-tie affairs are our right too, but are they really what we want?

I wonder how many femmes will dare to buy their Lammy fashions at the thrift shops; how many butches will cry, "I can't go! I have nothing to wear!"

I'll just hope for the best, put on my black tie and white shirt, iron my favorite jeans, and hunt for that pair of patent-leather dress shoes.

Lesbian Friends (1990)

It was a brilliant fall weekend in New England and I was visiting an old friend. We tromped around her quiet neighborhood on the edge of a troubled city and admired the blazing maple trees. We discussed the state of the world, as old friends do, and we visited our traditional haunts: crafts fairs, a former head shop gone legit, and—not so traditionally—we played miniature golf.

Old Friend is someone I try to visit once a year despite our three-thousand-mile separation. We talk by phone probably once a month. These facts led her girlfriend, who wore neon Ptown T-shirts all weekend, to remark, "We hear from you more often than from most of our friends around here!"

The three of us sat on the guest bed talking about the sad state of lesbian friendships. This seems to be a typical scenario: You're single. Friends are easy to find. One special friend becomes a lover. Your other friends drift away. Her other friends drift away. You commiserate over vegetarian chili. Why have you lost all your friends? Is it because neither of you is available now? Because she's totally obnoxious? Because you're too couple-y? Because the dyke community is so mobile and all your old friends moved to: a) Asheville, North Carolina b) a farm in northern Maine c) the West Coast? Or is it because you've gotten obnoxious?

And who are our friends, we of the Stonewall generation? I always used to make friends at work, but my present job is in a sort of a social services cottage industry so I work at home. Most of the friends I have locally are from my support group, or my writers' group, some are straight, some gay men. The lesbians, Lover and I included, are so incredibly busy when someone calls…

Then there are the same-coast friends. The women from San Francisco or Washington State or urban Oregon whom I see once or twice a year as they or I breeze through town, staying overnight. There was a time that I wouldn't even have called them friends because we don't bare our hearts on the phone daily. Twice a year qualifies as friendship these days.

Of course, there's another, and very prevalent, way to make friends when you're gay.

At the miniature golf course we were a foursome. Neon Ptown stayed home, but two women I've known for years joined Old Friend and me in our jokingly self-conscious foray onto the mini-links that are enjoying a mini-revival these days. I suspect we were also a little self-conscious about the strange lesbian way we'd come to cavort with golf clubs among the giant plastic elephants, giraffes, and apes which gave the course its theme.

Old Friend and I are ex-lovers. The women we were with are current lovers with each other. The quieter one of the two is another ex of Old Friend. The other, born the same September day I was, was a fledgling bookstore owner and I was a budding author when we met. I last clearly recall seeing Quiet One on another fall day when another foursome we were in had a pomegranate seed spitting contest in the woods. Same-Day-Virgo I'd last run into at a women's center tag sale. She's an ex of another of my exes, who I'll refer to here as XX.

Neon Ptown is also an ex of XX. Not only that, but Quiet One used to be lovers with XX's current lover. Got that? I'm not sure I do either.

But I do know that, despite my apparently tenuous ties with Quiet One and Same-Day-Virgo, all four of us playing miniature golf were extensively, intensively, and inextricably related by the uncharted lesbian in-law system. The rules of miniature golf are vastly easier to learn than how to relate to such a hodgepodge of new-age lesbo-relatives.

As I hit a pocked yellow ball across the astro greens, I was absorbed on the one hand by the game and on the other by the sticky web we'd all woven. It was like a trick math problem which I was half-consciously trying to solve.

The people around us seemed to lead such simple existences in comparison. A huge hairy father bellowed at his kids; two frizzy-haired young women flirted with their male escorts; a scowling straight couple silently hit balls as if they'd been condemned to miniature golf purgatory. They all knew where they stood in the scheme of their world. Society had formalized their relationships and they'd learned the rules, as we had, at their mothers' knees.

By the time we reached the tri-level eighteenth hole—the one where the sign always promises a free game for an impossible hole-in-one—I was thoroughly confused by the anarchy of lesbian relationship fallout, though grateful for the companionship I'd many times found among the exoskeletons rattling in my closets. It's kind of like the saying: home is where they have to take you in.

I write about lesbian friendships not because I have any answers, or wisdom in the matter, but because I've heard my confusion echoed in the words of many others. Actually, I feel like a miniature golf sportscaster, able to describe the plays and report the score, but enormously inept as a player. Old Friend and I—tied for last.

It wasn't for lack of trying that we didn't win. On the green or in real life. Has anyone tried harder than me to stay put and to consequently avoid collecting exes and exes' exes? On the other hand, if I'd scored a hole-in-one, succeeded at that impossible eighteenth hole of a forever-relationship, my store of lesbian friends might be sadly low.

Naming Ourselves (1990)

I love the names of railroads: Burlington Northern, Rio Grande, Cotton Belt, and my favorite, Erie Lackawanna. They conjure romantic destinations, adventure unbounded, a wealth of sights unseen.

Names tell histories, claim possessions, create futures. I'm not a completely passive name enthusiast; I also love naming. As a gay culture we recognize the power of naming. The Names Quilt is an obvious example. Outing is an incredibly effective weapon no matter who uses it. Calling ourselves gay publicly is one of the most freeing and validating acts available to queers. Then there are the great semantic wars: is it okay to call ourselves queer, dyke, faggot—is it all right if straight people do? Names that decimated us not too long ago are now defiant challenges to our detractors.

Gays often change their names. In rural areas dykes named Tree and Surf and Coyote and Mirth have sprouted like mushrooms in the woods. Name changes are part of our history. Drag names are still the queen's prerogative.

Sappho was writing "To Mnasidica" and addressing the subject as Dica long before Girl Scout Camps ever institutionalized nicknames. I was Grasshopper for the energetic manner in which I cheered the object of my affections at some sporting event. Then there were Dauntless, Shep, Little Mary, Sammy (a Brownie), and middle-aged Rocky.

My first lover conferred on me the dyke name Lee, very popular in the early sixties bars. She decreed that it would be my adult name and I couldn't use it until I went to college. The bar names weren't all that different from the Girl Scout names either: Duchess, Chopsy—I knew Crickets in both places.

Naming the products of our gay culture has been a reflective process. An early lesbian paper out of Washington, DC, *The Furies* was a great angry name. *Mama Bear's News and Notes* comes from the nurturing Oakland bookstore which publishes it. The Radical Radishes was a lesbian living collective in Vermont in the early seventies. Nomenus (No-Men-Us) is one name for the Radical Faerie sanctuary in Southern Oregon. Current periodicals carry quiet names like *Our Paper* (Portland, ME), or confrontational titles like *Gayly Forward* (Orlando, FL).

Sometimes I play naming games just for fun, or for more practical purposes like keeping myself awake while driving. My secret vice is naming kittens-to-be. I don't know what I was thinking of when I came up with the name Dogfood. Tunafish was a little better. One of the many ways I miss my cat Caunterbury Tailes is that I have no one to call Caunterbury Tailes.

Recently a matchmaker friend paired Lover with a stray dog. We turned on the naming machine and spent a weekend harassing each other and our friends. Should we use a gay reference, perhaps Mouse from *Tales of the City*? Her appearance: Apricot, Tawny, Coyote-Eyes? Did my runaway imagination even deserve to be listened to: Tailfeathers, Rootie-Tootie-Kazootie? We settled on Ginger for her wild puppy spirit, her gentle ways, and her color. Of course for me there's always the opportunity to embellish: Gingersnap, Gin-gin-ginger-good-bye after the old song, or Gin-Tin-Tin, the female counterpart of you-know-who.

Then another friend, who was planning a mural of our lesbian community, asked what we'd named our home. Weeks of poring though the thesaurus: dell, rill, knoll; the nature books: Shooting Star Hill, Robin Rill. Trios of tall pines surround the house, thus, Three Pines.

What do you call your lover? Lady—or does she complain that she's not a dog? Babycakes—or does he retaliate with Snookums? Does darling make you blush? Would you rather be called Teddydyke if only she wouldn't slip in public?

Public, every couple's stumbling block. At the annual condo-association holiday party, is s/he your partner, significant other, friend, roommate, the less plausible housemate, long lost cousin from Schenectady, best buddy, wife/husband, hubby, old man, mate, companion, lover, sidekick, straight man? *Straight man?* Or do you just say, "This is Mary Beth, my prhfysgvchsbhsvdte—can I get you a Calistoga?"

Fiction writers are twice blessed. Not only can we choose to name all our real-life stuff, our characters have pets, cars—you name it. Better still, they have names themselves. I found that I needed to introduce a character to my newest novel, *That Old Studebaker* (scheduled for release 2/91). I not only didn't have a name for her, I couldn't quite envision her.

So one beautiful spring day Lover and I walked to the river, about two and a half miles from Three Pines. We'd already hit the baby book and *Lesbian Lists*. As we walked we played with a character, hoping a name would follow.

"Her mother is devoted to her garden," said Lover, "and wanted to name her for a flower."

I take it from there. "The character's never been able to live up to the name. She doesn't feel pretty enough. Her mother couldn't display her like she could her garden."

On and on we walked, embellishing. The civil servant father. The mother's offbeat best friend. The character is wholesome, with a can-do attitude and no ambitions beyond a good life. She's a practical Yankee who moves to San Francisco because there's no fuss made there about queers.

Lover really liked the name Jasmine. I hated it until I began to pair it with last names. Something plain, I said, grounded yet individual. She's called Jasmine Jones. Lover hated the combination, but it was fun getting there.

Now I need a title for my next novel. The main character's a Texas femme adult ed teacher with a passion for Gershwin and a history of butches who are never quite romantic enough.

I wonder if I can name it *Erie Lackawanna*. Or maybe that'll have to wait for the next kitten.

OUTED! (1990)

The first and only time in my life that I was outed I was fifteen years old, barely knew what a lesbian was, and simply denied the accusation. The world was a lot less sophisticated then. People seemed to prefer not to know that someone they loved or looked up to, family or film star, could be so afflicted. Outing often served only to toughen willing denial systems.

In my case it was a disappointed rival who called the family and rudely dropped the bomb. Few were even capable of believing in 1960 that a fifteen-year-old could be sexually active much less seducing fourteen-year-olds of the same sex. And the gay people of my acquaintance then and for many years thereafter were equally incapable of the act of telling anyone outside the club. One simply did not. One, as a matter of fact, did everything in one's power to prevent that from happening.

Sometimes I like to think that my life would have been a lot more simple if the Rude Caller's word had been accepted. That I would not have learned to lie so facilely, or to hide so successfully. That by confronting society's stereotypes at an early age I would not have absorbed them myself and walked for decades with self-hatred a second skin on my body and soul.

That was romanticization. I would have been yanked out of my puppy love reveries and shoved into the offices of shrinks.

The first one I saw, when I was seventeen, loaded me up on new and improved addictive tranquilizers because I was having a hard time coping with the world. My college referred me to a second one who tried to persuade me to fight my Tendencies. The third was outspokenly Catholic. One visit was all he got outta me. It could have been worse, I know. I could have been locked up like my fourteen-year-old paramour. Diagnosis for her? Suicidal tendencies. You bet we were self-destructive. You bet we couldn't bear the pain.

Today, I have a suspicion of outing. A bit too much like Pandora's box for my stomach. The consequences of such radical interference with a human life are unpredictable and can be devastating. Which is more culpable? The police department that conducts raids on gay bars and publicizes names, driving the ashamed to suicide? Or gay crusaders whose more direct publicity has the same effect?

Outing is a natural consequence of the incredible frustration and rage of a people who have been subjected to raids and ignorant shrinks and rude phone calls since the beginning of time. I want the gay doctors and lawyers and sailors and politicians and actors and bankers and educators and writers and housewives and philosophers and musicians and construction workers and rabbis and athletes to come marching across the world's consciousness and conscience saying we are proud and you won't ever shut us up again.

I believe fervently that Silence=Death, although all too often it's the opposite we see. Obviously, if we ended the silences we'd end the shame and we'd end the death.

It's a quandary my poor little Virgo mind hasn't been able to sort through. I'm not at all sure there is one answer, just specific situations. Whether people on an individual basis can survive outing, whether mass exposures for the greater good of the gay masses is ethical, whether I personally would participate in outing.

On the other hand I cannot entirely condemn pulling the covers where it will do enormous good. A certifiable gay politician, for example, who is supporting heterosexist legislation. Once I accept that circumstance, however, which others become right in my eyes? Do the lines get fuzzy, does my judgment get shaky? Where do I get off making such judgments about others' lives?

The fervent and self-righteous rage of our front line outers, though one I am either generationally or constitutionally incapable of joining, is one I respect. These are our radicals. Society does not leave us many tools to defend ourselves, to make the world a better place for gays to live. Outing is a psychically violent means to end like violence and worse.

My Rude Caller was a wounded gay child like me. Unlike me she'd been battling in the straight wars for centuries by age seventeen, in jails and mental hospitals, on the streets—a knife-wielding, cop-stomping baby dyke. Society's silence did this to a kid who looked and acted queer. She knew thirty years ago that breaking silence would get her what she wanted. Except she couldn't break it alone. One screaming gay child could not call or shout or scream loud enough to out even one other kid who had the defenses of a whole culture protecting her.

Today the outers are grown up. They've got the media, the tactics of the sixties, and numbers. Would I condemn anyone who'd outed a Roy Cohn at the height of his power? I can't imagine that I would. I may be ethically confused, my heart going out both to the outers and to some of the outed, but I do acknowledge that the problem is silence. I just wish there were such a thing as a gentle war.

BACKWATER BARRICADES (1990)

I have demonstrated in New York and San Francisco for gay pride; I have marched in Washington, DC for a women's right to have an abortion; I have rallied in New Haven to take back the night; I have helped seize a radio station for feminism; I have circled against racism; I have been among those who have flooded, with their protesting bodies, plazas and parks; I have chanted and been maced, fled and bled for peace.

Never, never have I been so verbally abused, physically confronted, and obviously despised as I was when I stood recently with Lover and a hundred plus others on the steps of a women's club auditorium in rural southern Oregon. We were defending N.O.W. president Molly Yard's right to speak about keeping male legislators' opinions off our bodies.

Lover and I had imagined being two of a very few pro-choice people who would show up. We parked several blocks away because for once all the parking spaces in town were full. We read bumper stickers on the way: *Don't Believe the Liberal Media. Powered by Prayer. Jesus Is My Co-pilot.* We expected the worst.

When we'd threaded our way through the yowling picketers and signs depicting butchered fetuses, we found that the hall was packed full. Over one hundred would-be listeners stood on the steps, turned away. Would they slink off to cars whose bumper stickers read: *Arms are for Hugging* and *Freedom of Choice* and *If You're Not Talking Recycling, You're Talking Trash!* We stayed on the edge of the crowd waiting for it to melt away in the heat of hostility. But they didn't leave.

The Yard-protestors' signs read STOP N.O.W.! This injunction was all too apt. When our hardy group of mostly nongay women and men on the steps began to shout, "Equal rights!" the so-called pro-lifers booed viciously, very obviously more emphatically than they had at anything having to do with abortion. Their agenda was clear: keep the women pregnant and in the kitchen.

This made sense as most of the demonstrators were male, up to 80 percent by one tally.

The so-called pro-lifers lined the main street of town that hot Tuesday evening with hate-twisted faces, threats, and curses. Here are a few of the kinder words they shouted:

Murderers!
Why do you want to kill babies?
Stop sleeping around!
Get married!
You'd love a child you had by rape.
Go out with me—I won't get you pregnant!
Freaks!
Lesbians!
Stay away from the lezzies, they'll give you AIDS!

As if by design, we veteran marchers formed what amounted to a protective half circle around the high-school kids, the young pregnant women, the white middle-class women and men, mothers and daughters who looked as if they'd never been through anything like this before.

When the immoral minority tried to take our space away by crushing us together, we stood our ground. When they harshly shoved us, we dug in our heels. When they bellowed hatred in our ears, we remained silent, backs to them. Now and then they engaged the kids in our crowd in shouting matches and lurched forward to silence them. With the help of the police we held back their terrorizing fury-charged bodies. My knees never stopped shaking, and the police finally had to circle our circle to protect us, but it felt damn good to be back on the barricades, refusing to put up with bigoted bullying.

Though we were there only to attend a lecture, the anti-choice organizers had stoked up the loonies and purposefully sicced them on us, as it were. We pro-choicers repeatedly thanked the police, who did their job well. They'd obviously been trained with crowd-control methods developed against us in the sixties. What a switch: in 1990 it was easier to face five hundred screaming fanatics, to say what I believe, from within a police cordon.

After a while, demonstrators began to leave. Perhaps they were the more rational in the crowd, disgusted by the ignorant behavior of their allies. As they left they discarded the Stop N.O.W. signs. People on the steps tore the signs in two, displaying the bottom half: N.O.W.!

All that hot evening cars had been driving by, horns blaring to support the protestors. When our signs went up, the horns blared for us! We cheered the proof of our strength which had been hidden until this night.

Later, as we lingered on the steps while the audience, charged by Yard's speech, emerged from the hall, a friend stopped and said she'd heard all the noise outside.

"We thought it was the anti-choice people," she said. I imagined how she must have felt, packed into a small, hot building, sweating and anticipating walking into who-knew-what after the program. "We heard them yelling, *Molly go home!* But then we heard another chant: *You go home!*" And she grinned. "Our side was out there too!"

Very out there in this fundamentalist stronghold. Which is no longer quite so strongly held. Three weeks later the voters trounced a ballot measure which would have required parental consent to give birth control information to minors. Victory is sweet even on these backwater barricades.

A ZIPPO IN MY POCKET (1991)

Looking through the old jewelry box can sure stir up memories. Everything from the antique granny glasses of my long-hair radical days to my last and favorite Zippo lighter from the bars is piled hodgepodge in strange marriages.

First, in a great inextricable clump, come the necklaces. The dainty little girl atrocities that never succeeded in turning me into a dainty little girl are twisted with the worry beads from my hippy-dippy years. Some I bought at a wonderful bead shop down the block from Andy Warhol's Electric Circus: worry beads in the windows, worry beads on the walls, worry beads on whirling racks. There was a style for every freak, head, and lefty college kid in the metropolitan area. Each bead was a different color and under the right chemical influence had universes of significance.

My gym whistle, lying under the necklaces, is testimony to an earlier life. I bought it at the same time that I got my volleyball rule book in high school. I'd probably never felt more proud than the first time I walked across the volleyball court, Miss B. watching, to referee. I wore the whistle like a badge. Finally I had a place, some status in the world.

After school I was haunting the lesbian bars, foolishly hoping for a glimpse of my gym teachers, learning lesbian ways. Dykes smoked. Some lit their cigarettes with wooden matches struck on the soles of their shoes, but the ones I emulated used Zippo lighters. My first Zippo was the same clunky silver device my father had—too butch. I switched to the slender style that's still stored in my jewelry box, engraved initials intact. I carried it in my right front pants pocket and was eager for opportunities to ignite it in front of the cigarettes of femmes. When I gave up smoking seventeen years later, it was more difficult to part with the lighter, and the style lighters gave me, than the cigarettes. Now I carry a pocketknife in its place. Lover may not smoke, but many's the time that I've gleefully rescued her from knotty strings and overzealous packaging.

I loved cufflinks. In the sixties it wasn't unusual for women's shirts to be made with the French cuffs that required them. If it was possible to buy such items in women's jewelry departments, I never found any. That was fine with me. I grabbed any chance I could to cross-dress. Aside from that tinge of transvestite in my makeup I was very conservative. All jewelry must be silver because gold was femme-y. If there had to be a pattern, then I wanted the plainest I could find. My tie tacks or clips were subtle. That a woman wearing a tie wasn't anywhere near subtle didn't bother me at all. I had the fashion sense of a penniless, passing street urchin.

The rings in this magic jewelry box! Every relationship seemed to go through stages of rings. There are the first timid, silly rings, sometimes purchased from gumball machines. The dollar rings, now five dollars, found in the shallow bins or display cases of import stores that sprang up in the hippie era. The import shops were generally next door to the leather shop, down the street from the head shop. Who from that era hasn't had a collection of silver rings with tiny red or green or flat turquoise stones?

My homemade rings have disappeared. In the early 1970s, all the women in my living collective seemed to be stringing beads into bracelets, exchanging beaded rings, learning ever more complex patterns that evoked the feel of childhood summer projects.

In their lonely velour-covered boxes are the rings that have mates out there somewhere. Plain bands that promised so much at the time and now are sore reminders of ceremonies and certainties and ex-mates.

My pinky rings are happier tokens. The first one, with the pseudo-sapphire birthstone, was a gift. The second a signet with my dyke initials, L. L. Some are lost, like the one with the red stone, purchased simply because the heroine of *The Swashbuckler* wore one. Today, I wear yet another ring. The stone is purple because it's the gay color. I chose a pinky ring because it's a gay tradition. I always wear it because there are still women out there who look for it, who use that signal along with dykey looks and manner to confirm sisterhood.

Scrabbling around the bottom of the box I come upon my first crystal, a teeny thing, column-shaped with a pointed end. I bought it in the eighties when I was seeking self-healing and carried it briefly it in my pocket, the pocket in which I once carried a lighter. Did it help me? Who knows? Did the rainbow crocheted bag of "rubies" hanging from my car mirror help? Or the bag of protective herbs? I haven't had a car accident (knock on wood) since I hung them.

There's a collection of name tags too. My first women's studies conference in 1981 when lesbian publishing began to prove more effective in making lesbians visible than pinky rings ever had. Next to it lies a Girl Scout name tag from the era of invisible lesbians.

My grandmother's pocket watch! It still works, but it's slow. What was she doing with a pocket watch? Well, this was the grandma that made aprons by sewing together two of Grandpa the railroad man's red bandannas. The same kind of bandannas I carry, for equally practical purposes, in my back pocket today. This was the grandma who wouldn't allow liquor in her house. The grandma everyone thought was a little eccentric. Pocket watches are too butch for me.

What other treasures are in this box? Belt buckles from Provincetown. A mood ring like Mo's from *Dykes To Watch Out For* (would someone please tell her they're too, too seventies!). Key chains I keep without knowing why. A white braided rope bracelet like everyone had one summer at the Cape.

I may not wear these trinkets anymore, but my personal archeology reminds me who I've been.

I spent last weekend at a women's gathering high in the Oregon mountains. We pitched our tent alongside a raucously babbling creek. At the craft fair a woman sold natural jewelry, the kind we dykes like so much. I fell for a handsome necklace of hematite, a silvery-black stone reputed to have a grounding effect on its wearer. Later, I ran into a lesbian Realtor friend who'd bought one too. On the spot we declared it a butchstone. I'll wear it until it goes into my jewelry box. Like my gym whistle, my pinky rings, like the Zippo in my pocket.

No Place Like Home (1991)

Good-bye, Oregon. I hate to think of leaving, but come election day I fear I'll get a message that I'm not wanted here. Me and my kind. Less than animals, they call us.

The question, though, is where to go?

I'm on my way home from Texas, away from thriving gay communities in Dallas and Houston where I visited the two Crossroads Markets book-and-gay-culture stores. Away from lesbians at least as warm and enthusiastic as any I've ever met.

But it won't be Texas I move to if I'm not wanted in Oregon. For years they've been fighting a battle to get their penal code rewritten so that sodomy is decriminalized. It's too hot for me in the Lone Star State weather-wise as well as politically.

It won't be Colorado. Their Measure 2 is as dangerous to Americans as Oregon's Measure 9. Even though it looks like pro-rights Coloradans may win—their *No On Two* T-shirts sell like hotcakes, primarily to nongays—despite all that I wouldn't want to settle down where there is such a strong movement of bigots.

Do I want to live in Florida? Only if I can have the house next door to Anita Bryant. Just kidding!

San Francisco, our mecca, should be a natural. However, I've been told that men, who blend right in on Castro Street, are being trained in the South and sent to San Francisco to start storefront churches. From that position they establish grassroots footholds. For us it was a matter of daring to show our faces where we lived. This is conspiracy, this importation of trained missionaries with a political agenda.

Ironically, the Midwest and East seem like safe havens these days. Parents of gay transplants are waving the dusty *Come Home!* flags and tempting us. I know, though, that the Right plans to win the more politically ripe states and then deal with the crowded liberal cities on the national level.

It won't be the East Coast or the Midwest. Just the thought of New York brings the songs of my gay youth back to haunt me: "Nowhere To Run," "Town Without Pity," "Somewhere" from *West Side Story*. Will there never be a safe place for gays, for women, for Jews, for people of color in this world?

Meanwhile there is good news. People from all over are offering help. Even staunch conservatives like William F. Buckley are disowning this attack on human rights. Did the Republican convention, by going too, too far, show its true colors so brightly it opened previously closed eyes? I like to think of their current shenanigans as the death throes of the right wing.

I'd rather believe that this attack is survivable without surrendering an inch. My haven isn't a site across the mountains someplace I've never been, but a home I'm building right here. Looks like I'll stay and fight.

CULTURAL BOGEYMEN: CENSORS (1991)

Horror movies were a passion I shared with my older brother when I was in my early teens. He'd drive his little red sports car from New Jersey to Queens and spend the weekend with the family. After our parents went to bed we'd darken the living room and popcorn our way through the stormy landscapes and ridiculously terrifying traumas of some Goddess-forsaken town in the sticks. I didn't watch the most terrifying scenes, but Peter Lorre characters, among others, were priceless. It was a silly and satisfying pastime. Today, I still cover my eyes to avoid filmed violence and I never even enter the Horror section at Chuck's Video in town.

I'm not sure what changed to make the bogeyman come to life in a way that really threatens me. Perhaps, as a grown-up sixties' kid, it's my awareness of the true horrors of the world: crimes against people for fun, for greed, for power. Perhaps as the courage of my innocence wears thinner through the years, I identify too much with victims. Perhaps I've become aware of horrors that make me the victim.

As a middle-class white American woman, real-life atrocity is only a possibility, not the probability it is for so many others. Being queer makes life riskier, but being a queer writer raises the specter of a special horror, one that hasn't yet made it into Chuck's.

The horror is censorship. And I don't have to wait for late Saturday nights to see the presence of the villains, censors, on TV. I don't have to go the Horror section at Chuck's to find them. Ironically, despite the increasing violence of those films, that's where the censors seem to show up least frequently. More likely, they're lurking in Drama around some clean light bit of fun such as *Desert Hearts* or in Comedy around *La Cage Aux Folles*.

Life might be easier if these creepy censors did show their word-hungry fangs in the wee small hours of TV time. One horror show we used to watch had a host—was it Vincent Price?—who'd introduce the film and cackle ghoulishly. Now *that* would be a clever bit of marketing, wouldn't it, hiring Jesse Helms to MC a late-night gay series featuring *Personal Best* or a restoration of *Spartacus*.

Seriously, though, the thought of censors sends chills up and down my spine like no howling wolf or slavering ogre ever has. What would happen if a law passed saying, for example, that 2 Live Crew (to whom I've never listened) couldn't perform because I find them offensive? A month or a year later, someone would be in court telling a judge why my books are offensive to them and that the judge should throw the book—my books—at me.

In the midseventies I worked in a store that sold *Hustler* and a bunch of other magazines from behind the counter. There were a lot of lesbians—some feminist, some not—working for this chain, and for once, we had some perhaps illusory power. Men would come in and ask for a copy. We'd pick *Hustler* up by its corner, dangle it across to the counter, and drop it like a filthy diaper. Even we managers, whose income increased with sales from these high-ticket items, would shove the buyers' change at them and rudely turn our backs.

I was possibly the worst. As a trainer, for example, I'd teach sympathetic trainees to store the magazines not just behind, but under the counter. There, accidentally, they'd be covered up by layers of paraphernalia until the night crews couldn't even locate them. When the magazine vendor came in a month later there'd be the whole stack ready for credit. He—always a he—would cut the delivery for the following month. We'd fiendishly revel in the success of our campaign.

All those magazines seem so benign now. I'm told there are publications out there that depict acts more horrid than I can imagine. The movies I once watched were kids' nightmares compared to the pure evil available to those who, incomprehensibly, seek it. My books, erotic scenes and all, are innocuous. The censors who put lesbian love stories in the same category with victim-sex images have gotten something twisted in their values.

Yet they do it. And that scares me as much as anything else. My words threaten no one, though there are those who feel threatened by them. And my words, in the eyes of censors, are on a par with violence and acts that literally hurt living beings. This is what makes the issue of censorship so difficult for me.

Fear used to be something I watched on TV. Now, I fear my own bogeyman, the censor. As hard as it was for me to sell magazines that used women to titillate het men, it would be even harder to live with laws that gave the power to order those magazines out of my store. Yet if I denounce censorship entirely, do I accept that I must coexist, powerless, with printed, recorded, or celluloid unbridled violence against women, children, gays, and others?

What's the solution, if, in finally giving a lesbian writer freedom from censorship, others are free to sell the atrocities used to give thrills today? I want to ask what's happening to the world that there's even a demand for this kind of thing. But I know there are people out there who ask the same question about my work. Taste, harmless or not, can never be regulated, yet I can't cover my eyes to penchants that make people (or animals) disposable sex toys.

I wish for those old Saturday nights with popcorn and my brother. Horror movies may give me the creeps. I'm not exactly the audience targeted by cable channels devoted to the *Playboy* mentality. If, though, I should turn on the TV and should stumble across either, I'm unlikely to petition any politicians to amend the Constitution. So far I don't need anyone's protection. I can switch the channel. So far.

FOREIGN TONGUES (1992)

I recently read a book about a highly principled dyke who resists the political wave of her time, is arrested for exhibiting her sexuality, hounded out of her vocation for being who she is, and, for lack of a community, falls in love with a come-hither straight woman who doesn't have the guts to act on her feelings.

The novel, *Another Love*, by Erzsébet Galgóczi, is tragic, but even more tragic is the fact that the tale of a lesbian in Budapest during the 1950s Soviet occupation of Hungary should sound so startlingly familiar today. The concept of gay exiles is as ancient as closets. The most famous American lesbians of the first half of our century—Alice, Gertrude, Romaine, Natalie, Renee, Genêt—were literally exiles. Today we're holding our ground in DC and LA, in Dallas and Seattle, but we're no less exiles within our own lands.

How can we feel anything but other observing the presidential pseudo-election which speaks for us not one whit? How can we possibly feel *part of* when millions of moviegoers enjoy films that depict us as enemies of Decent People? How can we hold up our heads to be counted when voters cast ballots of disenfranchisement? This gay movement has been going strong for over twenty years, and sometimes it's hard to see through the backlash to the patches of space we've won. Sometimes it's downright discouraging.

A friend just sent me one of my old letters, circa 1963. I romantically wrote about my "life work," about the need to change my impending college major from phys ed to English so that I could follow the example of Radclyffe Hall. "Someday," I wrote, I would "try to help. One novel, maybe, but a step further. One poem even. I'm going to help. I swear."

Thirty years later I sometimes wonder if I should have stuck to girls' sports. Another friend who lives a closeted, apparently comfortable life recently confided, "I hate the word dyke." Right after that still another friend told me, "I hate that word queer." For at least ten years now many of us have been writing and talking about these being our words, reclaiming them from those who have made each queer term a curse. If we rejected every word tainted with jibes and insults and threats, we'd have nothing to call ourselves at all.

To remain visible citizens of the world we need to grab back what's ours, claim it, and stand up to be counted. Finally nongay society is feeling a little bit better about using the word gay, but it's become a male adjective. Lesbians are exiles even in our own language. The words we use to legitimize our lives become foreign to our tongues. As any oppressed people, we risk having not only no place, but no vocabulary that tells who we really are.

The dykes and faggots in my small town talked for years about introducing a gay 12-step meeting into a huge annual recovery gathering. The first response from the nongay organizers was, "No! That's too dangerous, you'll get hurt!" Read: the organizers didn't want those big, bad, threatening words, lesbian and gay, on a program. We blended for a few more years into the general populace. But we'd been to Living Sober in San Francisco and had tasted of freedom.

Last year's gathering hosted the first queer meeting. When I was told who led the meeting I tried to keep my mouth from falling open. "But she's not gay!" I protested. She's a kind, brave, wise woman who's been on the outside herself, but what does it mean when a nongay must lead us? That we need a protector? That we don't think enough of ourselves or our sobriety to take our own space? That we need a translator who speaks the language of our oppressors to stake our claims? That we really and truly don't belong?

During Women's History Week I attended a local celebration. The audience was primarily lesbian. The performers were lesbian. The exhibiting artists were lesbian. The history had been to a great extent made by lesbians. Yet the event dared not name itself lesbian and the keynote speaker was not a lesbian. She acknowledged that fact immediately (very immediately) and spoke of the accomplishments of the straight women in the community. Her words revealed a clear dichotomy: Us and You. Only three of Us walked out. Lesbians had invited her to speak. Lesbians gave her a standing ovation. The woman was well-meaning, but don't we respect ourselves enough to want to hear a lesbian speak? To recognize when we are, even unintentionally, being Matronized?

Something happened not long ago that took me right back to grammar school. I still remember the humiliation I felt when my best friend from first to sixth grade dropped me for a boy-crazy girl. Is it significant that I'd had my first lesbian experience with this lost friend? A few months ago Lover and I were hanging around with a nongay woman. She seemed glad to have our company. Then she dropped out of sight. The next time I saw her she didn't acknowledge me, though she appeared to introduce her brand-spanking-new boyfriend to everyone else in the group. Is there a message here about where lesbians fit into this society?

I'm feeling battered these days. Ultrasensitive. I see homophobia, internalized and free-floating, everywhere. Don't even ask me what I thought about the film *Fried Green Tomatoes* which demonstrated the most adept straddling of antithetical worlds I've ever seen. Yes, the lesbianism could have plucked at these queer little heartstrings, but my nongay acquaintances assure me that you didn't have to see it, wouldn't see it, if you didn't want to. If you didn't live in lesbianland, a country within a country, where women are still starved for images of ourselves.

And that's what exile is about. The heroine in *Another Love* didn't have to die escaping over the border. She could have gone into a quiet exile without leaving Hungary, the way so many of us live in exile right here within our hetero-totalitarian states. But she was highly principled, a resister, impractically out. Like, thank the Goddess, so many of us.

RADICAL ACTS (1992)

A friend called to tell me to watch the first night of the Democratic Convention. She described the moving speeches given by two people living with HIV disease, one of them a gay man. I flipped on the TV and caught a brief interview with Governor Clinton. When asked if he was concerned about negative fallout for his support of such an unmentionable subject, he replied simply but firmly, "We can't hide our heads in the sand."

"Oh, shit," I thought, also aware that he's supporting gay rights, "he's been radicalized." I was astonished that I could even entertain a fantasy that The People—the gay people, the poor people, the disabled people, the old people, the non-male, non-white, non-Christian, non-married people, and our very visible representatives at the Democratic Convention—might be heard again in America. I couldn't handle the upsurge of hope. Later, President Carter spoke, and I stood in front of my archenemy the boob tube with tears in my eyes, emotions like a tidal wave, and renewed faith that I didn't want.

How many times can hope be dashed? Idealistic spirits squashed? I have cast my queer vote in every election since 1966. Jimmy Carter is the only president who has ever represented me. Yet I vote on as if somehow this simple and powerful tool is enough to topple the Republican dynasty.

I talked to our activist friend Sky during the convention. "Don't watch it," she warned me, "it'll drive you crazy!" Perhaps it already had. I confessed to her that despite all my political disappointments, I'd been entertaining half-baked impulses of becoming active in the local Democratic Party. It was, after all, an organization that was in place and we need one to help us fight the relentless right wing bullies who have put on the upcoming statewide ballot a dangerous measure that would legalize discrimination against Oregon gays and set a national precedent. Sky admitted that she, too, had wondered if we ought to look at the existing political structures.

I made a phone call. As it turns out, some of the most vocal liberals in town form the core of the Party. In this Republican enclave, though, it's floundering for lack of membership, funding, and energy. What a radical idea, working with the Democratic Party. Is there really room in it for me?

Bill Clinton says he'll represent us. Can we turn America around? Sometimes I feel so persecuted, I discount the power I have. I dwell on the progress we're not making and ignore major achievements— like a candidate who's listening to the voters. I forget that if everyone who's been slapped in the face by Republican greed turns the other cheek and storms the polls with vengeance in their hearts, we can win.

The machines that count the ballots don't know female from male, or dyke from Mrs. America. Politicians can discount us, but our queer anonymous votes are powerful and binding. The voting booth is one sure place where a gay person will be listened to. Registering to vote now and casting a ballot in November may be the most radical action any one of us can take.

SOMETHING SNAPPED (1992)

The week before Halloween and the election I went to a fundraiser for a progressive candidate in my county. I was there early to help Lover prepare for her set. We carried equipment through the chilly, dark night. Inside performers bustled, doing sound checks, blocking the stage, running through their dances. The excitement level was high. It was a safe place and I was among allies.

But as well-meaning as that crowd seemed to be, I felt alien. I was, in those last weeks, suspicious of every nongay who didn't wear a supportive button opposing the ballot measure that would take away my rights. And that night, something in me snapped. Crazy thoughts, crazy acts drove me. Would snipers pick us off as we left? Our house, a half-hour away, was standing unguarded. Was it under attack? I fled into the night and sped toward home, maddened by fear. I switched on the radio to drown out my crazed thoughts. The oldies station came in strong. The Shirelles sang "Will You Still Love Me Tomorrow?"

I felt the excitement, titillating danger, and exaltation of a long-ago moment. This was the actual song that had played the first time I kissed a woman. This was what it was all about. Out of the night came a thousand nights, came a thousand feelings, came enormous gratitude for being gay. I cried with feelings of heartened renewal as I hurtled past the farms and the neat homes of nuclear families, through a county so antigay the statewide campaign had written us off in terms of votes.

I was no longer here at all. I was in New York, downtown, in the romantic, mysterious world of Greenwich Village in 1960. I was holding the hand of my first lover, that soft warm hand, I was smelling her perfume and her cigarette breath. We were huddling in doorways, making out in moments stolen from society, laughing at our daring and the sheer pleasure of our rebel kisses, entranced with each other, but also with being gay.

Can any nongay ever understand the rapture of coming out, of stepping that one small and infinite step beyond the world as we'd known it, a world where we'd never fit in, which didn't make sense to us? Can anyone but a queer person comprehend the transformation that comes with those first heady moments, months, years when the universe, which had been topsy-turvy, rights itself? It has nothing to do with sex, though that was once the only way we had to express it. Where now we exult in ourselves at marches and rallies, in art and song, then we exulted in shadows made bright by our intense joy.

In my car, thirty-two years later, all those early emotions rushed at me. I remembered my delight in being given a key to the gay world. It didn't matter that I was only fifteen and knew no gay but my lover. It didn't matter that we had nowhere to be ourselves but an ice-cream parlor on Sixth Avenue that didn't welcome us. It may even have enhanced the experience for us—normal teenagers—that we had to hide from our parents, teachers, friends. Who wanted to share what we'd discovered with those dull people who had tried so unsuccessfully to claim us? Nothing mattered but our gay world, the cautious looks of recognition we got from others like us, the hints from the square world that so many of us were shining stars in straight costumes, and the relieved, celebratory validation that comes with self-discovery.

Now here I was in rural America, tears streaming down my face as I rushed home for reassurance that my world had not been destroyed because I am gay. It was stupid to drive home. I was missing most of the performances, I was alone and more vulnerable that I would be in that crowd, yet I had to walk through my fear, had to cross my unlighted driveway to the house that shelters Lover and me, feeling blessed that it still stood, that I have survived to love this woman who shares it with me.

Sure, just before the election, gays, going out at night, put their animals in kennels for safety. Sure, even in our relatively safe town we would not let one another leave meetings alone but went to our cars in groups. Sure, lovers would wake in the middle of the night and whisper, what was that sound? Sure, friends shared last night's nightmares by day. Sure, toward the end, there was nothing to give one another but our presences, hugs, weak smiles.

Of course we turned to counselors to cope with the coming-apart feeling that accompanies the last moments before a bomb drops. Of course asthmatics went on inhalers, diabetics increased their dosages, gays with heart conditions found themselves in emergency rooms. Of course we felt terror, doom, rage, desperation. And there were stories, a thousand stories.

The lesbian grandmother: "I'm not normally like this," she says in her soft measured Southern accent. During the campaign a man had approached her, offering a slander sheet about gays that was put out by the vicious Oregon Citizen's Alliance. "I took it," she says, "because I wanted to see what they were saying. 'Are you voting yes on measure nine?' the man asked me. I said, 'Absolutely not.' 'Why?' he asked. 'Because I'm a lesbian!'" Incredulous, she says, "He told me, perfectly seriously, 'That doesn't matter.'" She shakes her head, her color high with indignation. "And then something snapped. I started yelling and screaming at him right there on the sidewalk."

We all snapped in our own ways. Yet gays have borne the unbearable since the beginning of time. No movement of hate and fear can erase the sweetness of loving and living true to who we are. Kissing in the shadows or in the full light of day, loving and being ourselves—that's what it's all about. Whether we're just-out teenagers dodging adults or lesbian grandmothers standing up for ourselves, we cherish our difference. And there is no question that, once again, we will prevail.

THE WAR ON GAY YOUTH (1992)

I've been trying to remember what it felt like to be a gay kid.
The effort is like forcing myself to walk, undefended, back into
a war zone. Though I almost immediately loved being gay and
enjoyed every moment of joy I could steal, there could have been
no more emotionally—and often physically—vulnerable feeling than
the abrupt reality of a world legislating, preaching, teaching, and
safeguarding against me.

I was only a kid! How could it have happened? Overnight my
very tender, new, deliciously overwhelming emotions had become
criminal. My tomboy clothes, illegal. My best friend judged a sinister
influence. I was in enemy territory with no rights but silence, no
sustenance but untried inner strengths, no peers but that fourteen-
year-old friend-turned-lover—and I knew no choice but to deny
myself or hide.

What kind of barbarity was this? I might as well have been taken
prisoner and tortured. My severe depressions, my escape into liquor
and drugs, my lousy school grades—what in hell did the world expect
from a teenaged prisoner of war? There are no Geneva conventions
binding anyone when it comes to a kid who falls in love with someone
of the same sex.

Over thirty years later the change has begun. Candace Steele
is Northwest Regional Director of Parents and Friends of Lesbians
and Gays. She's also mother of three daughters, one of whom is non-
lesbian. A licensed professional counselor, Steele is investigating
ways to serve children who have recognized their gay sexuality.

The problem Steele has encountered is the extreme liability of
professionals attempting to help this particular client population. One
clergyman she knows of has had to purchase an enormous amount of
additional insurance just to provide such support. How many brave
people can afford the risk of entering the war zone?

According to a 1989 US Health and Human Services report on youth suicide, gays account for thirty percent of the five thousand suicides committed in America every year by people from fifteen to twenty-four. That's a lot of dead kids, Americans who are obliterated in a war far deadlier and more insidious than any trumped-up invasion of foreign soils.

The same report found that conflicts over sexual identity force 26 percent of gay youth to leave home. Where do they go from there? How many of the runaways, the homeless, the institutionalized, the arrest statistics, the dying—how many represent gays who didn't make it out there on the streets?

I was lucky. My family could afford to send me to college. I immediately got in trouble, lots of trouble, but it's easier to learn to survive on campus than downtown. I lied, I hid, I used my talents and probably hurt people, but I somehow survived. There were two gay male teachers who befriended me, some dorm counselors moral enough to understand that my humanity was as precious as theirs, an old high-school gym teacher who acknowledged our commonality. That's all it took from the adult world, a few courageous people who were willing, each in her/his own way, to say *You're okay*.

All around me, though, I watched other kids fare less well. The boy who called himself bisexual and suicided from shame. The girl who proved she was straight by getting pregnant. The young woman who dropped out, confusion sapping her energy and study time. The dopers and drinkers so lost to chemicals it didn't matter anymore if they had a sexuality, or who they shared it with.

Some of us were nourished by our very defiance. Even as society disdained us, a rebel culture emerged. For gays it became Stonewall and those liberating nights propelled us into a new, if slowly evolving, world that produced such miracles as PFLAG.

In the early seventies I lived in a women's collective. One night two teenaged lesbians showed up on our doorstep. They were in love and had run away from home. I'd seen those two before, smooching in hundreds of ill-lit hallways, thrown out of gay bars, locked behind heavy doors in psychiatric wings, on the streets wildly shouting threats to kill themselves while friends calmed, dragged them away. Jailbait, we were called in the sixties, sisters in the seventies.

Those two made it to lesbian adulthood, though not together. But to this day gay youngsters marry from fear or convenience. Consume themselves with partying because the real world is too hard. To this day few can stay in relationships; if you hate yourself, how do you respect a partner? Garbage, they are still garbage tossed out by society, herded into closets, and told it's their own fault if they hurt. And they do hurt, daily they're damaged, mutilated by the scourges of isolation, scorn, discrimination, random violence, rejection, and self-images so low they don't register on any scale. How do they grow up at all?

This year Massachusetts has created the first state commission committed to reducing the gay teenage suicide rate. The consequences of such a move, initiated by Governor William Weld, may be enormous. If New York had had such an entity when I was a baby dyke, would it have made a difference? I think so. I grasped at every lifeline I could find. Just knowing a governmental body was concerned, knew I was out there, wounded, would have strengthened me. Certainly the commission will eventually have an impact on the hurdles faced by counselors like Ms. Steele. It's a big step in ending the war on gay youth.

I sometimes run into an androgynous baby-faced young woman in town these days. She wears an old coat that looks heavier than her. And boots, big dyke boots. When our eyes meet I imagine that hers go wide in mute recognition. It's terrifically exciting to be on the verge of living your real life. I want her to be able to enjoy being who she is. Finally I can, but it's all too easy, looking at her, to feel again all the bravado and terror of a gay youth, to, even now, feel the wounds of my own battle.

Changing the World (1993)

Here we go again. Oregon's radical right lost, but now it has carefully targeted twenty-four cities and eight counties for local antigay ballot measures. I live in a county on the hit list. In the newspaper a local right-winger claimed, "It's a foregone conclusion" that the gluttonous Right would win our little county.

He's wrong. With no opposition our county passed the 1988 antigay ballot measure only by 66 percent. After our active campaigning in 1992 the antigay vote dropped to 56 percent. The new measure is a silly piece of double-talk, tilting at windmills, and a desperate attempt by the Right to get something, anything, on the ballot to keep the funds rolling in and to gather more power. All we need to do is reach another 6 percent of the voters! I wouldn't have thought it possible a year ago, yet it is. And if we can do it in this depressed, politically volatile area, believe me, anyone can.

We've come so very far. Because Ballot Measure 9 radically increased hate crimes, Oregon's Governor Barbara Roberts held a Hate Crime Summit after the election. Out of that came a Bias Crimes Commission right here in Redneck City, USA This would have been unthinkable a year ago.

The divisions in communities were so huge after the election that our state Civil Rights Commission went around the state asking for testimony to help heal the rifts. As a consequence a civil rights agenda is being created that addresses gay issues.

The Oregon legislature has before it, for the twentieth year, civil rights legislation to protect us. Because just about every Oregon politician currently seated opposed Measure 9, and because this new attack is a slap at these legislators' stands, this could be the year the legislation passes.

The right has created a monster. It's not just Oregon that's been awakened; all of America is stirring. One has only to pick up a newspaper, gay or mainstream, to see us in action, from Queer Nation to the Episcopalians. The gay and progressive communities are an enraged whole now, and there's no such thing as isolating a county, a city, or a group. Our local organizations are in place. More volunteers are emerging every day. The whole world is still watching.

We've got a friend in the White House. However aggressive he feels he can be, President Clinton's not going to set us back like the Reagan-Bush vaudeville act did. Our friends have been seated in the Senate and House too. The scale is tipping toward us. I'm wired, like a hurdler at the line, waiting to fling my weight into the balance.

I've seen it work, this process of change. I particularly remember the peace marches in New York when I was part of the surge of people opposing the war in Vietnam, shouting with passion and conviction, intent on changing the world. And we did it. We stopped not only a war in progress, but the way the nation looked at war forevermore. That friend in the White House was one of us.

It's time to change the world again. I'm going to the March On Washington. Me and over a million others. April 25, 1993 will go into the history books right next to the Stonewall Inn riots. The nation's capital will swell at its seams with the largest number of protesters in history. Before Stonewall the gay nation was fragmented, hiding in closets without connecting doors, lines of communication, or even knowledge of our numbers. Twenty-four years later a fraction of us, one to two million, will march as one, shout as one, be heard as one. That ought to be enough to tip the scales.

I'm marching because everybody will count. I admit that I didn't want to do that grueling cross-country flight yet another time this year. I'd rather not worry about the dangers of exposing myself to homophobic nuts. I'd rather not crash with relative strangers on some kind host's floor. I hate to leave Lover, who's too ill to travel. I don't look forward to scrimping to pay off the airfare. Yet I know that if I'm there, thousands as hesitant as I've been will be there too.

Local skirmishes are the right wing's last stand. The conservatives' lies about special rights are wearing thin. It's obvious to all but the most embittered that the right-wing agenda has to do with backlash: against gays for emerging from the closet, against the civil rights movement for mortally wounding racist institutions, against feminism for setting women free. It's also obvious that if gays give an inch, the right will make straight for those other groups that fought before us.

Those who marched last time—minus the loved ones we've lost to AIDS, cancer, and too many other causes—tasted our strength and are returning for more. Those of us who stayed home can't be kept down on the farm another second. Whole coalitions of nongays and gays from Colorado and Florida and Maine and Oregon are reserving trains and cars and planes and buses. It's clear that this is not simply a gay issue. We're watching democracy as it's attacked from within. Even in America, champion of freedom, we're staving off enemies of human rights.

I'm incredibly excited. I feel like I did at age six when my parents somehow got tickets to a kids' TV show. I want to leave for DC now. I remember watering the garden during the last march, so moved that I cried as I listened to National Public Radio's coverage. I vowed not to miss this one.

For months I thought I couldn't go, and then the airlines—incredibly—dropped their rates for the march. The only barriers left were my fears. When I weighed my decision I realized that any one of us could tip the scales, that I could do it. We're changing the world again. Watch us.

AFTER THE MARCH (1993)

After the march, when we return to Shickshinny, Pennsylvania, Flathead, Idaho, and Wagon Mound, New Mexico, there will be no time to rest and regroup. Voices raw from chanting, slowed by jet lag or all-nighters on the bus, we will nevertheless be the clarions of an energy raised to explosive heights. A million marchers is more than some whole nations: Iceland, Luxembourg. A million veterans of such an exultation of power will come flooding home like soldiers after victory, certain that nothing can stop us now.

Nothing can—and nothing ever could. Like all oppressed groups gay people have been around since the dawn of civilization. We may be a built-in method of population control, and we may be a gift bestowed on earth to celebrate life through the arts and ceremony. With all the fighting about civil rights, I sometimes lose sight of our special place in the world, the magical plane we move through with our glorious purple pomp, our inspired visions, and gentle transformative touch. Unfettered, we bring a light to the earth no other people can claim.

The first time I was aware of being, as the drugstore pulp covers say, in that nowhere land between the sexes, I was old enough to feel ashamed, but young enough not to know why. I was thirteen when my family spent two weeks on a lake in New England. Children abounded in the cabins, trailers, and jerry-rigged shacks. I spent my time reading under the pines or clambering over rocks at the lakefront. The other kids were either in the water, swimming and water skiing, or in the rec hall, batting a Ping-Pong ball across a table. One day a little boy came up to me as I pretended to wait for a sunfish to interest itself in the baitless hook at the end of my bamboo pole.

"Are you a tomboy?" he asked.

I probably mumbled something adolescently assured like, "I don't know." That was the extent of the conversation. He went back to his friends and I to my dreams on the rocks.

My life was never the same.

To the self-consciousness of any thirteen-year-old was added a sense of difference. True, it had always been there or why wasn't I water skiing and playing Ping-Pong? But it had begun to take on shape, the shape of androgyny.

Over the next twenty years I never hardened to the taunts. Most of them were maddeningly repetitive variations of: Are you a boy or a girl? I couldn't, still can't, believe how seriously disturbed others would get over my appearance. It wasn't like I ran around in drag. It even happened to me when I was in skirts. I wasted hundreds of hours wondering exactly what it was that made me look so different from other girls and women.

Back on the lakefront it was pretty clear. I was lanky, had short hair which I slicked back every chance I got, wore jeans every waking hour, and, in one photograph, walked around with a chocolate cigarette hanging off my lower lip, the packet in the rolled-up sleeve of my flannel shirt. No wonder the other kids wanted nothing to do with me. We are marked young, and so are they.

Just as our in-between postures, gestures, and walks identify some gays, so does the discomfort of our challengers mark them. What is the signal we send out? What does it provoke in others that they react with avoidance, name-calling, and physical violence?

A friend suggested that we threaten the mandated urge to procreate. Do nongay people perceive us as a danger to the species, as genocide incarnate? I know the feminist theories about the patriarchal imperative to reproduce so that the male, by owning women who will make many sons and fertile daughters, has a ready-made workforce and protector of his wealth. Yet surely in this age of artificial insemination, alternative families, and overpopulation it's obvious that gays are not going to end civilization. (Except French civilization: recently a bill was almost passed there which would have barred lesbians from legal artificial insemination.)

I think this aversion to gay people goes deeper. Goes to the first human creatures roaming a volcanic, green planet, before thought went beyond food and shelter. Before any kind of moral code was created. Before spirituality was reduced to bowing to mirror images of males. Perhaps it had to do with envy of those who didn't need to hunt and gather for offspring. Perhaps it was resentment at "sissy" men who were taken care of by other men. Perhaps it was anger at "butchy" women who rejected sex with men while at the same time competing with them for scarce sustenance.

This enters the realm of racial memory, a concept not exactly generally accepted. Why else, though, should an innocently androgynous child trigger such deep antagonism?

As we return from the nation's capital to our communities, can we look squarely at the fact that we do scare our neighbors? We can thrash about in self-righteous anger and spew forth high moral platitudes till we're blue in the face, but those Americans we call our enemies are just like us inside. There is a common ground. We all speak the same languages. Most of the movement to strip us of civil rights is comprised of people convinced by a handful of power brokers that the solution to something—poverty? crime? drug use?— lies in shoving us back in the closet.

We need to learn to help the frightened let go of a fear that no longer serves anyone well. After our enormous show of strength at the march, those who went and those who watched will feel empowered. Based on 10 percent of the population, there are 24.8 million gay Americans spread across this country, each of us an ambassador. Perhaps we'll again accept the mantle of ceremonial roles some cultures have historically assigned to gays and bring our vision, our special light, our power home.

PERVERTS (1993)

Lover came home to me last night after a long business drive with two women coworkers. In the way women are wont during times of such involuntary intimacy, they had a great giddy time. Apparently The Subject came up and one of the coworkers, both of whom are nongay, shared that her initials gave rise in her youth to the nickname Pervert. As the other coworker is nicknamed Bert, the three cheerily dubbed themselves Bert, Pervert, and Invert.

Lover had to explain the meaning of invert, an old psychiatric term for queerfolk popularized in the days of Havelock Ellis and Radclyffe Hall. There she was, teaching queer culture to heterosexuals in the middle of right-wing heaven. Three people managed to respect one another's choices and even have some fun with their diversity.

That touched me. It helped me climb a bit higher out of the pesky melancholy with which I've been wrestling for a couple of months. The doldrums began to lift, I believe, when I canceled my subscription to the local rabble-rousing newspaper. I wrote to the editor and explained, among other things, that ours was the only paper I knew of to make a front-page story out of the Girl Scouts' vote to allow non-Christian members to pray to their own deities. Big fat hairy deal, right? Where I live that's sacrilege.

Colorado's Amendment 2 was a big part of my gloom. It was inconceivable to me that some man in a gown could hold the fates of so many of us in his probably heterosexist hands. I try not to dwell on Judge Bayless's rejection of the argument that we are a suspect class which does need protection. The very fact that Amendment 2 exists is proof of that unfortunate status.

Can you blame me and the rest of the queers in Oregon for a little despondency? There is another ballot measure coming at us this year. Maybe if we win this time, too, we can do it again in '95! Some of us are toying with the idea of refusing to participate in this rape of gay energy. What if we use all that campaign money, all that time, to elect humane politicians, or, for example, to bring Habitat For Humanity to our communities with enough hoopla to make the homo-haters hang their heads in shame? What, after all, would happen if the right wing gave a campaign and nobody came?

I know that I will survive all the political and legal wrangling, whatever the men in gowns and the uneducated, scapegoating voters decide. Heck, these relatively civilized battles, win or lose, are kid stuff next to what gays went through before Stonewall. It is the age-old heartaches that are the abiding losses.

We had another friend I'll call Subvert. For seven years Subvert, Lover, and I saw one another about twice a week. When I went through a painful breakup, Subvert was there to help haul me and my stuff out. I once even went on an all-women giddy long-distance trip with Subvert. When Lover and I got together, Subvert and her kids came over to visit. When Subvert had a near-fatal accident, we did what we could to help her and her family.

During the Measure 9 campaign, Lover and I both had bad, bad feelings about a group we attended with Subvert. Subtle we're-fed up-with-queers messages. It's-not-okay-to-be-different messages. It's-criminal-not-to-be-Christian messages. I felt as if I were lost in a blizzard, my sense of direction useless. I didn't know who to trust. Although we knew that Subvert and a few others supported us, first Lover, then I left. Where once we'd been open and accepted, I felt like an outcast.

After the election we learned from Jan, another nongay group member, that Subvert had voted for the antigay measure. Voted to strip us of our civil rights. Jan, who had worked on the campaign with us kept asking, "How could Subvert do that? How can I stay friends with her?" The months went on and Jan gave us reports of Subvert, who was becoming more and more involved in her fundamentalist church. Jan and another woman tried to reason with Subvert, reminding her of her old friendship with us, and getting in response a look that is becoming all too familiar as the right-wing virus multiplies. It is the look of someone in a *Star Trek* episode whose body has been inhabited by an alien being. A shutter in the eyes closes. The gaze is frozen. The face takes on a rigidity. The lips purse tight as a squeezed trigger.

Jan told me the other day that another lesbian from the group ran into Subvert in a grocery store. The lesbian, who had felt rebuffed by

Subvert during a previous contact, wanted to know where she stood. She walked up to Subvert and said hello. Subvert turned and, without a word, walked in the other direction.

"But what happened to Subvert? My Subvert?" Jan asks, mourning the loss of her friend. The new creed Subvert has adopted seems like a drug, an addiction that can only satisfy when it becomes stronger than reason, than compassion, than friendship. The latest news is that Subvert has become active politically, another soldier in the right-wing army.

Losing friends is not kid stuff. Nor is it a new heartache—ask any old gay. Yet if the pain of losing friends has always been one consequence of being gay, so has the joy of finding new ones. Thank the Goddess for the Berts and the Perverts.

CAMPING IN PROVINCETOWN (1994)

I have noticed that there seem to be two types of camping in the gay world. The kind the guys do is supremely portable and fun, like a tried-and-true recipe that can be counted on to cook up perfectly and please the guests every time. Women have our own brand of camp.

I never camped until I was twenty-five when I got together with a woman whose mother had been a Girl Scout leader. We were going to Provincetown for the weekend and could not get there until late Friday night, so I made reservations. Tried to make reservations. Maybe there are gay-owned campgrounds there now, but in 1970 the first one I called asked who made up the party. "My friend and I." The disembodied, sour voice on the phone announced, "This is a *family* campground." I knew what *that* meant, just what it means now: We know all about how you seduce children and steal wives. What could I do? The other campground got our business and we managed to seduce no one but each other all weekend.

Actually there was another time when I camped. Tried to camp. I must have been about thirteen, awkward and silent and at a loss about my place in the world. My older brother spent a lot of time with me then, treating me like a human being and not a gay adolescent, which probably saved my life. One Saturday he took me camping in his tiny red Austin Sprite.

That night he set up his pup tent. We dug a trench around it in case it rained. In case? When we awoke sometime before dawn we were in a pool of water. He did some baling and cursing until we finally put up the Austin's convertible top and slept in the car the best we could, soaked.

Twelve years and no camping experience later, my girlfriend and I arrived at the pitch-dark campground in Provincetown. We headed to the outskirts of the property (would they throw us out if they discovered we were gay?) and set up camp by the headlights of my VW. Well, to tell the truth, the Girl Scout leader's daughter set up. I busied myself digging a trench for the inevitable rain.

It wasn't that I'd never been a Girl Scout. You just won't find any camping badges on my sash. I belonged to a city troop and the closest we got to camping was a day trip to a park. As a matter of fact, other than my brother's soggy pup tent, the first significant use of the word camp in my life referred to the notorious Campy Corner in Greenwich Village, the meeting place for the underage crowd that thronged the Village streets at night.

Since the night we set up by headlights, I have chanced rain and outdoorsy homophobes dozens of times for the dubious pleasure of sharing a temporary home with pushy insects and messy birds. I am hardly nostalgic for the joys of camping in a Connecticut state park, anesthetizing the itch of mosquito bites with a case of Colt 45. Or of tenting in a muddy field reserved for gnats at the inaugural New England Women's Music Retreat.

The first time I went off to the woods for a weekend with Lover (Camper Extraordinaire and ex-camp counselor) about 75 percent of what could have gone wrong, did, from rain to a broken cook stove. A couple of years later we thought we'd get smart and buy a teensy antique Chinook which carries its kitchen. Off we went camping on a Memorial Day weekend. Trying to camp. After searching in the dark for our backwoods site and finding no one to ask directions of except an almost invisible cow chewing her cud in the middle of a road, we spent the weekend confronting local teens wielding boom boxes, siccing park rangers on men illegally driving ATVs in the shallow fragile river, hunting an appliance repair shop when our mini-fridge went out, dropping an exhaust pipe as we left the appliance shop parking lot, and losing both batteries—count them, two. We got pushed down the mountainside and didn't turn off the engine till we got home.

I've laughed till I cried at Suzanne Westenhoefer's tricked-into-camping-again shtick, and let me tell you, it's all true. Except for the part about the butches being the enthusiasts.

This summer the Chinook sits in the driveway, forlorn looking. We'd thought we'd repaired just about everything repairable on her, but darned if on a camping trip to see the sandhill cranes last winter her pop-top didn't develop an unplanned window right over the bed. I mean, it's no wonder so many lesbians come back from Michigan and gripe in *Lesbian Connection* about the Festival for the next twelve months: they've been camping!

Of course, the sandhill cranes and the weekends with Lover were worth it. Hey, that inaugural New England Women's Music Retreat was the first place I got to see real wildlife—dykes howling in abandon with Alix Dobkin under the moon. It's just that this city Girl Scout had a whole different idea of what camping entailed when I dreamed, at Campy Corner, of camping in Provincetown.

GENERATIONS OF GAYS (199?)

Anthony just called, in tears. It seems that her college class discussed values today. The instructor gave the class a list and asked for responses to various items like "a man in a dress." Anthony, a drag butch, told me, "I walked out. I couldn't listen to their homophobia." On the phone she kept saying, "They hate us. They just hate us."

Gay people are at an awkward stage on the road to independence. As difficult as it was for those of us who came out thirty or forty years ago, at least we weren't the victims of our own high expectations. Anthony has had the good fortune to have come out into an era when she could buy tapes of lesbian music and take her girl to a lesbian movie. She even has access to Leslie Feinberg on e-mail and has a college instructor who dares discuss difference in a classroom. But when he does, she is caught without her armor. Older dykes would have been ready for the onslaught of misinformation, prejudice, and contempt that she heard today. The young femmes and baby butches have nothing but the fledgling promises of gay liberation to comfort them.

I know they are taking care of themselves just fine, like we all do, but it's hard to watch yet another generation suffer at the hands of a twisted dominant culture. In this time of redefining moral good, I have come to believe that I have a moral responsibility to the young. Yet the old ways die hard, or not at all. Coming out is not an option for everyone.

How can we persuade John the local florist and Joyce the alluring pump jockey to poke their heads out of their closets when they are like groundhogs who never found spring? I asked Mean Norma Jean if, when she and her lover retired here, they had checked out the area for kindred spirits, for local attitudes toward gays, for safety. She replied, "No! We were too closeted." So closeted none of those things mattered because no one would ever, ever know. The gay groundhogs don't even believe in spring—fighting for it would never occur to them.

"I went back, though," Anthony told me, "and talked to the teacher. He wanted to know why I was so angry. He just didn't get it." I kept looking for words to comfort and support her, but all she really needed was to be told that she's okay. That a gang of heterosexists had insulted and degraded her—and they were wrong.

So I told Anthony she is okay. I hope it helped. The problem is, there's only one of me and so many Anthonys who need to be reminded that they're okay. Most of them have no one to call. Joyce and John are still sound asleep, not even dreaming of spring.

I don't blame our groundhogs. The reason I asked Mean Norma Jean about how she had approached relocating was because Lover came back from a trip to the Gulf Coast of Texas enthused enough about it to consider living in that area. I immediately started ticking off cons on my scaredy-cat list. Texas still has a sodomy law on the books. Texas just replaced Governor Ann Richards with George W. Bush. The Gulf Coast is filled with conservative retirees. Norma would call the moving van and play it safe once she got there, but Anthony, Anthony might not go there at all.

Anthony gave me more news on the phone. "This girl has been following me, trying to get me to run for student senate. I kept saying no, but I finally said yes. Then she told me that all the other senators are conservative. I don't need that." I agreed. Martyrdom is not a requirement for today's dykes.

But later, thinking about it, I decided maybe she did need it. Why shouldn't a gay kid be able to develop her leadership skills in college—whether she wears a tie or not. Why shouldn't a young lesbian find out if politicking is for her. The Victory Fund will need new candidates to support ten years down the line.

Beyond Anthony's immediate ambitions, there is the fact that gay hating is a societal disease just like child abuse is a family disease. All it takes is one generation to break the cycle. Not only is Anthony telling the straight world how wrong it is, but she is the future. When today's newborn comes out in twenty years it will be Anthony she turns to. Anthony's not going to tell little Sappho that she, unlike Mean Norma Jean, was too closeted. Anthony's not, like me, going to cautiously agree with her fear. Anthony's going to say, "Co-ol! Go for it!"

Even in the old days young dykes had their mentors. In 1963 I knew a gay gym teacher who spoke to me in code, at least letting me know she acknowledged me as a member of the club. She passed on the torch but dared not light it. My generation has set that torch ablaze.

And Anthony—Anthony called me back and said, "I'm going to do it. I'm going to run for student senate. Fuck 'em."

STONEWALL (1994)

I can only conjecture what I was doing June 28, 1969, when the faggots and dykes—oh, my!—showed the police how tired I was of hiding out in the apartment my lover and I shared in Bridgeport, Connecticut.

I wish I could say we heard the news and immediately caught a train to join in the next night's rioting. I wish I could say that I even remember hearing about the riots, but they simply were not significant to me. I have a lingering shame about that, about my lack of immediate insight into the importance of the riots. About the isolation that hid me from even a grapevine of excited, exaggerated reports that must have been just out of earshot.

It's likely that when I did hear some version of the events, probably from the straight media, that I at first retreated still further into our cozy closet, appalled. I had no qualms about marching for peace or demonstrating for civil rights—as long as it wasn't peace for gay people, as long as the civil rights were not my own. Drag queens tearing up parking meters? They'd ruin it for all of us! Never mind that it meant living with gagged mouths. Never mind that I was the one wearing drag: skirts and the rest of the costume required by heterosexist society. Never mind that my horror at the outlandish behavior of a bunch of gay men (it was years before I would hear that dykes were involved) was nothing more than a horror of my own twenty-three-year-old queer self. I know that I was not alone in questioning what Stonewall had to do with me and in dismissing the rioters as male troublemakers who ought to shut up.

Ironically, that night I was probably pecking away at my little typewriter, composing something or other for the lesbian magazine *The Ladder*. I could not see then that *The Ladder*'s voice was as loud and riotous and far-reaching as the actions the Greenwich Village cops were trying to censor. I couldn't see that those of us who made up lesbian stories and combed the works of women writers for signs of what was then termed variance were driven by the same spirit of revolt as were our counterparts in the bars.

I, who wrote under a variety of pseudonyms, could not have understood the words Audre Lorde had yet to say. Part of me still rejects that truth, that silence will not protect me. Even knowing that the more of us who are out of the closet the safer all of us will be, I cling to my little subterfuges. Silence continues to be a tool of survival for the majority of gays on this planet.

Where was I during Stonewall? I was hiding while I battered down my walls one keystroke at a time, lying out loud while I wrote the truth, fighting to love another woman while everything I'd learned had taught me to despise myself for doing so. On June 28, 1969, at my tiny desk stuffed into the corner of our bedroom, I wrote to pry open closets, then slipped through the dark to my twin bed. I never considered that we might have chosen a double bed.

When I heard about Stonewall, I weakly denounced my liberators, while somewhere inside, beneath the roiling fears, a thrill ran. I remember that thrill, that breath-holding *Could it be? Are we next?* Quickly stifled, hope and the vicarious taste of freedom would not be squelched. After Stonewall I worked harder at my little desk. Over the next months I became more alienated from my establishment job. By 1970 I was sleeping in a double bed, my job tossed to the heterosexists along with all my skirts. I was wild with that taste for freedom which had grown larger than myself. Come the first marches, I was out there on Christopher Street clamoring for my rights.

I still thought the drag queens were going to ruin everything for us. To this day I wish I'd known how to sign on for the revolution without leaving the lover with whom I'd shared my closet. I also wish I'd recognized my pen as a weapon back then, used more ink and fewer drugs. But those were apparently steps I needed to take in order to overthrow some of the chains of my fear.

Although my moment of Stonewall was obscured and denied, the glorious aftermath could not have been more clear. Twenty-five years later I am thousands of miles from the celebration, but those stomping bulldaggers with their exploding anger and quick fists, those nellie drag queens with their high-heeled rage and shrieks of protest—I will be one of them wherever I am for the rest of my life.

But then, I always was.

THE ONLY LESBIAN ON CAMPUS (1994)

Iwas the only lesbian at my college. When I read now about gay street kids, I know that back then I led a comparatively privileged existence, but at least today's kids have queer camaraderie. I opted for street life too, running away after two weeks of feeling like the only lesbian at school. I wasn't much of a runaway, though, and after some gentle persuasion, returned to four years of idyllic academe.

Of course in 1963 it wasn't idyllic at all, nor was I the only lesbian. I soon brought out a lover and we managed many a private sweaty session behind our locked doors. It was not a healthy relationship, but it was a necessary one for both of us.

Three years later I learned that one of the upperclasswomen was a lesbian. Wendy and her lover were always either locked in her single room or partying with their sorority. I wondered if the whole sorority and its attendant boyfriends were gay. It was the sorority that PE majors traditionally joined. I knew Wendy was gay because one night in the dorm hallway she advised me to play her game. After that she never had anything to do with me again. I was pretty out for 1966 and therefore dangerous.

I was not bereft of all support. The dean's intents were good when she referred me for counseling. The heterosexist psychologist drove me to a breakdown, then increased my visits as a result. Infirmary personnel renewed my tranquilizer prescriptions without question. My adult dorm counselor knew the signs of my deeper depressions. Pale, blond, wraithlike, she was kind and wise beyond her years, would invite me to the apartment she shared with her foreign-student husband and preschool sons, and would keep me until I had pledged not to do away with myself. I made sure I was out to the counselors on my floor, both of whom struggled within themselves to accept me. In the end they supported and defended me. Later, I became the floor counselor, a position that offered some safety and respect.

It also helped that I was the unofficial class poet. Everyone knew that poets were supposed to be queer or crazy or both. My habits of attending classes barefoot, tripping with cool people, and drinking with the older intellectuals seemed to take the edge off my deviance. The students would cruelly abuse "Mrs." Evans, the bleached-blond gay male drama teacher, but they left me, in my jeans and flannel shirts, alone. "Mrs." Evans was later murdered by two underage hustlers. I got out alive.

Sometimes I hurt too much to want to survive. One year the lefty-folk-singing-poetry-reading crowd—and every longhair with a guitar was either the new Joan Baez or the next Bob Dylan—brought culture to the dorms with traveling sing outs. I attended one gathering in my lounge. Folksinging, truth be told, bored the daylights out of me, but where else did I kind of fit in? I sat and looked intense along with all the other revolutionary teenagers and grown-up radicals. Then a long-haired boy strummed a Peter Paul & Mary tune on his guitar and substituted for their words a song that began, "Puff, the tragic faggot…"

I could not believe what I was hearing. This was the intelligentsia; these were the people who knew I was gay. These were supposed to be the sensitive ones who believed in equality, marched for civil rights, were America's future hope. Mortified, enraged, frightened, literally in shock, I reeled out of there and fled to my room where I shook and cried for hours.

I have never written or spoken about this to anyone. It is still painful twenty-eight years later. I never dared wonder about why, but as I finally let it out, I see that the song, the moment, the laughing crowd of peers, blew my world apart. The proud poet-butch, the gay child-rebel, the peacenik-poseur, the little girl deposited in an institution that literally taught normalcy—"the only lesbian on campus"—couldn't pretend any more. I was really, undeniably, unbearably all alone.

I was never beaten up. I was taunted and insulted. To this day I avert my eyes in public bathrooms and in the vicinity of women in states of undress, a habit based on old dormitory fears that I'd be accused of voyeurism. Regardless, more than one door slammed on me back then as I walked along the hall. There were so many incidents. Once a group of girls on my floor dragged me into a room and held me while one, who I had thought was a friend, tried to kiss me, I presume on a dare. Once a male student grabbed my arm and forced me onto a bed where he was making out with his girlfriend, who had risked being my friend. I call these acts psychological terrorism, and no gay kid should have to endure such treatment.

The women longhairs, the bisexual and even straight men, were, one-on-one, intellectually exciting, adventurous. My small group of dorm pals, none gay at the time, accepted me. We didn't talk about my sexuality, we just had fun. One gay male teacher treated me like dirt, another was an inspiration. My lesbian teachers, mostly in the physical education department, ignored me as hard as they could.

When I got desperate I went to New York and drank at the bars. I wasn't of that world anymore, so there was nothing for me there but liquor and the wordless companionship of anonymous queers. Even so, it was terribly hard to leave the bars and sober up on the gritty, rocking train, often packed with raucous, besotted male baseball fans. It was hard to walk the miles from the midnight train through the dark downtown, past the hulks of smoking factories, along the loud and littered housing projects, and finally into that alien land, the college, which sought to impose conformity as much as it sought to educate, where I was neither welcome nor comfortable.

There is a snapshot of me in my college yearbook, a barefoot, androgynous blur hurrying across campus, as if pursued and trying to escape. That style, the style a gay kid sometimes needs in order to survive, never entirely disappears. If I learned nothing else in college, I learned not to linger some places too long, or look at some people too closely, lest I hear the laughter, see the hard truth of closed minds, find myself lost, the only lesbian on some new campus.

WITHOUT HER (1995)

Only for two weeks. We're not talking major breakup here. As a matter of fact we'll celebrate Valentine's Day when she gets back and a sixth anniversary this year.

Just two weeks. Not even two weeks in a major metropolis fraught with danger and temptation. Two weeks with her mom to bird-watch. But, see, that's why it's a matter of survival. Even if she calls nightly, this half of the couple is susceptible to the lonelies without her. And there's no sadder phrase than without her.

I'm not saying I won't enjoy batching it. Briefly. There are certain advantages to living alone, setting one's own schedule, not having to accommodate anyone else's needs. Aren't there?

Already I've got my menu planned. If I don't have enticing tidbits to anticipate, I'm likely not to bother feeding myself without her. Boca Burgers and tortillas and maybe I'll make myself a big ol' pot of baked beans (we have different food allergies at the moment). How about some ice cream with carob chips? Maybe I could even get to the point of looking forward to my solitary meals.

Meals are the least of it. I'll finally have time to put up the new birdhouses. Then, when Lover returns, we can watch all the little bluebird couples move in together. I'll bet some of them have six years too. And maybe I'll visit people we never get to see when we're home together enjoying each other's companionship, too content to go out.

I'll write more instead of cozying up to the woodstove with her, maybe do a short story to surprise her when she comes back. I'll fix that squeaky drawer so I don't wake her on the rare occasion when I get up first. I'll read! I'll catch up on all the review books languishing on the to-be-read shelves, but she won't be around to listen to my complaints and raves. I'll work more hours at my job to buy her an extravagant Valentine's Day gift.

I'll have a Sonic the Hedgehog Spinball marathon with the handheld game she gave me for the holidays. I'll run over to the coast, though I can't imagine walking on the beach without her to show me the rare agates and jaspers she spots.

The truth is, I probably won't do any of it. I'll be lucky if I get my usual stuff done without Lover here. I'm even writing this column early to make sure it gets written at all. Without her, how would I know if it's any good?

The real scenario goes something like this. Remember hearing about those rains in California? Roads closed, people evacuating, killer creeks? Well, we're just north of California and the rain isn't respecting any borders. Lover leaves in a few days. I expect I'll keep doing what I've been doing all week—playing in the mud, black boots up to my knees, rain-suited from head to boots, trying to divert rivers of runoff water from our gravel road, and building a little dam (no dykes allowed in Oregon) to keep our well house from flooding. With two more major storms predicted, I'll barely notice that Lover's gone.

Then, it's the time of year when I sequester myself in my office all weekend to pore over columns of numbers, bundle up hundreds of receipts, and trundle it all through the wet streets to share with the accountant. Lover's lucky to miss my tax season.

The worst of it is, it's not just gloomy outside. If disaster does strike—doesn't it always when Lover is away?—and I'm stuck at home with the roads and electricity out, trying to heat up canned beans on the woodstove and mopping up the melted ice cream from the freezer, where's the fun in it without her? I actually love the rain, the raging waters, the whipping winds, the brute power of nature humbling her tormentor, mankind. Still, rain or shine, I miss my mate, my keel through life, my shelter from the storms.

It's the little things that make it rough. Like the things that go bump in the night when Lover's not here for me to reassure—or to reassure me. Like taking a break from a long, long day of work and knowing her hugs left with her. Like silently discharging the endless weekend chores because no one's around to grumble to. Like being reminded constantly that Lover may be femme, but she's the one with the strong arms. Like listening to the evening news on public radio when Lover's not around to share the horror.

The good news is that, in the vast scheme of things, even the horrors are a blip, and winter storms always end. The sun comes out. Lover returns safe and sound. And suddenly I'm bobbing and grinning at the window, then running to her, stumbling all over myself to carry in her luggage, tell her everything, and soak up all the hugs I can get.

COUNTING QUEERS (1995)

In the newest the-public-will-believe-anything and then vote on it sex survey, gays came out shy once again. Shy in the sense of fewer, lesser, missing. As in, "The count was shy a few million." Shy, we can assume, in the sense that the subjects fell suddenly shy when confronted with an intimate and historically punishable question like, "Have you ever done it with someone of your same sex?" And shy in the sense that their interrogators—sitting right there with them looking at them, or toying with their writing instruments, or blushing, or bored, or whatever—were asking questions the subjects may have found invasive.

One of the results of this scientific assessment of the numbers of our people was to indicate a lack of rural lesbians. As I recall, none showed up in the survey. Zero. Zilch. Nada. In one critique I read on the survey the writer said something like, "Tell that to rural lesbians."

Yeah. Here I am, one of that zero, invisible, belittled population, to tell you all that the numbers, as per usual, lie through their forever-clenched teeth.

Proof that we're here in the sticks? The nearest city has a population under 20,000 and most of us live out in the country. More proof? I just sat down at the computer after hauling in wood for our woodstove. Proof upon proof: last night, in order to get lesbian culture to our community, Lover held a house concert in which rural Wyrda Atowl performed Carolyn Gage's *Joan of Arc* (a rural peasant) in our living room. In order for me to receive broadcasts of National Public Radio, I have to stand still in one spot and drape the antenna across my shoulders. For company and entertainment when Lover is out of town, I listen to a scanner. The clincher: we get two TV channels clearly. Is this the boonies or what?

Not only am I here, but so, obviously, is Lover. Our next nearest dyke neighbors are probably four miles away. When Lover produces a house concert it is not unusual to get women from, oh, sixty miles away. And the variety of us! No survey could ever define us—even if it could find us in the first place.

I know a country dyke who works on a small newspaper. We have realtors and teachers and entrepreneurs and hosts of retirees. We have countless artists and writers. We have women who perform at festivals and women who travel the US for corporations. We have bus drivers and hairdressers, social workers and firefighters. We have housepainters and store owners and department managers and office workers, accountants and attorneys and physicians and therapists. We have women with independent incomes and women on SSDI and welfare moms. We have machinists and farmers and architects. I could continue this inventory for another page or so. Don't tell *me* that there are no dykes in the country.

Yesterday we went out hiking with a nature group. The majority of participants were lesbians. New friends in the group were telling us about their friends who are active in another nature group. We went to a gathering not long ago where, after over a decade in this community, we met yet more women who'd been here all along. At the play last night we learned of a couple who moved here within the last few years who only met the women we know because they became neighbors. A dyke who called for directions to the play said, "This is Lydia." I asked, "Oh. Lydia of Lydia and DeeDee?" "No. Lydia and Geri." Two *more* lesbians.

We crawl out of the woodwork, as that unfortunate but accurate saying goes. Or at least many of us do. The more country dykes we meet, the more we hear about.

There is an underground beyond the underground. These are often old lesbians who have little interest in contemporary dyke culture or have lived with the closet habit so long they're simply not comfortable out and about. I always feel honored when they reveal themselves to me. They are only a small percent of the under-underground in rural America.

I know lesbians who aren't even interested in meeting other lesbians because they've heard that country dykes are too weird and witchy. Wrong, but that uncovers still another hidden group. On the other hand there are droves of urban dykes who come to the area to retreat to local women's land, or the lesbian bed-and-breakfast spots.

Why do we live here with our homemade culture and our isolation from the riches of more urban life? Speaking for myself, it's cheaper and I can spend a little more time writing. The air is clean. It's easier to be a hermit. I like the distance from gays and straights alike. I like the independent spirits of my peers. It smells like pine trees out here. There's a creek up the road. We have a resident pileated woodpecker.

If lesbians are invisible in this great nation, then magnify that times ten for country lesbians. We may not be hooked into the great white able-bodied middle-class wave of dykes-about-town, but we are pumping out our own newsletters and putting on our own shows. If we're not getting counted by hotshot surveys—getting defined as a lesbian market—you won't see us out there hooting and hollering to be included. Exclusion has always made dykes tougher. We'll survive the survivors. Don't forget, survey-takers, we're here, we're queer, we're too busy to answer your questions.

CROSSING THE LINE (1995)

One by one, holding hands, the men, some in suits, and the women, some white-haired, crossed the line to be arrested. Three to four hundred protestors broke the stillness of the old-growth forest with applause. I photographed the historic crossing through tears. A woman behind me broke into a searing scream, giving voice to the mutilation going on around us.

This was a protest against the timber "sale" called Sugarloaf. People who love the trees, the earth, and the life both sustain, tried to stop the greed that was, at that same moment, powering chain saws that severed the trunks of trees so old only wild animals and the ancestors of Native Americans had seen the saplings.

On our way up the Caves Highway in southern Oregon, truck after truck roared past us, most carrying no more than three logs apiece. These trees dwarfed even the logging trucks. At Sugarloaf the rent-a-cops were waiting, paid for by the timber company, Boise Cascade. We stood in a respectful circle asking the forest to welcome us.

It was another day of shame for America. The same radicals who refuse to recognize their common humanity with gay people refuse to honor nature itself. They snuck Sugarloaf and many other sales through. The courts had held back the forces of greed and destruction with the strong arm of the law. The radicals chopped off that arm—undid the law. They knew legislation to take the timber would never pass on its own, so they added a so-called salvage rider to an appropriations bill. Neither profit nor competitive bidding was required. We taxpayers not only got nothing from the dirty deal, other environmental laws including the Clean Air and Clean Water Acts were also lifted for these sales.

Many of the right-wing politicians who gave away Sugarloaf were elected on platforms which included antigay provisions. Now that the Oregon Citizen's Alliance and its confederates in other states have amassed enormous mailing lists and funding through the use of gay-bashing propaganda, and have built political clout by demonstrating that they can influence the vote in Colorado, Cincinnati and Queens, New York, they are using that power to feed corporate greed and irreparably damage the quality of life provided by these last untouched American lands.

It's not just Oregon. The Everglades in Florida are being smothered in concrete. A bill before Congress would allow a huge coal-mining operation on twenty million acres of federally-owned land in the Red Rock Canyon country of southern Utah (near Bryce Canyon and Zion National Park). More legislation would allow oil drilling in the Arctic National Wildlife Refuge in Alaska. Are there any wetlands left in your town? Where do all the wild critters go? This ecological holocaust goes on and on.

Out in the Sugarloaf woods, everyday people, kids who'd stayed out of school, politicians and environmental advocates crossed that line to protest lawless logging. I stood beside heterosexual folks I'd met while fighting the antigay ballot measures. It seems like people who respect life, respect life in all its forms. And I was far from the only gay person there that day.

In this time when so much I hold dear seems to be on the line— the right to health care for the old and poor, the right to jobs and housing for gays, the right to clean air and water—I greeted this informal coalition of human rights and environmental activists with jubilation. We need to acknowledge that our bottom-line goals are the same whether we champion salmon, education money, a decent minimum wage, or freedom from persecution. We can accomplish great things, those of us who value all of creation, with a currency called respect. Our power comes from honoring the dignity of one another and of the planet that supports us.

I remember the old woman from the wildlife refuge who came to town for help. Laws allow farmers to use water from the refuge for irrigation. It was a drought year. When the pelicans came, as they always did, by the hundreds, to birth and raise their young, there was no water. The baby pelicans, forced to march miles to water with their parents, dropped and died. The woman got no help from the regulating agencies. Alone, she carried some of the babies. She exhorted us to write letters, to make phone calls. When the pelicans returned the next year, there was more water, partly because one woman spoke out and reached out.

We do not know the extent of our careless cruelties, nor can we imagine the breadth of our concerted power.

At the Sugarloaf demonstration, the police refused to arrest those who had crossed the line into the sale area. The police waited up the hill, around a bend, out of sight of the media. As the morning wore on, ninety-five people crossed the line. A few at a time, they went the whole distance up the hill and disappeared.

We cheered them. We pressed against the rope. I had traveled there with two local environmental leaders, levelheaded people. We had no intention of getting arrested. Yet at one moment, we looked at one another and nodded in unison. If the crowd crossed the line that denied access to our public lands, so would we.

There was some negotiation with the media. This would only be worth the risk with witnesses to bring our action out of the forest. But if the media went with us, their equipment would be confiscated. One reporter went up the hill only to be tackled by the police. A white-haired woman was maced trying to protect him. The moment for the crowd to surge forward into mass arrests passed. Later, another old woman tried to be arrested. The police wouldn't take her until she returned with a group of younger women and stood in the shadows, where no cameras could reach. They wouldn't arrest kids at all.

The giant Sugarloaf trees are at the mills. The baby pelicans are dead. Gay kids are still killing themselves and poor people are scared. The old women cannot stop the radical right alone. We can't either. In the chain of life we all need one another.

CAUGHT IN THE NET (1995)

Listen, I don't have time to do a column. I just went online and it's too much fun to stop. Oh, sure, I've read the warnings that the information superhighway can be harmful to your health, making you stay up all night, neglect food and daylight and exercise. I've heard about the online anonymous groups forming all over the world to deal with the addiction. But I've been there, done that, bought the 12-step T-shirt, so I know I'm not likely to develop a new dependence.

I suppose that's what they all say. See, for you nonusers, it's not the machines or the electronics. It's the sudden widening universe in terms of access to information while the world of communication shrinks. It's the promise of new people in one's life without the complication of messy interpersonal relationships. It's the ease of connecting with people already in my life, like my-brother-who-never-writes but I suspect will e-mail like a songbird.

It's that, with the expensive paper shortage, I can return to frequent communication with my safe-fax buddy, Sky. It's that I do all this from my desk, looking out the window at the bluebirds nesting in a birdhouse.

It's partly, too, the promise that I'll be able to zip this column to editors in the blink of an eye (if someone will tell me how), saving paper and postage and eliminating the need to wade through the right-wing petitioners outside the post office.

It's feeling thirty years younger to be joining the kids who can send e-mail from their college dorms and who take the wonders of computers for granted the way my generation did political activism. It's communicating with people in the kind of sound-bite/abbreviated stream-of-consciousness language that seems to evolve from frequent use of e-mail.

It's the constant flow of up-to-date political information through the Rural Organizing Project in Oregon or the Victory Fund in DC which makes me feel a part of things even though I'm not a meeting person. Last night I learned from e-mail that Oregon has a new nondiscrimination bill stuck in a legislative committee. I got that information into our local human rights newsletter so local voters can call the appropriate politician. I feel like an activist again!

I also feel like I've joined a new community. When I went to the local woman-owned bookstore to buy an electronic how-to book, it was like going to my first Girl Scout meeting. I was welcomed to a group eager to help me join and full of a camaraderie that comes with distinctive rites and initiations and skills. Later, when I e-mailed my address to people who had been encouraging me to go online, I got immediate enthusiastic responses back. In a kind of hushed, co-conspiratorial voice, I exchange e-mail addresses with others of my new ilk.

While I'm on co-conspirators, an e-mailer just let me know about a poll which showed that about 75 percent of people using the information superhighway are of the Republican and/or conservative persuasion. Presumably some of the reasons for this are economic.

Other than that, are gay people really more traditional in methods of communication than nongays? Liberals more hesitant about cyberspace than conservatives? Today, information is power. Communication, in the hands of anti-human-rights activists, is a weapon, not a tool. We don't have to organize sit-ins at radio or TV stations anymore to take back power. The technology is ours for the using!

There are ways to get online even if your income looks like that of a lesbian writer. It took some patience, but I'm hooked into a local network that costs fifteen dollars a month for a hundred hours. No long distance fees either. It saves me money.

It's kind of nice, too, to always get mail, one of life's little pleasures. And it's much easier to delete junk mail with a keystroke than to open, sort, and lug the stuff to the recycling center. I love to get messages without an insistently ringing phone. If I want to log on I can. If not, see you later! (So far, of course, I always want to log on.) My ten-channel scanner once kept me company on long lonely nights when Lover was away. Now I'll just cozy up to the computer and communicate!

Listen, I gotta go. In the time it's taken me to write this I haven't checked my e-mail box. I know there's something in there. It's this feeling I have, almost a compulsion. I don't have to look, I could not look if I wanted. I'm not one of those online addicts or anything… :)

REAL DYKES DON'T DRIVE FORDS (1996)

After it was all over, someone told me that buying a car is one of life's major stresses, not far down the list from marriage and buying a home.

Now they tell me.

Some people can turn in a car every few years, or buy old clunkers to run into the ground, but for me, we're talking best-friend status. Constant companion. Freedom to roam the world.

All these months later I still get choked up talking about my '76 Volvo sedan, Spock. He was with me for nineteen years, longer than any lover to date.

In the end, though, I couldn't care for him the way he deserved. The one good Volvo mechanic in town retired. The next best guy ran up a thousand dollars in bills that last month, and my health insurance wouldn't cover Spock. I had to buy a car.

But what? I really loved that Volvo but couldn't afford a new one. After two years of heroic rescues by Lover, emptying my bank account, and fearing to wander farther than Super AAA would tow, I wanted nothing to do with used vehicles.

That decided, I faced the nightmare of car payments. Fortunately, my employer pays me instead of giving me benefits. So it was simple. I don't get sick or take a vacation for the next six years and bingo—the car is paid off. Well, it made sense at the time.

What would I buy? My only idea was the no-haggle cult-car, the Saturn. One day I parked Spock around the corner and slunk into the dealership. The Saturns were really cute. And about two tons lighter than my glamorized Sherman tank. Cars quickly lose their cuteness in a collision with a logging truck.

I had a feeling this wasn't going to be one of these deals where I walk into a showroom, fall in love, and drive home in the car of my dreams. I spent that hot summer month memorizing *Consumer Reports: New Car Buying Guide*. I lived, breathed, and sweated cars. What I really needed was a kind of car-parent to tell me what to buy. My stepdad-in-law counseled me but confessed, "I'm a GMC man." My mechanic echoed him. So I reported with great hopes to the nearest GMC dealership. No match. GMC must be a guy thing.

Lover is very out at work. Her old boss Molly has always taken a motherly interest in us. She teases me about spoiling Lover when I bring flowers. She gives us gruff mini-lectures about appreciating each other. Now this wouldn't be strange except that in our radical-right town, queer couples don't get many straight mentors. Molly goes her own way. "A Ford," she pronounced, in her best I-don't-want-an-argument manner. I couldn't explain that dykes like me don't drive new Fords.

Back to haunting the car lots, amassing stacks of slick brochures, and mercilessly interrogating salespeople.

Lover, who had quietly gone out the year before and replaced her old car with its updated twin, introduced me to after-dark window-shopping. It seems there's an American ritual of meandering acres of auto barrens after the harassing sales staff goes home. We scanned price and options stickers by the light of the summer moon. Soon, I had it narrowed down. Safety—at fifty, mortality becomes very real. Low repair costs—lesbian writers don't keep cars nineteen years for no reason. Roominess—I'd always had difficulty fitting bookcases and multiple pet carriers in my economy cars. I'd entered my station wagon/minivan years.

The Toyota people took one look at me and wouldn't let me past their tinny Corollas. I was warned to avoid the local Dodge dealership. Honda wagons are as teensy as Saturns.

What was left? Lover's choice—the lesbian national car, the vehicle with a life span of several lesbian owners and an advertising campaign aimed at gays—a Subaru wagon.

I drove one, loved it, and went to talk turkey with the salesman. Then his manager (this is the only dealership for a hundred miles) arrived for a good-cop/bad-cop routine. I walked.

More research. Big-city brokers. Test driving. Internet queries. I was so exhausted and confused Nixon could have come back to life and sold me a used car.

So I gave in. I went to car-mom-Molly's Ford dealer. They had what I wanted and made it affordable. Molly even called during the negotiations and told me to get the pretty blue one. As soon as I saw that minivan, I knew her name was Large Marge.

Car-mom knew best. Menopause is no time to be politically correct about air conditioning. Middle age is no time to resist automatic transmissions or the power options made for bad shoulders and knees. And pride goeth before rejecting dual air bags, antilock brakes and antiglare windshields that improve my fading night vision. For the first time in memory, even my own mother told me, "Daddy would have been proud of you."

One evening I pulled up in front of Lover's office. She's now on the management team with Molly. The employees filed out, ogling Lover's friend in Large Marge, and climbed into cars decorated with Christian fish magnets and Free Willie '96 bumper stickers.

In a minivan I literally sit above the crowd. Encased in such a symbol of economic solvency, I felt very adult, very respectable. When Jed, one of Molly's underlings, came out, he looked at the car, averted his eyes from mine in the usual I'd-rather-not-know manner, and conceded, "Nice van."

With the smugness of a black sheep who's the favored sibling anyway, I boasted, "Thanks, Molly picked it out." Jed stopped in his tracks, a look of total confusion on his face, then scurried away.

It was suddenly all worth it: the conflicts, the expense, the political embarrassment of driving a shiny new Ford. I began to understand why buying a car is a major life stress. It's a rite of passage. A common initiation. Evidence of achievement and, even for a lesbian, of belonging.

I can't wait to show it to my in-laws!

THE INVISIBLE LESBIAN (1996)

Sometimes, in this figurative Kansas that constitutes Lesbian Nation, I get the feeling I'm not in Kansas any more. When I see lesbians in the limelight I wonder, what is this tattoo craze? When did gender issues get to be more important to lesbians than femme/butch? How come dykes do things to their hair that I associate with queer-hating adolescent boys?

I suspect that the problem of lesbian invisibility has not been resolved by lesbian chic. That the media image of Everydyke is far from a mirror reflection. And that what may be this week's rage in the lesbian ghettos loses momentum as its shock waves reverberate into the rest of America where most lesbians live.

The truth is, most lesbians are still invisible—and like it that way.

The invisible lesbian is the librarian who won't meet another dyke's eyes to check out Martina's new mystery. The invisible lesbian is the scruffy gas station attendant who turns out to be a girl. The lesbian who goes back to live with her parents because that's the only way she can afford to fight her breast cancer. The women who stay married to men and make love with their best friends while the kids are at school. The quiet couples, one a nurse, one a bookkeeper, who only socialize with their straight neighbors.

Aren't these women lesbians too?

Some dykes actually cringe at the sight of body piercing. Their tastes in leather run to purses or billfolds, pumps or Birkenstocks. Sex clubs are an alien concept. Personal ads are a source of entertainment or fantasy, not sex partners, although they may subscribe to one of the quiet newsletters that connect women-loving-women.

Rather than nude posters on their walls, many lesbians tack up cute puppy pictures and, if it feels safe, their favorite *Dykes to Watch Out For* cartoon—though some don't even relate to the word dyke.

They may be moved by flirtatious femmes, but the butches clam up within a yard of one. Cuddling is a fine form of foreplay as far as they're concerned and campfire smoke the most potent aphrodisiac they've ever experienced. Some dare to buy lesbian videos, but many get all romantic just singing Girl Scout songs. Sex toy demonstrations aren't their cup of tea.

Lesbians can even be prudes.

Though they like the idea of dyke community, a lot tend to be stay-at-homes. Their only links with other lesbians, if they're really brave, are the Naiad mailing list and a subscription to *Girlfriends*. If some like to observe traditional holidays with their birth families and can't bring their lovers, there's always one couple that holds open-house barbecues or cooks turkey for fifty—and welcomes the strays.

Despite the radical-right hysteria about gay marriage, lots of lesbians wouldn't think of it. They don't believe in it, don't feel they need it, or fear to be that out. On anniversaries they go to the Red Coach Inn and celebrate with wine or ice cream sundaes for dessert.

Even if they're only an hour's drive from lively dyke scenes in New York or Seattle, Chicago or Dallas, try and pry them from their horses, bridge groups, hiking, gardens, bowling tournaments, or volunteer work with the women's shelter. Far from the big cities there might be a Halloween or Valentine's Day dance, but who wants to drive at night and the music's too loud, and the dance starts too late or they can't get a sitter. They'd rather watch *Star Trek*. Any generation.

Lots of us are in the slow lane.

They're as likely to be at an environmental demonstration as a queer one. To donate money or time to animal rights as gay rights. To vote Republican as Democratic—or not to vote at all.

One National Coming Out Day an invisible lesbian might agonize through telling her best friend at work who'd guessed years ago and vow never to go through that again.

Leather and lace may be the fabrics of choice for many dykes, but many more wear flannel shirts bought for two bucks apiece on clearance at Walmart with J.C. Penney's jeans, the ones that were a really, really relaxed fit even before relaxed was in.

Do they get to be dykes even if they wear dorky clip-on sunglasses? If they've got about as much desire to go on an Olivia cruise as they have to go to war? If even the thought of watching the Dinah Shore Golf Classic bores them silly? If on vacations they stay in RV parks chock-full of straights and have a great time? If they never learned line dancing, and outdoor music festivals exhaust them? Yep, they count.

Some dykes just want to be cool in the Castro. Some want to change the world by marching on Washington. There are those who want to sweep women off their feet. And others who'll fight to add lesbian literature to the curriculum.

But what about those who spend Friday nights clipping Safeway double coupons? And Sunday afternoons, after church, sealing their foundations to stop the skunks from settling under their houses? Who work their butts off to keep their jobs and health insurance and to pay off their Fords?

Can they keep their dyke cards?

The invisible lesbian may have no tattoos, no causes, no gay community. She may not even have a lover.

But she's loved a woman somewhere, sometime. She's a lesbian.

The Joy of Us (1996)

We watched from a window of the small restaurant as seven men pulled into the parking lot, assembled, and headed in the door. They were a motley-looking bunch, clean-shaven, bearded, in neat work clothes or polka-dot shorts, long-haired, balding, from twentysomething to fiftysomething.

I felt a twinge of aversion. Here we were, celebrating Catch's birthday, and now we'd have to put up with a clump of beer-guzzling loud guys having some kind of stag blowout.

The waitress brusquely presented our food just then. I barely noticed that the men took a long table almost adjacent to ours as Lover and I toasted Catch and dug into our various delicacies. It's always fun to discover a restaurant as good as this on the Route 249s of America. These are the roads littered with gun shops and struggling used-car lots, carpet outlets and welding supply stores. This divey-looking eatery is smack in the middle of a U-Haul empire. The ambiance is not exactly your trendy gay watering hole.

There was something about that long-haired fella, though. Naw, a blond surfer-type with a wide feminine streak.

A woman swaggered past on her way to the ladies room. The three of us looked at one another, looked over to the booth where she'd been sitting. Yup. Another lesbian.

"Sure," said Catch matter-of-factly, "you see a lot of dykes here. The food's good."

Was that boy wearing nail polish?

Another woman went by. Short haired except for the long thin pigtail down her back, but she was in retro hippie garb. Could be anything.

And then four of the men began to sing. Why, they were a barbershop quartet! They rolled out an exquisitely rehearsed "Java" and not a face in sight was without a smile.

"Hey!" Catch said. "That's the group that opened when the Portland Gay Men's Chorus was down here."

We applauded. So did everyone else. Including the end booth with two old heterosexual couples. The men went over to serenade them with "Blue Moon." A singer fell to one knee and extended an arm, crooning with gay abandon. "Happy anniversary!" we heard them say.

By this time there was no doubt. These guys were good, they were generous with song, and they were gay. Their meals came and things quieted down, but we joked about having hired the group to celebrate Catch's birthday.

After dinner the men were primed. The little dive was transformed into a scene from a fifties musical where the numbers are done in outrageously unrealistic settings: hay wagons, the streets of Paris, a rooftop in New York. Well, why not Route 249 in a dingy mill town?

They were up, by then, and singing an old rock song at our booth. One of the old straight men was headed for the cashier, dipping at the knees, silently sha-booming with his lips. His wife came along the aisle after him and the songsters whirled on her, fingers cheerfully pointing as if in this musical, she was the star.

The woman, obviously in her eighties, didn't miss her cue. I could see the spotlight swerve to her. She did a quick, studied double-take and pointed at herself, eyebrows raised, then grinned and danced in place.

By this time, our fellow diners would have to have been from Saturn not to notice the show had turned camp. The countertenor with the glittery nail polish and long curls, Aaron Logsdon, I later learned, was not shy. Nor were Dave Deller, Tom Walker, or Al Robins. They were swooning in one another's arms, dancing together, and getting pinched by the waitresses.

They were unstoppable! In the parking lot a group of young couples, newborn babe in arms, had an encounter of the queer kind with these high-spirited carolers of gay goodwill. The U-Haul empire was transformed into yet another set for this standing-room-only musical. *Rent*? *Bring In 'Da Noise, Bring In 'Da Funk*? Who needs Broadway? Right there in the town where two lesbians were murdered less than a year ago—for being out lesbians—gay men were reaching out to the straights.

Even musicals end. The anniversary couples drove off. The newborn was carried inside. The crunchy-granola dykes got into a car with California plates—how had they heard of this gay hot spot? I got serious with the guys. Some of them were on their way to the annual Radical Faerie gathering farther north. They were all locals clearly singing for the sheer pleasure of it—and vocalizing in yet another way what a special, talented, and joyous people we are.

They're called Delusions of Grandeur. Their card claims, *We're the best barbershop quartet in the entire universe.* Their T-shirt admits they're *Legends in their own minds.*

I suspect Catch won't forget that birthday dinner for a while. Especially after the Delusions sang her their birthday song on that hot August night—"White Christmas."

I hope the nongays won't forget either. Like all our choruses, the men of Delusions of Grandeur are musical ambassadors.

THE SHAMEFUL TRUTH (1996)

I never thought I'd be the kind of person who would pay money to look at pigs. Yet every year, in the same week that throngs of lesbians celebrate at the Michigan Womyn's Music Festival, Lover and I visit our County Fair.

I've never been to Michigan, but I've been to the Fair at least a half-dozen times. Surely there must be something wrong with me to stay here with those adorable suckling piglets when I could be frolicking with a multitude of bare-breasted, body-painted, hand-holding women.

The shameful truth is that I'm a homebody. Oh, I've heard the stories of enlightenment through sisterhood and spiritual recharging and mass menstruation. I've been at other festivals for the proud construction of stages and the strutting of security patrols and the cheerful mingling on interminable scrambled-tofu lines and the midnight howling as Alix sings.

In the Northwest I've chopped my share of onions and picked up my tons of trash. At Bloomington I've done the workshops and attended the candlelight 12-step meetings. I've walked the miles from tent to dining hall, and I've tried to sleep through nights reverberating with drums. I've endured gnat invasions in New England and pitched my tent in mud. I've watched for wildfires at Yosemite.

I've blocked country roads on ticket lines where every driver wondered whether she was creating more pollution by repeatedly turning her car on or by letting it run. I've been shouted at by local boys with itchy trigger fingers. I've sobbed with Festi Stress Syndrome. I've left for home with requests for souvenirs as well as a year's supply of must-have T-shirts I wouldn't dare flaunt. I've read the festi-flaming letters in *Lesbian Connection* with feelings of validation as well as annoyance.

But tomorrow night Lover and I will hitch up the ol' Subaru and mosey on over to the County Fair. With any luck the feature will be Big Wheel, the monster car that thrills audiences by crushing a line of vehicles as long as one waiting to get into a small women's festival. Not that we'll be in that audience. The midway clears for Big Wheel and we'll be practically alone in the garish neon glow of Ferris wheel and Tilt-A-Whirl. We'll tempt ourselves with silly games of chance and wish we weren't too health conscious to eat cotton candy.

While lesbian comediennes tickle the crowd at Michigan, we'll admire Lover's coworker's third-prize string beans and Joanie's candidate for Great Pumpkin. Instead of avoiding the body-piercing demonstration, we'll wander the craft building to ogle intricate needlework and lust after racks of glorious quilts. While amazon night-stage stars tune their guitars, we'll meander through the art show, disagreeing with the judges' choices and marveling at Hazel's watercolor. Although we won't spend a cent at lesbian craft booths, it's likely the Fair won't empty our pockets either. Well—I do have to replace that five-buck straw hat I picked up a few years ago which now looks like a 4-H goat thought it was dinner.

It's true that I find some of the Fair booths offensive. The right-wing politicos strong-arm passersby and the Gideon Bible people proselytize the kids. But the Seventh-day Adventists do a real service with their blood-pressure monitoring and the Girl Scouts are always there. Not to mention Smokey the Bear.

There's no accounting for taste. I know lots of women who enjoy the festivals, but I'm no adventurer. Fighting the Fair traffic is challenge enough for me. I'm glad I've had the chance to be knee-deep in lesbian culture (as well as mosquitoes), but I got to see Ferron at an outdoor concert really close to home this summer and that satisfied me.

I guess I'm just a little old-fashioned. It's neat to watch the square dancers, although I know what would happen if Lover put on a flouncy gingham square-dance dress, I a string tie, and we tried to join them. It's easier to be a vegetarian at a women's festival, but being around well-treated horses and bunny rabbits has its good moments. Maybe it's growing up in Queens that makes County Fairs just a little bit exotic. Maybe it's the American in me. Maybe it's the need for a balance—steeped in lesbian culture as I am through my work—a balance among all the cultures that I claim for my own.

Or maybe it's just the new crop of adorable piglets that draw me back year after year.

You Always Remember Your First (1996)

Gay Pride march, that is.
I didn't march that first year. The significance of the Stonewall riots had not yet become clear to me. Gay Liberation was suspect. Civil rights were for minorities. I didn't feel like a member of a minority group back then. I had a lover, a job, an apartment, a car. I simply accepted that I had to lie to my family, my coworkers, and just about everyone else in my life in order to get and keep what I had.

For me, it was *The Ladder*, that monthly declaration of lesbian independence that opened my eyes. For others it may have been a simple yearning for freedom, or telltale ulcers—some tipoff that living in closets wasn't good for us.

Then there was a women's dance held in the basement of some sympathetic church. A small group of lesbians met every week to talk, not drink. At a party some exhilarated gay man described a fabulous march in the city with more gay people than he could have imagined. Mainstream newspapers reported crowds of hundreds, thousands.

There was something in the air beckoning, challenging, daring us to all to come out for a few hours, one day a year. We were too young or too oppressed to know that the taste of freedom was more addictive than any substance we'd ever used to dull the pain of living condemned and in hiding.

Those slow, early years of liberation may be a jumble of memories, but not my first march. It was big. We filled the streets as far back and ahead as I could see. You're not really aware you're making history while in the midst of it, but that day I knew, I think we all knew.

We were a force of nature, a river of queers overflowing our banks, a tidal wave of agony splintering a hundred thousand closet doors, the human spirit rising in a tide that would never recede, right there on familiar streets.

Before, we'd walked those streets only at night, always frightened, whispering, hypervigilant and timidly defiant. At my first march the sun shone. We sang, "Here come the les-bee-uns!" Didn't we bellow, didn't we strut and sashay.

Oh, the bulldykes and the guys in cowboy hats, the bedazzling, bedecked femmes of all genders! The long-haired boys, the short-haired girls, the costumed, and the barely dressed. The chants that blew the roof off the city, the visions that were born and grew. The laughing cops who couldn't guess that we'd be walking beats beside them.

The massed excitement would carry so many of us into then-unthinkable queer careers: organizers, politicians, singers, historians of the gay culture. That day we were, unknowing, carrying not only banners and posters, but America's future. While we thought we were having fun, we were creating a revolution, spawning everything from protective legislation to gay credit cards to rural gay sanctuaries. We were laying the foundation for the Supreme Court to rule against Colorado's Amendment 2.

Deep in the shadow of the citadels of respectability thousands of us marched. There were bar floats and fun floats and religious floats. We were not only educating those who watched, but ourselves. Imagine, gay people in organized religion. Could we change even the major institutions of our oppression?

Drag queens blazed in their finery, moving sparks of angry, exultant life. They sang their own songs, the cheerleaders of our parade. I remember feeling torn: we'd be damned for their stereotypical antics, but they were at the very heart of queerness. I wanted to hide them and was ashamed for wanting that. I feared they'd ruin the revolution and knew their fierce defiance was the revolution. I wanted the drag queens to go away and I wanted to be a drag queen. Next year I'd wear a tie.

Next year. Once part of our great upheaval, I had no doubt that there would be a next year. I looked around that day and saw, by sheer numbers alone, that we could not be vanquished. Strangers smiled at one another. Before, in the bars, in a store, at work, we had used highly evolved signals that involved ducking the head, averting the gaze, and telegraphing recognition all at the same time. It was a double-survival tactic: we risked no overt confession and were strengthened by acknowledgment.

When the ticker tape began to float down from windows full of cheering, waving, smiling people, I felt that we were being blessed. We were war heroes. Outer-space pioneers. We were presidents that day, and Olympic champions. We were the toast of the town. No one who has been so celebrated can ever go back into hiding.

A woman I'd known in college rushed out of the crowd and hugged me. I'd suspected, but now she told me, told the world, "I'm gay!" All over the streets the silent sister- and brotherhoods were shouting in welcome and appreciation of one another.

We were thirsty and too excited to wait in line for sodas. We were tired, and too buoyant to rest our blistered feet. We were hot and too euphoric to seek shelter.

Shelter found us as we reached Central Park. We showered ourselves with water-fountain spray and flung ourselves onto the cooling grass. As the speakers praised our numbers, a prowling straight woman tried to pick me up, eager to come out, to be a part of us.

Like the drag queens, the religious queers, the butches with beer bottles, and the women and men who stepped off the sidewalks to swell our power, we marched because everyone deserves a pride day, week, month—a life of pride. You always remember your first.

WIRELESS (1998)

My pal the CEO and I were chatting about computers. Just that morning I'd unsuccessfully downloaded a media program designed to give me animated answers to some research questions.

"Ha-ha!" he laughed. "My brother couldn't get that to work either. He downloaded it, but he didn't extract it and then wondered why he couldn't use it. Ha-ha!"

"Duh," I said, feeling clueless—wireless. Extract? Why don't they ever mention the little details? If women or gay men ran the computer world we'd have recipe-like instructions that included the electronic equivalent of add two teaspoons, stir, combine, cook at 350 degrees. Then extract from oven. We wouldn't ever leave out that last essential step.

It's a darned good thing Lover is not only a techno-wiz, but smart and patient. She extracted the program for me that night (I still have no clue what that means) and went back to her needlepoint. I stayed with my neato-keeno new toy which enabled me to relive the Yankees World Series win and hear the cheering again and again.

I happily twiddled away, deciding after that successful installation to play with the settings. Lover had increased the number of colors; I would increase the number of pixels! This, I thought, would give me a clearer view of my triumphant team.

"Not a good thing to play with," was all Lover said when I sheepishly broke it to her that I'd destroyed my computer. The screen had gone black, I told her. Yes, the machine was still running. The prognosis, Lover's face said, was poor.

Did I freak? Naw. New computers only cost money. Naw. Replacing everything on a machine only takes time. Hundreds of dollars. Dozens of hours. Just because my eyes glaze over when I try to read a computer manual or understand something Lover's explaining, why should the small detail that I'm totally wireless stop me from reckless experimentation?

Lover came barefooted and nightgowned to my room and struggled mightily. She turned the thing off, then on. Nothing. She pressed some keys and the screen lit up. The corners of the screen were marked SAFE MODE.

"Wow! How'd you do that?" I asked eagerly.

She shook her head and sagely pronounced, "It's better if I don't tell you."

I couldn't argue. I'd probably have tried it out when she returned to her sewing.

In any case, she saved my machine. Not that I deserved such a miracle. Especially since I just found out that I lost more than my urge to fool around—with my computer, not on my girlfriend—after last night's fiasco. My speakers now emit an annoying hum instead of all the cute little jungle sounds that normally blare throughout my day.

It'd been such fun, talking on the phone with Someone Important like my computer-incompatible boss, who is not to be confused with the computer-literate CEO. He'll be saying something weighty, like, "Good work, Lee!" when a chorus of crickets or a raucous jungle bird screams into the phone. Slight pause, image of boss wondering if he really heard the strange sound, then a hurried good-bye. Just one more weirdness coming from his satellite office.

Hey, some people are good at computers, some at…Uh, I wonder if I perform any practical miracles around our house.

There are the spiders, of course. Lover accepts that I catch and evict them, though she's more than willing to spot for me when I climb, lean, or otherwise contort myself to reach the little guys. The worst is the bathtub. Have you ever balanced on the tub's edge in order to stretch to the corner where ceiling and wall meet, and then try to coax a spider from its web fortress? If you haven't, I'll bet your partner has. Somehow, though, this little specialty of mine doesn't seem as valuable as saving spendy equipment.

Nor does my other achievement. Until recently I was the unrivaled champion of kitty litter cleaning. I won't go into detail, but no one could argue (why would anyone try?) about my aptitude there. Recently, though, I was replaced. A litter box with electronic eyes came to live with us. It scoops the stuff up and dumps it into a closed compartment within moments after a deposit is made. The kitties are loyal—they won't use the thing. Yet. As soon as they get used to it, I know what will happen. Yep, I'll be downsized. And you know who had to assemble this high-tech gadget. Yep, Lover. By wiring the potty she's reduced my repetitive stress syndrome—known in nongeek circles as litter elbow—by 25 percent. Now I can spend my newfound spare time assembling custom techno-music CDs to my heart's content.

Last week I stayed with web virgins. Honest, they didn't know how to search, outside of a mall, for the Barbra Streisand album they wanted. I taught them. I hope Lover feels as good about her techno-rescues as I did about leading my friends through the wires of the web. Or as I do after I deliver her from preying spiders.

When my computer lost its sound she quickly fixed it, explaining, "One of the kitties unplugged the speakers."

No wonder I was wireless.

THE COUNTRY MOUSE (1998)

My mother used to read me a story about a city mouse and a country mouse. I thought the city mouse was much cooler. Those country mice wore gingham and overalls. No contest.

Thirty-odd years later I moved to the country. I lived with mice. They did not wear gingham or overalls. They ate my lesbian pulp paperbacks, then nested in the leftover shreds.

Everything seemed shabby, compared to the city and the suburbs. There was nothing interesting to look at, like cornices on an old warehouse, or neon lights flashing reflections onto wet midnight sidewalks. After a while even majestic mountains can get a little humdrum.

I pined for the city. Any city. During those years I visited New York, Galveston, Chicago, Reno, Tucson, San Francisco, Seattle, Houston, Greensboro, Boston, Las Vegas, Portland (OR), Norfolk, DC, Corpus Christi, New Haven, Dallas, Concord (NH), Los Angeles, and on and on.

All I wanted was to walk the streets, ride the buses, look at the architecture. To visit the shops and museums and galleries and restaurants. I wrote about cities. I photographed cities. I dreamed about cities. I wondered if I could survive in mousey towns the rest of my life.

Little by little, something changed. I guess that something was me. I'd drag myself back from the bright lights and crowds and collapse. Goddess, it was good to get home. I'd say I never wanted to leave again, but a few months later I'd be hungry for the excitement, for romancing the concrete villages.

Meanwhile, back in Mousetown, I found that I had some friends. I got involved in The Audubon Society. I volunteered my time. The shopkeepers knew me by name. I could leave messages and packages for people at the bookstore or the natural food store.

I began to appreciate the quiet that five acres could bring. Or the cacophony that often greeted me when I got home: chickadees, nuthatches, doves, grosbeaks, wild turkeys, juncos, towhees. Birdsong, not taxi horns. Our land sounded like an aviary, but the creatures were free. I was free.

The idea of living in an apartment building became anathema to me. Layer on layer of boxes stacked toward the sky? Those things could collapse, for heaven's sake. And to get in an elevator, a mousetrap that ran up and down on strings—had I ever really thought that was a good idea?

Country isn't neat little squares with life hidden behind screens of brick. You kind of get used to spilling over onto the land you share with critters. City sprawls too, but now that sprawl looked shabby. The teeming streets of summer with every stoop filled, lawn chairs on sidewalks, kids hopscotching—I felt crowded instead of neighborly, they sounded loud, not exultant.

I was changing. Every year I had looked forward to going to New York. Then I realized all I wanted was to see the skyline. Then I didn't even want that.

The sights I loved are overwhelming. The sounds I barely noticed are confusing. The dangerous what-ifs are too numerous to defend against: those snapping elevator strings and collapsing buildings, muggers and pedestrian-hating cabbies, gangs and terrorists and neighbors going postal.

The city was a wonderful place to grow up. Museums were my playgrounds, parks my Sherwood Forests. It was a lot easier to come out with Greenwich Village a subway ride away and Valerie Taylor's novels in the bookstores.

I know it's not age that's doing in my love of cities. There are plenty of fiftysomethings thriving in metropolises.

I've been seduced. Lover was surprised today when she watched me pick up the lizard in our canning closet and reassure it that it would find the move outside beneficial. I've come to be quite fond of lizards. They don't eat lesbian books.

Yesterday I hiked with publisher Renee LaChance and poet Ila Suzanne, two transitioning ex-urbanites. I was chilly in the clear morning air, excited at the sea lion Renee spotted. We all had binoculars at the ready for glimpses of every bird we could find. It's taken a while, but I learned there's something interesting to look at in the country.

My friends weren't wearing gingham, but I was in my blue-and-white striped OshKosh overalls.

Later, at home, I read an old *New York Times* I'd been hoarding, finished up the latest *New Yorker*, and came across a great Lower East Side photo from *New York Magazine*. I cut out the photo. It's on my desk, plucking at my heartstrings.

The Country Mouse, that's me.

DANCING IN THE STREETS (1999)

Y2K means a lot of things to a lot of people. For me, it will mark thirty years since I became a card-carrying member of the Women's Movement.

We didn't build bombs or plot government downfalls. We didn't subvert kids or put stealth candidates on school boards. We met to unburden angers and confess stifled yearnings. We sang together like Girl Scouts and comforted one another. We parceled out chores and planned demonstrations. We tried to invent alternative housing, we tried to share money, we tried to get along. We held dances.

The hub of all this hopeful activity for me was the Women's Center in New Haven, Connecticut. Housed in two castoff rooms in the basement of a Yale dormitory, we had a couch, pillows, chairs, desks, lamps. We took turns staffing the Center, answering the phone and rudely turning away curious men. We had no useful strategies, only dreams. Our models were created by powerful males and disenfranchised males. Books about communism in China were popular. Dealing and struggling was the phrase du jour, and stealing The Man's technology a rallying cry as women took up electric guitars and learned to do their own sound.

While a women's band played "Dancing In the Street," we drank buckets of sangria from lined thirty-three-gallon garbage cans. We socialized with one another in lefty working class bars, ignoring the stymied menfolk. We alienated our old friends and our families. The women who were not yet out alternately lectured and hectored male lovers. Lesbians either hated all guys or pitied and befriended the gentle ones. Gay men were dismissed as the lowest of the low, belittling women with drag and stereotypical effeminate behavior. The Radical Faeries were still but a gleam in the eyes of Harry Hay, and the first stirrings of gay liberation seemed like a rip-off.

When we danced in the streets, church basements, college halls, and bars we were dancing to Anne Murray and Linda Ronstadt. We despised the Rolling Stones, who sang "Under My Thumb."

In great powerful circles we held hands and group-danced to Sly and the Family Stone and the New Haven Women's Liberation Rock Band.

Laughing and conspiratorial, we sang along with Todd Rundgren's "We Gotta Get You a Woman" and Stephen Stills's "Love the One You're With."

We made love by candlelight and incense to LPs of Jethro Tull and Joy of Cooking.

We scorned the Carpenters, never guessing Karen needed to be with us. Elvis was lower than gay men.

We cried for all the lost women when James Taylor sang "Fire and Rain," Neil Young extolled his "Cinnamon Girl," and Simon and Garfunkel wailed "Bridge Over Troubled Water."

Janis Joplin was a martyr. Joni Mitchell and Aretha Franklin were goddesses. We were goddesses, just discovering the labrys, that double-sided ax with which the Amazons smote their enemies—and were just discovering words like labia, that double-sided flower of our sexuality.

In the shadowed women's center we felt the kind of excitement that changes the world. We daringly danced without men. We danced on the campus, in the parks, in moving cars as we drove back and forth to Manhattan. We took over straight dance floors.

All of us were exploding with liberated energy. Working nine to five was out of the question. We were in the midst of a revolution simmering with sex and danced till we were sweaty with sweat we never knew we had. We had never heard ourselves speak out loud and now screamed with Janis. We thought Angela Davis of the Black Panthers was the greatest woman in the world, and we sang inspirational songs on the New Haven Common with our black sisters and brothers. Indian bedspread drapes hid revolutionary women fugitives from the law. Our phone was tapped.

This new breed of women crowded into New York and Boston gay bars, danced in circles, and met other women afire like us. The old gays were lower than Elvis. They obviously wanted to be men. The butches oppressed femmes in makeup. The libbers secretly wanted to dance like the butches, dirty and possessive. And like the femmes, safe in another woman's arms.

We wore jeans and cotton harem-style pants, long skirts, sandals or ragged high-top sneakers, T-shirts, flannel shirts, and peasant blouses. Jewelry was silver or wood and bought in head shops. We grew our hair long or cropped it radically short. The colors of our revolution were bright reds and yellows, deep blues and seductive purples. Everything else was lavender.

We ate vegetables, fruit, brown rice, yogurt, honey bought through our co-op. We split rent so many ways we paid forty dollar a month each. Our homes were run-down houses whose rooms we painted in bright orange or other vibrating hues.

The Women's Center, nestled on the training ground for the future military-industrial leaders, was the place where we invented our feminist selves. It was the witch's mouth which spewed us forth into the world like lit torches. Soon women's centers claimed territory in every large city. We were joyous with our anger and our demands for equality. We danced around bonfires in the night and we were the bonfires.

PARADE PERMIT (1999)

I just went down to the savings and loan in town to get our lineup number for the parade tomorrow. What a zoo. The bank manager is one of the organizers, not just of the parade, but of our little town's annual bash. Besides the parade there'll be slug races and public-figure dunking and a band concert, a boot contest (last year it was hats), and princesses whose hair will be done by the local beauty parlor, and two dances, a boat decorating contest, and a street fair and a strawberry festival, though the strawberries are said to be late this year.

The bank manager had phones in both hands. She was delegating with her eyes and tosses of her chin. Customers were trying to cash paychecks in order to have enough $3.50s to buy pancake breakfasts at the Elks Club for the whole family. The fellow ahead of me wanted an application to drive his vintage car in the parade. A bunch of kids were across the street polishing up the 1962 good-for-nothing red fire engine.

It's a really big deal in a small town, this parade thing. Being hooked into it makes me feel bubbly inside.

I've been trying to recruit marchers for the library contingent. Do they call them contingents in nonpolitical marches? Not that this is a politics-free tradition. The Republicans and the Democrats both march—and I suppose any parade with the National Guard in their lovable Humvees can be called political.

My participation, however, is not political. Well, maybe a little since I'm trying to give the library a higher profile. It's a piddly-sized library, but the staff makes it feel big. I think I can get any book in the world I want through interlibrary loan. The facility itself might be all of eight hundred square feet. Every time they get a new book an old one has to go.

If I were in a political space, I'd be in one of the big cities parading for gay pride. I've been calling dykes, trying to corral them into marching for the library, but they're all going to gay pride. This ought to be a very big year for gay turnout. Meanwhile I'll be striding along Main Street under a banner that should read: THE ONLY FRIEND OF THE LIBRARY. Not very impressive.

But fun. How surprised I've been at the delight I can take doing small-towny, civic pride activities with the straight people. Last year there were only a handful of us library boosters, but we were so high-spirited, and silly, wearing ridiculous hats and costumes, that we won a first prize. I wore a lion costume. At one point a little girl approached me in wonder and I playfully growled at her. Whoops. She switched into reverse and looked as if she might cry. I had no idea a kid might believe in my rag-tag costume. What a learning experience for me.

This year I'll be more benign as the White Rabbit, complete with a floppy-eared, bunny-faced beanie that friends loaned me. I'll hop around and look frequently at the oversized pocket watch and rainbow-colored chain I'm making tonight. Anything for a good cause.

It's been important for me take Parade 101. For decades my only experience of a parade was marching through city streets with defiant thousands protesting this or that, and celebrating with the rainbow people. Such gatherings were as serious business to us as this town's big day is to the bank manager. Peaceniks in beads and major hair, wimmyn in the armor of androgyny, pretty boys in extravagant queen-clothing, those were the good old days. Even when we were having fun, we were aware that our very presence was a, sometimes illegal, Statement. March in a parade just for fun? What a concept!

I honestly didn't know what to do with myself the first time I simply paraded. The march adrenaline was fierce, but I had no outlet. I was demonstrating the importance of the library to the town, but people were enjoying my presence. The police marched with us not because of us. There wasn't a whiff of tear gas. Strange.

Even stranger, I don't feel a bit guilty about high-stepping with the once-enemy. It's not such an us-and-them world today. Tomorrow—I'll have to see—as I go hippity-hopping along Main Street for all ten blocks of the parade route, a silver-haired woman in androgynous costume carrying on an old, old tradition that brings wonder to the faces of children and goodwill to the hearts of adults. Can't be all bad.

THE TAO OF BUTCH (1999)

It's time to speak out. My patience has worn thin. The tao of butch is being misrepresented.

Normally I ignore these online questionnaires that help one evaluate how femme or butch one is. This one came as a semichallenge from friends. The attorney who sent it bemoaned her score, lowered by the nylons requirement that afflicts female practitioners of her craft. Her entrancingly femme partner racked up a satisfying minus score, commenting—or bragging—"I guess you can't pass every test you take."

I innocently plunged in but was almost immediately stopped in my overconfident tracks.

"Does the vehicle you drive most have standard transmission?" (3 points) Well, no, I just bought my very first automatic a couple of years ago. Shifting was too hard on the aging body, although I suffered through twenty years of tendinitis from sheer pride and unwillingness to accept my disability.

"Do you regularly wear men's cologne or aftershave?" (2 points) Well, no, not anymore. Both Lover and I are severely allergic to artificial fragrances and have difficulty being in the same room, even on the same planet, with people who perfume themselves.

I lost two points because I don't lift weights. I was never that anxious to spend my life in the chiropractor's office, but now I'm under strict orders from the doc to avoid heavy lifting.

I appealed to the attorney. She ruled, "Okay, I agree, some of the questions require a slight modification: *Do you* should be read throughout as *Have you ever*. Fair enough?"

Fair enough. Of course I've owned foreign cars. Of course I've worn steel-toed work boots—I just discarded the beloved shit kickers I bought in 1970. When I was a romantic youth, wearing keys on my belt was indeed a major pride. I never tried to tie a cherry stem into a knot with my tongue, but you bet I used to drink shots.

So, as the lead singer melodically boasts in Carolyn Gage's musical comedy *The Amazon All-Stars*, I'm a big bad butch! I admit to some amused ego gratification at my score which put me in the (surprise!) *decidedly diesel* category. But I have some questions for the Questionnaire.

Why would anyone do anything that hurt her body for twenty years, whether shifting gears with an injured arm or drinking oneself silly? Because that's how I demonstrated my identity? Do femmes have their own torturous rituals? High heels come to mind. Hard to believe as femmes are generally more sane than silly show-off butches.

Do the newly out, say the forty-three-year-old single mom who's just left her hetero marriage of twenty-one years, take these jesting questions as standards? Who will teach her differently? I learned by example, aping my elders, but that kind of imperative isn't as powerful as seeing "Do you ever wear a leather collar ?"(5 points) in print. Of course, she may read fashion rags and think collars and leashes are alluring. Naive me, I thought that was an SM practice, not butch.

I hope no baby butch concludes that her native talents and what she's born with aren't enough to please her girlfriend and that a dildo (1 point) is required rather than optional equipment. Or that she'd be a sissy to shave her armpits (minus 1) if she's trying to make a living as a ballerina.

It may be all in fun, but these things stick. They enter our culture or, if already there, are reinforced. Don't we already know from the dominant culture that it is not okay to be too old or too disabled to want to climb mountains and raft rivers? (10 points per event) Some expectations are our own fault. Butches don't crochet. (Like heck we don't.) Butches carry knives with four-inch blades. (Only at Girl Scout camp.)

Yes, I'm making too much of it all. It's a holdover from the days when highly politicized women tried in vain to teach me how to be a lesbian after I'd been doing it since the first time I rolled a packet of candy cigarettes into a shirt sleeve.

The way to approach these things is with my retired friend's sense of fun. "Do you own more than three flannel shirts?" (+2) She answered, "Of course—sixty-nine. How about a point for each one?"

There's also, I'll admit, a bit of butch arrogance speaking here. "Do you have a black leather jacket with lots of zippers?" (+5) Well,

I challenge any leather jacket any straight girl can buy at any Target store to out-butch my cracked, faded, fleece-lined brown leather authentic flight jacket which I bought years ago in San Francisco. But then, as Lover says, "It's not the jacket, it's the way you wear it."

Now that's the tao of butch.

Y2Gay (1999)

When I think back to that first moment at age fifteen when I leaned over and kissed Suzy, and how frightened we were of being caught, I remember the terror mixed with excitement that became a part of my being. Hypervigilance settled deeply into my very muscles.

Today, that tension is ingrained, that caution a part of me. I still find it difficult not to lower my voice when I speak the words lesbian or gay. Often I use the phrase *s/he's family* rather than blow anyone's cover to eavesdroppers, even when I'm speaking to someone who's not stuck in the closet.

The phrase *the damage done*, from Neil Young's "The Needle and the Damage Done," rings in my ears when I think about us. A different kind of damage was done to my generation than to that of my elders. We were the ones torn between the old ways that are a part of us and the brazen new freedom that was ours for the taking the moment those bulldykes and queens outside The Stonewall shouted, "No!" I'm aware in every muscle and nerve that I re-hurl their first brick each time I come out to someone by saying *My partner, she*. The thrill and bone-deep apprehension of that adrenaline surge has lessened, but never completely gone away.

And why should it? The Republicans are accepting our political donations, the administration holds meetings with us, the military takes baby steps to protect us from dishonor and heterosexist violence, but the disenfranchised guy on the street keeps a baseball bat handy for bashing our queer heads

Despite him the times are incredibly different. The new, appealingly reviewed lesbian film *Better Than Chocolate* isn't banned even in Boston. Our local small-town theater had no qualms about airing *In and Out*, with Kevin Kline and très butch Tom Selleck—possibly the most gay-positive film I've ever seen.

The Radical Wrong is not gone, yet growing numbers of Americans now understand it's comprised of silly overreactionaries. I'm amazed how quickly the global coming-out party of the last thirty years has revolutionized attitudes and erased much of the ignorance. Enlightened religious folk may believe in hell, but they don't automatically expect to see us there.

Hate groups and their followers aren't going to disappear anytime soon, if ever, but there seems to be a general sense that they're over the edge. Sure there's the lady at the Laundromat, squinting over the cigarette hanging from the side of her mouth, who complains we're everywhere, taking the jobs from real men. And there's the tight-collared CEO who wants us screened out of his company.

When I came out, people like these were in the majority; now they're a dying breed. Within the next few years the Laundromat Lady's going to quit smoking and let her daughter's girlfriend come for Easter dinner. The CEO will be let go when gay-friendly stockholders protest his policies, gays boycott his products, and gifted employees go where they don't have to work in closets.

At the same time the lady at the health-food store asks how my partner is today, and the new owner of my company doesn't just market my job-related skills, but brags that I'm a gay writer. This is the second job I've had where I've dared to be out. It's been years since I've wished I'd used a nom de plume.

New York Magazine just ran a feature on Evan Wolfson, legal Boy Scout and gay-marriage champion, titling it "Family Man" and affectionately highlighting his quest for a husband. This is some change from the days when magazines with serious gay content were available in a grand total of two stores in the country.

Is anyone incredulous besides me?

Of course there's so much more to be done, but we've integrated the revolution into our lives. We change minds every time we move in next door, or ask for the right to marry. Nongays can see that we're too busy mowing the lawn to be recruiting. They already know marriage takes the danger out of sex.

The next generation should be even more schooled in who we are, when many gay-raised children reach adulthood and marry people of another gender.

I'm filled with hope today, buoyed by what I see around me in the last months of the millennium. When I kiss Lover in public now, I sometimes have to stop myself from looking over my shoulder, but just as often I forget.

Some new young Lee, somewhere, is leaning over to kiss some new young Suzy. They're still scared, but it's mostly the fear of exposure experienced by any young couple in lust. The excitement of freedom is eclipsing the daily terror of the outlaw as we approach the year—the century—of Y2Gay.

Deviant (2000)

In the early sixties I spent a lot of time, like most teens, trying to figure out who I was. My best resource was the library. The section where I found the most relevant information was Criminology.

New York, where I lived, considered me a juvenile delinquent because I was a gay kid. Never mind that I was well brought up, didn't skip school and/or carry a switchblade like some of the nongay girls.

Nevertheless, I was a young criminal and the studies of female deviants in prison were all I had of literature about myself. Often, their criminality was attributed to their variant natures. Occasionally they were granted a kind of forgiveness. After all, the women studied were in jail, without men, poor things, so they had to make do. I was suspicious of these studies—if researchers studied women in prison, then all the lesbians they studied would be—Guess what?—criminals!

I admired these bad women. It never occurred to me that they might actually be criminals. They were gay; if they stole it was because they couldn't get decent jobs, and if they assaulted it was because they couldn't control the circumstances of their lives.

Living happily ever after was not to be for them. Inside, they fell in love with and fought for straight women who might go back to men. I can't imagine why I was so proud and happy that I was queer like these women, or why reading about them gave me such a thrill. If I was sick, then it was an illness I treasured. If I had to survive in their world then I would—and by my wits, not by my fists, although I was perfectly ready to use those if I had to. My brother, as if sensing the vulnerability of my difference, had taught me long before how to box.

Despite my queer attraction to these lesbians, I knew I'd never be quite like them. Sure, I could talk kind of tough, but I was better at keeping my mouth shut and getting teased about being the strong, silent type. Sure, I had to walk like I had no fear, but I'd never exactly mastered a girlish sashay in the first place. And of course I had to learn to drink, a talent for which my genes showed great promise.

Oh, and I was a criminal. I'd fallen in love with my best friend—that made me a menace to society, right?

Since the film *Boys Don't Cry* opened, several women I know have come back looking shell-shocked. I can't bear to see the movie, and I guess they got a bigger dose of reality than they'd paid for.

Brandon Teena may have been trans, or may have been a lesbian in drag, or may not have used those terms at all. However he identified, all that I've read and heard has taken me right back to my baby butch days. It's important that this film is out there because it apparently graphically demonstrates that nothing's really changed; there are still women who are attracted to other women, act on it, and are punished by society one way or another, sometimes by vicious men like Teena's accused murderers.

I certainly had gender issues as a kid, but I didn't want to be a male. I found them foreign creatures, too large, too loud, and so arrogant. Why should they always get the last say? I remember thinking. And they did get the last say—at least the last Teena ever heard.

When I came out, some of us were really into drag or even into passing—at age fourteen and earlier. This wasn't the same as wanting to live as a man. For a little while each week or each day we felt strong in our boy clothes. We didn't get stared at when we put an arm around our girlfriends. We walked more freely in the world.

Somehow, my friends and I managed to stay out of major trouble—and to stay alive. I remember lying on a bed fully clothed, a fascinating young woman beside me, when her boyfriend came upon us. He started physically bullying me. I was good at the squirm and run maneuver and managed to plunge into the thick of the ongoing party where he couldn't get at me. How many of us have had these close encounters?

It may now be legal for women to wear men's clothing and to make love with women, but both can still get one killed. If Teena had done male hormones and surgery he might still be alive.

Who knows what will be standard forty years from Brandon Teena's death and after forty years of gender exploration. Maybe we're evolving toward blended genders. Or will kids, trans or gay, still be reading criminology texts to find themselves—as victims?

DILBERT DAYS (2001)

Is there anything more uncomfortable than a new job?
Of course there is. I could crash-land in a foreign country and be a prisoner. I could be homeless and hungry in freezing weather. I could have a painful disease or disability.

I'm thankful to have a job. Seventeen months ago the company I worked for closed, and I didn't have the heart to go job hunting, nor could I face the prospect of another first day at work. The very idea gave me the creepy-crawlies. So I struck out on my own and built up a little business that kept me out of the poorhouse. My hours were long and I filled out job applications to ease my insecurities. One day I realized that the worst was behind me and I'd succeeded at my microbusiness. What was next, joining the Republican Party?

This month I traded in being my own boss, which was a capitalist illusion that I loved, for the illusion of safety I have at my new job. (At the least I may be eligible for unemployment down the line. If there's still unemployment after Bush.) It was the right decision, but now I have to live with the first-month blues.

I have a great employer, one I got to try out as a subcontractor. Instead of staff meetings, I talk with her by phone. Instead of meeting with clients, I e-mail them. I'm off the front lines, providing services to service providers, so I'm in a help/help position, working for both the clients and their providers. Best, I work at home where the dress code requires baggy jeans and oversized cotton pullovers. When I get on firm financial footing, I'll buy one shirt in each available color, including frosted blueberry, teabag, gumball, and pimento, to make my country dyke power wardrobe complete.

I have the ideal job. But it's a very new job. It doesn't fit yet. It's as if my shirts and jeans are wet and I'm waiting for them to dry to size in a humid climate. Yet this is more comfortable than crying at the cash register over a first-day multi-million-dollar error. It doesn't come near the excruciating self-consciousness I felt (a lesbian wolf among the innocent sheep) on meeting the women at council headquarters the day I became a professional Girl Scout. It couldn't outdo being tossed with a raft of other new college grads into a nascent antipoverty program and being told to make it work. It's nothing to being literally flown out of the sticks to a multinational in the big city and getting a caseload to work while simultaneously receiving training and reading twenty-five-pound manuals. Or getting the oldest boat of a cab, the one with steering that made streets feel like sand dunes and squishy brakes, then being dispatched into parts of the city even armed cops avoided.

For someone that never felt like she belonged anywhere, starting a new job was—and is—confirmation of all my fears. Yes, I'm inadequate. No, I'm not trainable. Nobody likes me, everybody hates me, I'm going to go eat worms! This would be comical if it weren't happening to me.

Taking a job was supposed to mean that I wouldn't have to do clerical work and bookkeeping long into the night. In order to stay employed, I'm burning more midnight oil, not less. Taking a job was supposed to make me feel more secure. There is no way I can measure up to the impossible expectations I expect my new employer to expect of me. She tries in vain to reassure me and to make these early days less torturous, but I'll prove my worth if it kills me. Fortunately, there's health insurance.

I keep hoping each new job will be my last, that the mythical concept of retirement will turn out to be real. Or that one of my books will find the brave producer who understands that it's The Universal Lesbian Story which will end homophobia for all time and make a blockbuster movie out of it, paying me handsomely. Or, more likely, that I'll win the lottery.

I really like my job, and I know the awkward stage will end and I know everything has always turned out fine before—but it's still a job. Discomfort, insecurity, overwork, miserable first days. In my experience, that's the nature of the beast.

Can you imagine? It was like wearing a virtual burka twenty-four/ seven. Out to my family, friends, to neighbors, teachers, employers? Forget it. You just did not tell. Or ask.

And gay people still do this. I still do this. My early training went deep.

It's a lot more complex now. In my twenties I knew I could only be out on weekends, around other gays. During the week the gay part of me (all 99.9 percent of it) simply disappeared. Pouf! I'm a normie. Navigating the world was like walking across a checkerboard and knowing that some of the red squares were too dangerous to step on.

My general policy is to be out to everyone. Doctors, lawyers, the accountant, these kinds of people have to know. But the bank tellers? Does one describe one's beneficiary as a friend or domestic partner? Loan officers? Realtors? I'm still a little nervous around these folks.

I was looking for a place to live with a Realtor recently, and we drove by a house in a *nice* neighborhood. I explained the geography of gay to her. Sometimes, nice neighborhoods are family-value neighborhoods. If a butch lesbian shows up on moving day with a continue of little red dyke trucks and women who stack cartons of books three high in their arms, the welcome mats get pulled inside. The Realtor said, "But I thought we were good about that kind of thing here." "It only takes one," I told her, "and I'd rather live in a quirky old fixer-upper than a neat closet."

I've left many closets behind. The newly out closet where every square looks red. The post-Stonewall closet where danger was just another word for excitement. The bar closet where I almost drowned in alcohol. The job closet which required incredible maneuvering between overly curious straight ladies, oblivious men on the make, and little power-hungry bosses for whom difference was a weapon. In the nineties the right wing tried to herd us into closets the size of concentration camps.

Adolescence was a closet all its own where by turns I cowered and flaunted my newly discovered gayness. Now I'm in the grayed closet where I have to practically carry a queer badge to be noticed, much less threaten anyone's sexuality. Yet I read a horror story about a lesbian in a nursing home. None of the staff would bathe the dyke.

That makes me want to build a vault. Or tear down every closet on earth.

THE GEOGRAPHY OF GAY: NEW YORK CITY (2001)

Really my hometown was my first lover. New York City embraced me, educated me, somehow shielded me from its hidden threats. Long before I came out and learned that it was the gay capital of the world, it was like a glamorous woman, resplendent in Christmas finery, elegant in bright colors that sparkled in the black velvet nights. I fell hard for her, with her rushing trains and movie palaces, infinite number of circus rings and her siren voice, half cacophony, half symphony.

On the day of the attacks I spoke with a sister New York City expatriate. When I told her that I kept thinking the words, "My city, my city," she cried, "That's exactly what I've been saying!" When I got to the anger stage of my grief, I found that I was incensed. "How dare they mess with my town," I thought.

We can't help it. Educated in New York City schools in the 1950s and 1960s, we were taught that New York was the best city in the best country in the world. I spent years studying its history, geography, and culture. I was told that there were other important places in the world. But in my heart only New York mattered.

To this day I love to read books set in New York. I collect art books about New York. Lover knows she has to sit through all the titles of a video if they're, as they often are, superimposed on camera work depicting New York. I guess I've never fallen out of love.

This is all very foolish; I haven't lived in New York for over thirty years, haven't visited in a decade. The city doesn't age and I can't keep up with her anymore—she wears me out. I love her from afar, she who has been beloved by more lesbians than she cares to recall. Yet I notice my accent, never before strong, is reasserting itself. Is this an unconscious gesture of my devotion? I am heartsick that I am not among her healers. Yes, I sent a little money, but she's been wooed by billionaires and her wounds will require their ministering.

Sometimes I think that I might not have come out at all had I not been seduced by this vamp of a femme. But then I am appalled at the thought—a breeding life as a heterosexual is completely unimaginable to me. No, I would have come out, just later. I am so grateful to have started my conscious gay life where even Beebo Brinker lived. I walked in the streets Willa Cather and Gertrude Stein once walked.

I wonder if people who grew up in Kabul are as chauvinistic and proud about their hometown.

NYC was my playground. As kids, Suzy (my first human lover) and I could—and did—spend fifteen cents on the subway, swaying at the front window of the cars, to travel to the harbor, to Broadway, to an airport or ballpark. We could ride underground or walk the canyons of Lexington Avenue. A nickel got us a romantic ferry ride. We slid along the slick floors of Grand Central Station and hung out in the greatest museums of the world and shadowed the dykes of Greenwich Village.

Although my parents saw New York as the enemy, I think it's the best gift they could have given me. Of course they were right, I was sucked into the underworld of gay life. And I was right—it was a glorious underworld. They thought the city was dangerous, but I found it safe. Suzy and I were never evicted from museums for making out. No gay adult so much as spoke to us. No bar let us in. We learned through experimentation like all baby dykes did. The difference was that I knew from day one that we were not the only lesbians in the world, and from day two that lesbians were as happy and productive as anyone else in New York. I knew these things because I could see my future self diddy-bopping down the street, and I was in love with her too.

The World Trade Center was built after I left, but I went back and rode the tourist elevator to the observation floor. I remember that the huge windowed room, like the city, easily absorbed the crowd. I remember hearing many languages spoken around me as I went from window to window. I remember marveling like the non-natives at my own hometown. I wanted to brag that I'd grown up there, to somehow claim as mine the vast majestic sight of the busy little island surrounded by her blue, blue waters. But that's the magic of New York, we all fit in there, we can all be proud of the imperfect democracy that thrives on our wealth of languages and cultures and allows us to come out as whoever we are.

CLOSETS I HAVE KNOWN (2002)

When I came out, everyone was in the closet. It would h occurred to me to ask someone, "Are you out to so You only came out to people you suspected might be a littl

The bus driver was one of them. I was in college a wheels, so if I was going farther than my bike would ta grab the bus. If I timed it right, the woman driver would I I say "the" woman driver because in the midsixties wom hired for strenuous jobs like sitting in one place all day ste This driver was so butch I imagine the personnel offic have dared to discriminate. I mean, she was tough-lookin pants and uniform shirt, mumbled out of the side of he gave me the look like she was inviting me into a club.

Which she wasn't. After months of getting up stuttered out some inane question to her probably alon "Is there a gay bar in town?" The woman didn't eve It was as if my words turned her to stone, which she anyway. Never looked at me again, never mumbled to slammed her closet door so hard I could feel the draft.

Another time I found someone in our queer under; when I went for driving lessons. I got a guy instructor good-looking, and very, very friendly. I looked kind androgynous Harry Potter. I was totally shocked whe me out at the end of the first lesson. What was he thi

I found out. He'd been scoping me out for the gi took a few lessons for Joyce and me to murmur en to each other to come out. When we did I not only l getting inspected by an intermediary to enter her ci actually been married to the guy who owned the c still used his name. Walk-in closet.

I Was a Gay High School Student (2002)

A tiny article in my local paper announced that the National Education Association has encouraged schools to adopt policies that punish harassment and discrimination against homosexual students and teachers. "About time," I grumbled over my breakfast muesli. Later I tried to remember what it had been like for me in high school.

I Was a Gay High School Student. Sounds like a tabloid headline, but in reality, I had a great time. It wasn't exactly a bed of roses, but I was a tough little dyke, at least I thought so, and I thrived on the adversity that came with being special.

At fifteen I barely knew what the word homosexual meant. At fifteen and a half, I knew I was one. This was in 1960. Don't ask me how I came to be so proud of being gay. I agonized over the stigma for two weeks—and I clearly remember that it was two weeks—before I embraced being gay with a convert's fervor. Many years later I reconnected with a friend from high school who came out as an adult. She told me that I'd always looked like I had a wonderful secret. I had a big crush on her at the time, so I imagine she saw an eagerness on my face to share that secret. I must have strutted along the hallways like a baby butch rooster, cruising for my kind.

If it was that hard for me to contain my ebullience back then, I can't imagine the challenge for gay kids these days, some of whom may go from the high of a gay pride march on a Sunday to the downer of an early morning math class on a Monday.

It occurs to me that nongay teens also move in an underground world. Sex, goth, drinking, whatever the current vices may be, drive all young people to hide their pleasures. Was I any worse off than the straight girl who needed birth control and feared to seek it out or the young guy who couldn't speak his love for girl or boy because of raging acne on his face? It all feels the same at age fifteen.

Except straight kids had a support system. There were adults they could choose to talk to. It was okay to be in love with someone of the opposite sex, unrequited or not. Gay kids had no such luxury. Proud as I was, half of me was continuously, silently defending my life choices, my existence. The verbal slurs hurt. Standing upright under a crushing load of disapproval left its scars. Energy I could have used to write to my full potential or succeed in sports or to help others was wasted in strategizing to survive. If just one teacher or Girl Scout leader had reached out and said, "You're okay, kid," what a weight would have been lifted from me.

Other than that, I didn't suffer much. I had one tormentor, a young man who I later learned had been dealing with his own sexuality issues. He called me names and did a lot of smirking and whispering with his friends. At the time I was terrified of him. The first rule the gay child learns is to protect her/his secret. Exposure was about the worst thing I could imagine. Better to die silent than live in shackles, no longer able to be my gay self.

As it was, I was banned for a period of time from seeing my girlfriend. My parents suspected… I learned that closets are filled with lies; telling tales became a way of life. I'd jump on my bike, ride like a messenger on speed to a distant part of Queens for a brief spell of bubblegum kisses and heart-to-heart laughter. We were in love, but even better, we were outlaw lovers, making out in doorways, in elevators, basements, empty subway cars. We were like Macy's Thanksgiving Parade balloons, bigger than life, better than ordinary life, flying above the crowds.

And completely unprotected. What a nightmare if we had been caught. What we did was proscribed by law, by religion, by culture. We could have been locked in jails or mental hospitals. We could have been beaten or murdered. We could have been shunned by our classmates, punished by our teachers. We lucked out. Other kids didn't. They were buried young—in dishonest marriages, in an avalanche of alcohol and drugs, in the ground.

What I fear for the kids whose peers and teachers get sensitivity training is that more gay kids will dare to come out and be crucified for their trust. I fear there will be a backlash from straight kids, that conservative parents and teachers and preachers will intensify antigay training. What I hope is that by shining the light of day into the closets of gay youth, their spirits will be stronger. It was exciting to be defiant, but also a burden that took energy a growing mind sorely needed elsewhere. It was intoxicating to be young and gay, but I'll never know what acceptance would have given me.

I'm glad gay kids will know the benefits of this greater acceptance. I'm glad a few of them will be able to take their puppy loves to the prom. I'm glad they'll be able to grow up with the kind of support that will enable them to become the teachers and writers and leaders we need. It's about time.

THE OSCAR WILDE BOOKSTORE (2002)

Sometimes I hate hets. Excuse, me, my mother tried to teach me never to use the word *hate*. Instead she recommended *intensely dislike*. Whatever. I try to be this positive, loving, accepting, nonjudgmental person, but heterosexuals—we can all name exceptions—and their pervasive culture sometimes sorely try my patience.

I realize that it's not directly their fault that Oscar Wilde Bookstore in New York City, the world's first gay bookstore, may be forced into bankruptcy just as I realize it is not entirely the fault of George Bush that the US appears to be chomping at the bit to get at Iraq. Blame is easy to assign; responsibility is a much more complex matter. It may be true that some gay writers are putting links to Amazon.com on their websites, and that most readers, myself included, generally will take the easiest, least expensive route to reading a book, but I wonder if our inability to prioritize our purchasing decisions is not deeply rooted in our heterosexist upbringing.

It is so easy to participate in the culture of the majority. Turn on the TV and what do you get: 99.9 percent het programming. Go to the movies and what do you see: 99.9 percent romanticized renditions of het life. Peruse the library shelves and what can you select: 99.9 percent are books, videotapes, and CDs by, for, and about people who experience the world very differently than do most gays.

When the Oscar Wilde first opened in 1967, I was living in the closet in Connecticut, a new college grad with seven years' experience in quietly haunting libraries, straight bookshops, corner drugstores, and newspaper stores in search of gay literature. The thought that there could be one physical space that would house what had taken me years to find was incomprehensible. That there were people in the world brave enough to risk their lives staffing such an emporium of variance just blew me away.

It took a while to work up the courage to visit the Oscar Wilde, but my need for it overcame my fear. The store was not on Christopher Street then. Christopher Street as we now know it wasn't even Christopher Street. The Stonewall riots had not yet changed the face of the gay universe, and no magazine bore the name of that still sleepy street. The Oscar Wilde was some blocks east, a tiny storefront that I found awe inspiring, comforting, and terrifying all at once. I was very nervous, not only that I'd be seen, but that I wouldn't be seen, wouldn't be able to make some connection with other literary warriors. Here I was, surfacing from a life underground—I wanted to shout my existence while I muffled myself.

Life has never been the same for any of us since the Oscar Wilde took its stand at the portals of gay liberation. I have always associated its opening with the Stonewall riots. Having a gay commercial enterprise in the greatest city in the world legitimized us in a way nothing else could in a capitalist country. The founders of that bookstore sold not just books, but courage and strength.

And now the Oscar Wilde may be closing. It's a matter of being careful, as they say in 12-step groups, what you pray for. Back in 1967 I was not alone in wanting acceptance, a safe place in the world. When gay lib came along, although I walked the gay pride route giddy with excitement and a feeling of empowerment, something in me was uneasy. Would normalizing gayness lead to demystifying it? Would being gay be viewed as normal instead of special? Because I have always felt special and, yes, I admit it, superior, to the hets with all their privileges and blood ties and mini-mes.

While I, and many like me, came out early enough to have roots in the old secret-society kind of gay world, others threw themselves wholeheartedly into the new era. Coming out to family and society now became as much a rite of passage as coming out itself. Sustenance was suddenly available and encouraged in the form of an accessible gay culture that included books and our own politicians, dances, and our own church. We became a people, a sometimes romanticized and ennobled tribe. We claimed our place in the sun.

And then we got swallowed up. The lesbi-gay businesses are shutting down one by one. What were we thinking to give nongays control of our culture by letting them distribute, then sell, then record or film or publish us?

There's a lot of talk about assimilation these days. About how we've made it into the mainstream and have become so complacent that we don't support the very institutions which got us to this place. And it's all true. Many of us don't have to struggle today. For every ten lesbian teachers who play it cool in school, there is one who teaches gay lit to her English classes. Which of them is more invisible? Which of them is most likely to buy a book at the Oscar Wilde? Ironically, neither.

And that's why I, at times, intensely dislike hets. Either way they're still calling the shots. Whether I'm scared and suspicious of them (I'm both) or basking in their acceptance and approval (I want both), I am Other. It is not time to let go of the infrastructure that has given birth to a fearless generation any more than it is time to give up an inch of the bloodied ground we have gained. Some highly visible nongay people may accept us, but that doesn't mean they've let go of seeing themselves as the norm and gay people as deviant. They may invite us to their parties and give us domestic partner benefits, but that doesn't mean they want their kids to come out. I am so tired of their arrogant chauvinism, their assumption of having the correct sexuality, of their sexual imperialism. I'd almost rather be reviled than tolerated and, in truth, believe for all their liberal posturing, that deep down I am reviled.

It's hard for a marginalized people to reject the crumbs of safety and privilege tossed by those who haven't let go of an ounce of power. It's hard not to leave icons of struggle like the Oscar Wilde behind. It's hard to resist the seductiveness of the unwitting benevolent despots we call family of birth or straight friends or accepting coworkers. We probably won't. It'll take inevitable het betrayals before we understand that assimilation is just another closet. We can reverse our losses—and our deceptive gains—by taking back our culture now.

The Dyke Who Kept Christmas (2003)

It always surprises me to learn how many, many lesbians celebrate Christmas. Whatever winter holiday we observe—or don't observe—Christmas and its rituals always peek through. The other day Lover's mom was remembering aloud her childhood visits to downtown Chicago to see the Christmas decorations. My parents took me into Manhattan to see Lord & Taylor's window display and Rockefeller Center. This is a vivid memory. Whether its roots mean anything to me or not, Christmas flows in my veins and surrounds me. I guess since Mr. and Mrs. Claus and their retinue are part of my cultural heritage, it's a matter of if you can't fight 'em, join 'em.

So I do. It's too hard to hide from the season and too exhausting to be angry, like Alison Bechdel's Mo, at everything about it. Even public radio joins the national glut of Christmas music. If I had any desire to donate coins to The Homophobic Salivation Army, that desire would die with the first clang of the Army's irritating and inescapable bells. If I watched television, I would ask Santa to bring me a rock under the tree to throw at the greedy advertisements. If I see a crèche decorating a town's common space, I feel personality assaulted by such flagrant violation of the principle of separation of church and state.

Yet come Christmas Day I am very grateful not to be a lonesome rebel. I chuck my principles to the wind, kiss my girl, and say, "Merry holiday." I call my far-flung family. I give the gifts I've been buying since last January. I open presents.

The central social event of Christmas Day has become for me an annual visit to the home of our friends, the Pianist and the Handydyke. For many years they've invited the community at large to bring potluck goodies and gather around a metaphorical groaning board. Their living room is literally stuffed with dykes. It's the kind of scene I used to write into stories, dreaming. I didn't know it could really happen. Have lesbians always done this?

In earlier years I traveled through blizzards and traffic, leaving my partner behind, to celebrate with my birth family. It never occurred to me then that I had a choice not to; everyone I knew did the same. Whenever I could, I'd leave the relatives on Christmas Day and drive three hours to spend the evening at home by my own tree. Even when I stopped commuting north for the holiday, my then partner and I went to her family's home both Christmas Eve and Christmas Day. It was exhausting, but where else could a dyke go?

It wasn't until I moved to the West Coast that December 25 began to take a shape that reflected my life, or the life I wanted. I found other lesbians and gay men out here who wanted to be part of the festivities, but with our own people. There were always queers, usually a long-standing couple, who turned their homes into shelters from the Christian blizzard. Those of us driven to make merry by nostalgia, loneliness, or even a desire to observe a holy day could do it together.

I'll soon pull out my carefully neutral winter holiday cards and make funky little catnip mice for the cat people I know. I'll wrap up the gifts and mail them in my stead to my relatives back East. Lover will prepare her famous cranberry relish. The lesbian family we've become part of will jingle the phone lines to decide who'll bring what to their gathering.

It's just astonishing to me how far I've traveled from isolation to community. Is having a gay home for the holidays a byproduct of our noisy antiestablishment gay liberation movement? Does the radical Christian right suspect that their day of days is now ours too? Do the legislators understand that these gay families who come together for the holiday are yet another kind of lawless civil union? Whatever. I'm just glad that this season, yet again, there's room at the inn for me.

SCRUFFY LITTLE DYKES (2003)

When my friend the Innkeeper told me she was going to an art gallery opening a few weeks ago, I asked if I could tag along. She paused for a long moment and a thousand reasons for her hesitation raced through my head. "If," I offered, in a very small voice, "you don't mind going with a scruffy little dyke." Immediately, she said, "I've been living with a scruffy little dyke for thirty-four years."

We went on to plan the excursion. A few minutes later it hit me. I told her, "I just realized what you really said," and got off the phone quickly because I thought I was going to cry. I was feeling a huge wave of appreciation for the good femmes who stay thirty-four years with their scruffy little dykes (SLDs).

And what is an SLD? It's a woman who is not tall, but not necessarily short, who's inclined to live in blue jeans, but has a good pair for dress up, or at least a clean pair. Some people might look a little puzzled about why my good pair deserves that description. She's likely to dress very simply, in T-shirts with short sleeves and maybe long sleeves if it's chilly. In my case I like to have a few denim or canvas shirts or work shirts, to protect me from the sun and because I think a collar looks spiffier on those occasions when I need a little spiffing up. Like art shows.

I know many lesbians no longer believe in femme and butch because they think this is role playing, but I have never played a role in my life; I simply know where I fall. Was it something in my baby formula? Was it because I adored my big brother? Is it in my genes? Or maybe it was because my mother taught me that comfort is one of the greater virtues. She, of course, talked the talk and did not walk the walk, but her daughter took her at her word and is a bra-phobic woman who dresses like a skateboarding teenage boy. Aka, an SLD. And proud of it.

Yet I have to wonder why femmes put up with us. The Innkeeper with the SLD partner could hardly complain if she wanted to. She tells the story of the guest who asked if she always wore T-shirts. The Innkeeper said, "No, in the winter I wear sweatshirts." The difference is that she wears pretty-yet-interesting sweatshirts decorated with abstract designs or other arresting graphics, and her partner generally goes for solids and handsome illustrations embellished with house paint or sawdust from her many handydyke projects. Sometimes they share. They both wear jeans most of the time. The Innkeeper disdains the time it takes to "do all that shit," like makeup and fancy girl clothes. But does any femme ever look like an SLD? No way! She looks well put together. How do femmes do that?

Having recently been thrown over for the dominant society, I am painfully aware that some women do not put up with us. They want to change us or they give us a wide berth. Some lesbians are otherwise fine partners who were perhaps brought up in a way that makes living with an SLD a trial. Some women are bi and straddle both worlds with amazing dexterity including the world that comes equipped with SLDs. The women I most admire are the ones I call the good femmes, the women who love us partly because we are scruffy little dykes. They will straighten a collar with tenderness in their eyes, walk down the street alongside us with an unconscious protective defiance, and gladly avoid places where we might be made uncomfortable.

They seem to think, the good femmes, that we are beautiful despite a society that finds us repellent. Some of them enjoy nothing better than spending time with a gaggle of admiring SLDs. They are a special breed, these femmes, created to love and be loved by the special breed called scruffy little dykes.

The concept of the SLD has become a family joke now, but we've talked seriously about it too. The Innkeeper is careful to use the words self-proclaimed before she uses the SLD term. The best news is that this good femme doesn't see us as SLDs at all. Rather than describing us as little, or scruffy, she sees us as women who dress for comfort, practicality, and for our situations, whether we are painting houses, dancing till dawn, or cooking breakfast.

What she hasn't acknowledged knowing is, of course, that we dress for her.

DYKE STATUES (2003)

I met a really sweet young lesbian not long ago. By young, I mean that she was in her thirties. She let a mutual acquaintance know how welcomed she felt by our community. In her own, she felt discounted and rejected because of her relative youth. I'd really thought things had changed since the days when Suzy and I trailed the grown-up dykes around New York. We, of course, were jailbait at fifteen in the era when to be a lesbian was a crime, and the women we so admired, emulated, lusted after, and copied had no choice but to shun us.

Why would any community today be anything but enthusiastically welcoming to those who will carry on our spirit, our work, our histories? Surely we don't fear that the young whippersnappers will in some way supplant us? I think the generation of gays that created a liberation movement, gave name and form to women's and gay male spirituality, started our publishing and music industries, put positive images of gays on TV and in films, accomplished the impossible with ACT UP and similar groups, is on the verge of being granted some form of legal recognition akin to marriage, got the Supreme Court to outlaw sodomy laws and Justice Clarence Thomas to call such laws "silly"—I think my generation of queers doesn't need to worry about getting credit where credit is due.

I've been thanked many times for being a pioneer and for recording the present that was becoming our history. I'm pleased and grateful when a younger person recognizes and values what s/he has inherited, and I try to pass back the baton. If not many of them are taking up the reins, could it be because we're loath to hand them over? I'm not involved in activities like planning marches or providing health services or even keeping one of our few remaining bookstores running, but I suspect that there are hordes of twenty- and thirty-somethings who are quietly learning the ropes. I was way surprised when I found myself one of a smattering of suddenly mature women holding the lesbian pens that would endure. The young gays will be surprised too, when they wake up to find themselves in charge of fundraising galas or managing gay-friendly motels in resort towns.

There is also an army of gay kids in their teens that has the energy and vision to do its part to sustain our community. Maybe the next revolution needs to be generational. We can't just rack up victories, then sit on our laurels, complaining that purple-haired twenty-five-year-olds with nose rings shouldn't be canvassing for votes, or that no one wants seventy-two-year-olds at the Halloween ball. Nor can the new dykes and gay men take their relative freedom for granted—the right wing is never going to go away. How can we combine the strengths of all ages to do what needs to be done to make the planet safe for our people?

A warm welcome apparently goes a long way, according to that report from my friend. We don't have to become best pals with someone decades older or younger, but, oh, the thrill of seeing the young gays strut and prance and my seniors dare to live outside the closets they were born to. When I am with a peer, how our eyes spark with laughter and pleased self-consciousness to break into a duet of some Meg Christian song.

I'm no organizer, but I host a potluck at my home on Thanksgiving and the Fourth of July. This year there was no one under forty, but we ranged well into our seventies. The sense of continuity and of family I experience when I look around the boisterous bunch of us is inspiring and sustaining. It took all of us to get this far, and it'll take all of us to maintain the gains we've won.

One night at a potluck heavy in the category of what a thirtysomething lesbian called "short white-haired women," I was brought to tears of pain as they discussed a memorial to the women in the group who had died. There was no question of putting names on the plaque—even in death the anonymity of these women must be preserved. We weren't going to spell out the name of the organization because, daringly, it contained the *L* word. There was great sadness in the plan, and although I sensed pride, it was a queer pride that we needed to hide.

What if, that night, there had been some young women with blueberry-colored hair and Doc Martens shoes, one with a skateboard parked at the door and another wearing leather pants and a T-shirt that ended just above her navel. What if a third, in goth black, had sprung from her supple, cross-legged position on the floor and cried, "Who are you protecting? Not me and not yourselves. If you really loved these dykes, you'd get enough cash together to hire a sculptor and put up a damn dyke statue!"

"Cool!" the other baby dykes would shout.

The rest would have had a choice: quietly ignore these fearless pups or soak up a little of their outrageousness. The mute memorial could have found a voice, and while that voice would have been quieter than the kids', it might have broken some lifelong chains of silence.

CRUISING EYES (2004)

There's this little couple around town that we keep bumping into. Both women are small, one with short, thick stark-white hair and the other with short hair dyed a light red. Sometimes we see the white-haired woman alone, never the redhead.

Usually, when I think someone is gay, I smile in recognition. Responses vary, from a wide smile or knowing eyes to abruptly averted eyes or a blank wall. This couple is of the blank-wall variety. I am always eager to meet new dykes and tend to go bounding up to introduce myself at the slightest encouragement. These two act like my girl and I are invisible.

They dress in neat, perfectly fitted shorts and T-shirts, their hair crisply styled, and the white-haired woman has small sparkling things in her ears. I wondered if they hung out with the moneyed lesbians who live in gated communities. I tend toward shaggy hair and an oversized mix of Goodwill and L.L. Bean clothes—pretty obviously I don't live behind gates. Is there a gay caste system that encourages shunning? Am I so naive that I never noticed our lack of democracy before? Couldn't be.

I thought if we could see them in a social context we might be able to divine the reason for the couple's unresponsiveness. Last night we found ourselves at a table next to theirs in a noisy dining room in a seaside bar. By this time they were such familiar figures I automatically smiled. One looked quickly down and the other switched to blank-stare mode so fast I wondered if she took us in at all. Then I saw their dinner companions—a nongay couple.

Maybe I've been jumping to conclusions. Maybe two women who dress alike, go everywhere together, walk with an independent spring to their steps, and sport short hair aren't lovers. Maybe they're—not sisters, they don't look a thing alike. Roommates?

Distant cousins? Kissing cousins—no, there I go again. But, darn it, they feel like dykes. I would be astonished to find they aren't.

How do I know this? Once upon a time it was easy. There were pinky rings (I still won't be caught without one—like you couldn't tell otherwise). Then there was *the look*, sometimes bold, sometimes shy, sometimes just a spark of recognition in the eyes. There's even a voice that goes with being a gay woman. It has a certain depth, richness and maybe a hint of smugness, like we're sitting on a secret that, if we cared to use our powers, would change the world radically. And it would—else why this panic about gay marriage?

But that's not my immediate problem. How do we, in the twenty-first century, tell a lesbian from a het woman? Lipstick lesbians look like straight girls and straight girls dress butch. A lesbian the age of these women, who are probably in their seventies, could be someone's great grandma—and I'll bet the redhead is.

I'm making another assumption. Maybe the butch is a grandma too? With so many women coming out in middle age or later—I met one recently who didn't see the light till her seventies—who knows what gay women will end up looking like in later years. We're not going to change much, I would imagine, except for the latecomers who may cut their hair to the length they always wanted and stop curling it. Or not.

What I notice about this older couple and others is the lack of defiance in their walks. There's something uppity about the no-nonsense yet alluring way a femme walks. Neither did the term stompin' butch come out of thin air, though there are definite degrees to stomping. Is a defiant walk something that belongs only to green-haired, nose-ringed youth these days? Is there something about decades of moving in a society dominated by nongays that wears down our queer sharp edges and smooths out our gaits? How will I know my sisters as we age?

I'm learning. Women in couples seem to resemble each other more the older we get. My partner and I look nothing alike to gay people, but the hets ask if we're sisters. It's partly our silver hair, but also a melding of styles. I used to wear T-shirts with political slogans, but in recent years I find that I, like my girl, choose neutral graphics like blue herons or Steamboat, Iowa. And then there's what's missing: it would seem so natural to see some women walking down the street holding hands.

It's a lifelong habit, this scanning of crowds for dykes and gay men. I'd sure miss it if my eyes found nothing gay to light on. That's why I have great hopes that I'm right about this couple we've been running into. Maybe they're just new in town and kind of bashful— after all, the locals, more savvy about the weather, don't dress in shorts, that's for tourists and recent transplants. I don't want to think we lose our gay style at any age or in any century. My cruising eye can't be failing. I'll betcha we're right about these two and that someday we'll be sitting in that noisy bar—having dinner with them.

A FARMERS MARKET ROMANCE (2004)

When all the rest of my life is in transition, there is one thing I can count on: the farmers market.

The burgeoning growth of farmers markets has been a joy in my life. There's something about going out to buy produce and plants on a Saturday morning which brightens my whole week. Tables of dark leafy greens laid next to baskets of glowing tomatoes, tents of sugar-speckled baked goods that somehow seem healthier for being sold outdoors, lines of nursery pots sprouting light green lettuces and yellow daylilies, stands filled with raspberries, blueberries, strawberries, blackberries too tempting to pass up—this is the fruit of the land , the richness of America.

Farmers markets serve another purpose in our society. As my girl said the other day, they're a good place to meet lesbians when our dogs stop to sniff. "Somehow, people know what to say when attached to a leash."

We didn't have dogs with us, but we, too, met at a farmers market. I was staffing the Audubon Society booth and she, with her late partner, stopped for information. The booth might as well have been lavender. Excited to be approached by a couple of dykes, I went into such an energetic song and dance about Audubon meetings and field trips, I'm lucky I didn't scare them off. They showed up at the next meeting, and the next and...That was ten years ago.

In every town, the farmers market seems to be the place for liberals as well as lesbians to meet and greet one other. Markets draw those of us who reached our maturity in the days of the back-to-the-land movement, when college graduates were dropping out to try and make a living with leatherwork and pottery. There was a street in every town back then with a food co-op, a head shop, a leather-goods store, a woodworker, a jewelry maker, a gallery or two, and a hole in the wall that sold smoothies and carrot cake. Now these reluctant capitalists have long gray hair and sell at the farmers markets.

It's true about the dogs too. At a market of any appreciable size, the dog owners stop to admire one another's canine friends, and there always seems to be a dog food or pet bed maker who's giving out treats. Sometimes it takes a pass or two before the twin boxers or the growly Belgian shepherds move on and the border collies and cocker spaniels can get their turns. Tiny terriers sniff shaggy sheepdogs, and a Corgi leash gets tangled in the rope some kid's got attached to her new Lab puppy's collar.

Not every market is carnival sized. In the small town I'm moving to, there may be only two vendors parked in the lot next to the tiny natural food store, but what vendors! Their trucks are heaped to the brims with fruits and veggies. The farmers market is a cooperative roadside stand.

Farmers markets may not be strictly an American tradition, but they're definitely democratic. Not only do sales keep some small farmers going, they are a means for the grower to deal directly with the customer. Entrepreneurs other than craftspeople show up too, hawking salad dressings and jellies, herbal massage oils and barbecue sauces. Political tables often dot the entrances, proselytizing for every persuasion. During the ballot-measure wars in Oregon we sometimes had the antigay table across from the pro-gay table. It looks like it'll happen again with the gay marriage issue. The farmers market is a town square.

Eugene, Oregon is known as a spot old hippies go to die, and dozens of them gather at the huge Saturday market downtown. Not only are they pushing their crafts, they're making music on the grass or at the bandstand. The smell of pot has been replaced by the smells of a food court that outdoes any indoor mall. From falafel to burritos, spanakopita to fried rice, the crowd—and it's truly a crowd—keeps the cooks busy. There are two full blocks of crafts in mazes of covered tables. Growers line four city blocks with fresh and homemade goods. Though I love to imagine what a market in New York would be like, I can't visualize a better one than Eugene's, which is colorful, festive, and busy and tends to sell at fresh market prices.

So it was only natural that when my girl and I were unwittingly falling for each other, just friends, we'd travel to visit the biggest, oldest, and most authentic farmers market. We took our time and wandered the mazes admiring and laughing and buying and just having a great time together. When we dress up now, she wears her tie-dyed poncho and I wear my tie-dyed button-down shirt—I can see in her eyes the memory of that day when everything began to change for us. Cupid had a stall there, I swear.

A PLACE OF PEACE (2004)

I live near a lake and often go there with my dog to stand on the shore and just look at it. It's a small lake, but I can't tell that from my sandy cove. At those moments, that lake is my whole blue-and-green world. I find myself silently singing an old Girl Scout song about asking peace of a river and breathing more deeply than I can anywhere else. My last home was near the ocean, another across from a river. I've wondered why it's the lake that brings me peace.

When I was a kid—a pre-baby dyke—my parents started taking two-week vacations on a lake in New Hampshire. Lake Winnipesaukee was an eight-hour drive from New York City, longer when you figured in the cat and me getting carsick, picking up a passel of relatives north of Boston and then a whole cooked turkey from a venerated institution called Harrow's in North Reading, Massachusetts. The trunk would be too full and someone would hold the turkey on her lap, its smell filling the old green Hudson with promise the rest of the way north.

Days at the lake were lazy, but full. There was time to swim and fish and tootle around the water in a rented aluminum boat with a 1.5 horsepower motor. And to read, read, read to my heart's content. In the mornings, part of my family might walk to Melvin Village where I'd get an allotment of penny candy. At night we'd walk to the ice cream place down a leafy road by the lake, and I'd crunch the powerfully peppermint bits in my pink ice cream. Little did I know these days and nights with my family were, even with personalities clashing and money worries (it cost two hundred dollars for a week for a lodge that slept twelve) and conflicting needs and too much drinking, this would be as idyllic a time as I was to experience in my life.

Looking at pictures of little Lee at the lake, I am astonished that my mother let me carry on like that. There's one shot of a skinny, prepubescent girl with short hair, dressed in a loose flannel shirt with sleeves rolled high up her arms, muscle-shirt style. Dungarees, as they were called then, and white sneakers finish the ensemble. The only difference between that little girl and the dyke of today, besides a few years and pounds and updated glasses, is the candy cigarette hanging from the side of my mouth in the picture. Oh—and the fact that, back then, I'd never even heard of lesbians, though clearly I was a lesbian child.

In another picture, I'm on some rocks that jut into the lake, in shorts and a polo shirt, holding up the fish I caught. One day, as I fished from those rocks, a little boy scrambled out to me and asked, to my great embarrassment, "Are you a tomboy?" I was still too innocent to understand that this implied that jaded adults were also questioning my gender and my sexuality, my androgynous James Dean style.

My annual idyll continued undisturbed. In other pictures, my family even looked as if they might be getting a puzzled kick out of me. Obviously, anything went up at the lake. I got to try out my little butch. It would have been silly, after all, to force me into a dress or take off my beloved sailor hat when I was thigh deep in water while pulling the boat to shore. Or while I baited hooks or built trails through the fragrant pine needle ground cover. At the lake, magically, it was okay to be me.

That's where my present sense of peace comes from when I visit the little lake near my home. Those vacations were the only time I was truly comfortable and happy, because my family let me be myself. I could breathe. Later, when I was a counselor at a Girl Scout camp on another lake, I sang, sang like I could, like I knew the words to life that everyone else seemed to have by heart.

The last two years that I went up to the lake with my family, it was too late. I was out and had learned to hide myself as best I could. They were, by then, expecting me to act like the young lady I could never be. I visited the campground post office daily, before anyone else could beat me to it, to pick up love letters from my girlfriend, and then I'd read them in a secret grove of trees and stash them away from the eyes of my family. Being myself meant hiding.

I stopped going to the lake the summer I was seventeen. Apparently, I left my sense of peace there, left behind my family and my innocent, forbidden self. Now, visiting this little Pacific Northwest lake, I feel rusted parts of myself clunk back into place where they're starting to move freely again, oiled by the everyday love of my girl and the decades of lessons that led me back to a place of peace.

Are You Married? (2004)

Every now and then something happens that makes my world shift. The ground tilts and great heavy doors open to the light. I know I will never be the same.

This time it happened in a pretty mundane way. My girl and I are refinancing her house because, without the ability to get married, it's the only way to legally arrange for it to belong to both of us. It's an expensive solution, but maybe cheaper than the wedding we can't have. Of course, we don't get the honeymoon either.

I've been gay a long time, though, and usually just go along to get along. So it was a shock when, sitting with my girl at the title company, the nongay escrow officer looked at both of us and asked, "Are you married?"

There was a pause before we answered, "No." In that pause was the weight of history, gay history: a thousand beatings, a million firings, an army of gay kids thrown out of their parents' homes; hundreds of marches, dozens of attempts at legislation, a universe of hopes. I thought of saying, "We can't!" but stayed silent as I felt centuries of fear flush out of me in that moment and realized how very far we'd come.

I have a running dispute going with my friend the Pianist. She tells me how much has changed for gay people, and I tell her that nothing has changed while there are people who blindly hate us. Well, my friend, you're absolutely right, something has changed. The escrow officer was just an ordinary middle-class woman (she made sure to mention her husband) who, ten years ago, one year ago, would never have asked that question, but today she has not only to consider that we might be married, but in doing so has to acknowledge that gay people exist.

And we have to deal with not being invisible any more. In the twenty-first century we can't be trembling in our clogs with fear that an escrow officer will Guess. All kinds of clerks behind counters and desks need to know our status, and we need to be able to be up front about it. We're losing the choice to live in closets!

This doesn't mean no one hates us. And if the right wing gets to write its obsolete scriptures into our Constitution, the escrow officers of the world won't ever have to ask again. But meanwhile, they've been forever changed by our liberation movement. And that's what's different. They may be Fundamentalist or Republican, but same-gender couples are in their world. We're here, we're queer, get used to it is more than a rallying cry, it's become a reality.

Whether my girl and I would marry or not if we had the chance is beside the point. Part of me rejects the whole gay marriage movement as frivolous and not the issue I'd have chosen to take a stand on. Part of me is elated at the exposure we're getting, win or lose. Part of me wants to smash the patriarchal institution of marriage, and the rest of me wants to drag my girl to the altar so I can pledge my troth publicly.

No matter, the word gay is being shouted from political podiums, splashed across front pages, and talked about in straight homes and religious meetings. Gay! Gay! Gay! There's no escaping us. The governor of New Jersey couldn't escape himself. "I am a gay American," he said and those were no cowering words. It won't be long now before there will be an openly gay governor who doesn't have to resort to infidelity to be true to himself. It's important that Governor McGreevy has not apologized for being gay, only for being unfaithful. Perhaps the straight public will learn—those who are open to learning—what a mistake it is to enforce compulsory heterosexuality.

"Are you married?" There is something about those words that implies more than the question. It has echoes of "Shouldn't you be married?" I can't imagine the escrow officer was thinking any such thing, yet the implication was there. She made a point of her concern about protecting us in the wording she used, in giving us a document that recognized the seriousness of our commitment. Perhaps the true union is between the words *gay* and *marriage*. That shocking proximity may have done as much to stretch minds as the thousands of recent photographs of two women in bridal veils and two men kissing.

Something has finally changed, my Pianist friend. There is now a global consciousness that includes the unthinkable, and there is no turning back from that. Our escrow officer was the voice of an expanded universe that is large enough to include the once abhorrent thought of two women, two men, finally getting their honeymoons.

"Are you married?" What a lovely question.

I Do—Not (2004)

What if I don't want to get married?
　　Well, of course, it's my choice. I don't have to marry my girl. But then again, I only have the one choice: I can either not marry her or…not marry her. What's wrong with this picture?

As it happens, neither of us is chomping at the bit to hear wedding bells; we hear bells whenever we're together, it's that good between us. I have to confess that I feel that what we have is sacred, and I worry that formalizing it would expose it to the profane. When I tried to picture us standing in line in Portland, Oregon, with the religious zealots threatening divine wrath and the media filming us, I didn't want to expose my girl to marriage at all. At the same time I was terribly excited about the opportunity and completely supportive of those women and men who thus publicly proclaimed their love.

What a big step. It seems very sudden to an old gay who remembers when we had to disguise ourselves—checking our walks, dressing like hets (for women this meant appealing to men), and deleting most references to our lives from conversations. In those days it was really special to recognize someone by her pinky ring or to find gay people to socialize with. Now, we're registering with government agencies, testifying on paper that we're gay, and signing our names to make it official. Given that there are still people in this country who shudder when they think about us, I think that's pretty darn good.

Is this an efficient way to get on the list many gays still fear? We're so brave, so trusting, so eager for acceptance, so hungry to belong that we lined up by the thousands to sign on for whatever. I understand that impulse; part of me wanted to join the lineup because marriage is a language I understand. It's fine to know that my girl and I have a deeper, truer bond than any piece of paper can bestow, yet I am the marrying kind, a one-woman woman, a nice middle-class girl. The temptation to seriously propose is great. It's how I learned to express my love: by my parents' example as well as from the books I read and from the enthusiastic movies I watched.

I admire Phyllis Lyon and Del Martin for being first in line. I also admire my friends the hotelier and her poet lover who made a statement by waiting four and a half hours to get a certificate—and that's all. They are not following it up by finding a little wedding chapel or turning the thing in signed; they just wanted to be counted. I was impressed when a gay man in town wrote a proud letter to the editor about how he wanted to marry his partner right here at home. I just ran into him and his young son at the co-op and he said he hadn't heard a thing from our county commissioners. Surprise. A few days ago, two musician friends, who have been together at least twenty years, did go the whole route and were married by the minister father of one partner. That brought tears to my eyes. When it's right for a couple, it's right.

I've tried to imagine what bothers nongays so much about us getting married. Their protests are thin and passionless when couched in words like "destroying the institution." No, it's got to be more visceral than that, like disgust or horror or fear. I wonder if they know what bothers them. I think they've been brainwashed by obsolete religious beliefs. Somebody needs to tell them, hey, we have enough people in this world, guys. There's no need to keep marriage laws written to insure that men go forth and multiply—and keep track of their progeny. Or maybe they need to hear: Can't imagine a feller in a wedding dress? Gay people love, we're getting married, get used to it!

The urge to marry, rather than a perversion, shows just how very normal we are. If committed relationships are to be encouraged by tax breaks and benefits, family and peer support and sincere pledges to one another, then let's make sure these rewards are available to everyone who wants to make the move. Gay marriages haven't destroyed civilization in Canada, Belgium, or the Netherlands—what's holding the US back?

My girl and I don't want to get married today, but you'd better believe we want the option tomorrow.

Queer Families and Hospice (2005)

I didn't know how I was going to cope with my girl's last days. At the end-stage of ovarian cancer, she's been growing steadily weaker, increasingly sicker. It was bad enough knowing I was going to lose the kindest, gentlest, wisest woman I have ever known, the woman who found it in her heart to love me just as I am, and who thinks it's pretty special that I love her. How was I going to give her the care she needed? How was I even going to find the time to tend to her and keep my job?

As it turned out, I wasn't as alone as I thought. Her two daughters and a faraway friend arrived. This covered some of the cooking and cleaning and allowed me to work a little bit, but none of us are health-care professionals. We didn't know titrating drugs from a Harris flush. We'd all had a little experience with being around the dying, but not quite this intimately, twenty-four/seven, and not with the woman we all loved more than anyone else on earth.

All through the processes of diagnosis and misdiagnosis, CT scans, blood, barium, and urine tests, surgeries, chemotherapy, a gastroenterologist, an oncologist, a urologist, and a superwoman gynecological oncologist, I felt confident and supported by professionals. But there came a time when it was just us, suspended between the last physician and the last breath.

Fortunately, my girl had spent several years as a hospice nurse. She asked the last doctor, "Am I hospice appropriate?" He answered yes. We live in a small town, but hospice is here. They had us signed up and receiving services within the week. When it came to filling out our paperwork, the case manager asked for my relationship to the patient and we both answered, "Partner." He wrote it down as if he registered queer families every day. All the hospice folk have been like that, never questioning my involvement, sharing information freely with me, making sure I was included in discussions and decisions.

One day the case manager, who is nongay, turned to me and asked, "So, how did you two meet?" I was so startled that this straight guy would be interested it took me a moment to answer, "Through the Audubon Society." I gave him some details and he looked distressed. Uh-oh, I thought, here comes the homophobia, but it wasn't that at all. He had never heard of Audubon and thought we were members of some weird society formed around the autobahn, a German road. We all laughed about that.

When the volunteer coordinator interviewed us, she asked if we had any special concerns, and of course we wanted reassurance that we wouldn't have to deal with a volunteer who was uncomfortable with our relationship or whose agenda was to proselytize for some religion. It turns out that hospice, even though this one is affiliated with a church hospital, takes diversity training very seriously. The volunteer assigned to us could not have been more respectful, kind, or sweet. I had no idea there were so many people like this in the world.

Even with my girl so ill, working with hospice has been a pleasure. They take over the prescriptions, give us instructions, send a bath aide three times a week, one or two nurses daily, a volunteer twice a week, supply us with equipment from a commode to baby monitor to chucks (bed protectors) and, most important, are available to us day and night, seven days per week.

Hospice work takes a special breed of human being. Their job is to make dying people comfortable. Can there be a greater—or more demanding—service in the world? They need to be continually compassionate, vigilantly protective, able to adapt to any environment or personality, and enthusiastically creative. One day, for example, my girl had terrible stomach cramps. Daughter #1 caught the nurses as they were leaving the driveway, and they returned on the double. The nurses decided on a procedure which involved one getting into a kneeling position on the bed with my girl, the other standing at the other side of the bed, Daughter #1 half lying on the bed supporting her mom, and me at the foot of the bed to run for whatever was needed. That made five of us in a room already filled with bedroom furniture and bookcases.

Then we noticed the dog was missing. She'd last been seen crawling under the bed where the cat was hiding from her. I peered through the puzzles and other stored items to find that the kitty was fine. We called the dog's name and heard scrabbling toenails toward the head of the bed. Beastie is pretty small and very devoted. She'd just wanted to be close to my girl, so she'd crawled between the frame and the wall—and got stuck. Here's Daughter #1 under one side of the bed, pushing, me under the other, pulling, both of us cajoling worried little Beastie. All the while the competent, calm, adaptable hospice nurses kept their focus, did their work, and took care of their patient while we two idiots hung out under the bed with the dog.

Later, Daughter #1 and I laughed until tears came to our eyes at the ridiculous scene, but it was also the laughter of relief—the nurses' simple, jerry-rigged procedure had been successful and my girl was comfortable again. If Hospice has anything to do with it, she'll be comfortable for the rest of her life.

MY LESBIAN APPRENTICESHIP: THE BARS (2005)

I heard about gay bars in the city shortly after I came out. They were definite destinations on my baby dyke itinerary, but it was the Hayloft that really intrigued me and my small set of underaged cohorts. The Loft, as we so urbanely referred to it, was out in the suburbs and completely inaccessible to us. Not only were we too young to go to bars, we were too young to drive.

In my desire for gay authenticity, the unattainable Loft was replaced by the city bars. The Swing Rendezvous—or the Swing Lounge, or the Swing, as it was variously known—was my first triumph. It was a dive only saved from the reckless depths of sailors' bars by the lack of sailors in uniform and its distance from the wharves. The bar itself was up front with the jukebox, while the tables and tiny dance floor were in back. It was dark, smoky and the uneven wooden floors, where we did the outlawed bump and grind, were sticky with spilled drinks and who knew what else. Yet, even now, when I hear the first beats of certain rock 'n' roll songs, I feel a tremor of nervous excitement in my gut and the exhilaration that went with my right foot pushing out to dance in that room where the music became like water to a high diver.

It was my first bar. My ID was borrowed from an eighteen-year-old who was such a regular at the Swing she wasn't carded anymore. I was in! I slipped the ID back to her once I'd passed the bouncer and tried not to worry about a raid. Liquor held the same romantic appeal as the bar, so I lapped it up like a pro. Of course, after the festivities, I had to get back on the subway, take two trains to the end of the line in Queens, then walk the two miles to my parents' apartment, a majorly sobering trek. Why my mother never asked the reason I smelled like an ashtray filled with whiskey, I'll never know. Once in my bed, I was jubilant—a real lesbian who went to gay bars!

After my first bar, I was so sophisticated that I didn't bother with fake ID. I tried to mimic the rocking walk, the tough, sibilant way of talking out of the side of my mouth that seemed to convince bartenders and waitresses—mostly straight—that I, at seventeen, was a vetted butch barfly. I was starved for identity, for validation by my own people, and the bars gave me that even though, once inside, I was too young to mix with anyone but the girl I was with. At the same time, I was beginning to learn that the bars were a rip: boring, expensive, scary places that drew preying men as much as they drew lesbians. Still, I ached to enter more gay bars—Googie's and the Music Box, Pam Pam's and the Sea Colony—the castles in my lavender sky.

Then I moved to Connecticut, where you had to be twenty-one to get into a bar. I lost all memory of disillusionment and yearned for gay people and places with a constant intensity that made me feel like I was on fire. In the city, I'd at least observed my people from inside. It wasn't long before I heard about a place down by the railroad station, but it came with warnings. It was supposed to be a tough, dangerous dump which drew from the seamier side of town. I had so romanticized the Greenwich Village bars that I never figured out, until I went to this forbidden watering hole several years later, that what was considered tough in Connecticut paled against what I'd already survived.

I was usually in enough trouble in college without chancing a visit to such a purported den of iniquity. I had a new destination bar: The Cedar Brook, or The Brook, as the in-crowd called it. Again, it was way out in the burbs, in affluent Westport, Connecticut, across the Post Road, irony of all ironies, from the state police barracks. It's celebrated as the second-oldest gay bar in the country now, but then it was just a rickety old roadhouse that regularly soaked up as much of the flooding brook as it did spilled beer.

By this time, I had doctored a copy of my birth certificate. One Saturday night, a bunch of us took over a booth at the Brook, where we worked up the courage to get onto the empty dance floor. The trouble was, we had a curfew back at school, and an hour's drive. It was much too early for anyone but the serious, all-male drinkers at the bar and us silly kids, pining to belong. By the time the gay girls started arriving, it was time for us to leave.

What did that matter? I'd spent a couple of hours in a place where I could once again dance a lesbian dance.

STRAIGHT PEOPLE (2005)

Straight people aren't all bad. They'll never completely understand us, but most of them seem to have good intentions. Of course, we know that one bad apple can spread its fear and hatred to many others. We also know that most of the bad apples are closet cases, so afraid of their own sexuality they lash out at ours. That's a very small comfort.

When I moved to this coastal town, tolerance was not a lesson I expected to learn. My girl was already established here and had managed to find a half-dozen gay people because she knew I was going to miss my gay family. As it turned out, we didn't see much of the gays, or much of anyone. Since my girl died, our lesbian friends have been right there for me, but incredibly, so have her nongay friends. They made it their business to keep tabs on me, spend time with me, and get me through the worst early days.

For the first time in years, I found myself hanging out with straight people. Although it's been like traveling in a foreign land at times, our languages are similar enough that we communicate well. To my delight, I found out that my girl's rock enthusiast pal and I had birthdays one day apart. We are so similar we trip over each other's shared opinions, common backgrounds, and mirror-image neuroses as well as our rock collections. Who knew that behind that neat, short-haired exterior and carefully styled, slightly offbeat clothing there lurked a sixties kid, an ex-hippie graduate of Haight-Ashbury. We walk together a couple of times a week, and she introduces me to lakes and trails that are achingly beautiful.

Then there's the retired elementary school teacher. One of the most accepting, least judgmental people I have ever known, we mostly talk by phone, but go on and on, babbling about our days and ups and downs, offering and taking one another's advice, giving comfort. She has just started attending computer classes and lets me play expert to her novice. Both of these women are obviously glad to have my friendship, as I am theirs, and are sad that I am moving back north. Neither has ever said anything that made me feel patronized or inferior or weird or hit on as an experiment. Both are single, so there are no men in the picture to feel threatened by our attachments. The rock hound makes a point of having single women friends, straight and gay, like some sort of feminist. She takes my lesbian chauvinism in stride and announces the arrival of every new dyke, or newly out dyke, in town.

In this same period of time, my college roommate tracked me down through a gay paper. We are somehow both thrilled to be in each other's lives again, despite our very different lifestyles: Manhattan het and West Coast gay. We are also both button-bursting proud of each other's accomplishments in the decades since we've been out of touch—she is an artist. I remember, way back when, how we'd lie across our darkened room dreaming our creative dreams aloud. The artist lives with a guy but seldom mentions him. She is much more discreet about her lifestyle than I am about mine. Once again, our lives are more alike than not: the artist works and longs for more time to paint; I work and long for more time to write. She sent prints of her work to hang by my girl's hospital bed.

Are these new connections typical for postmenopausal women? Are we now secure enough about our identities that nongay women don't worry that having a lesbian friend makes them lesbian and lesbians don't confuse passionate friendship with sexual attraction? Have I come to appreciate friendship more, having seen so many come and go, and have I learned to respect and treasure these bonds even when they stray from the culture where I am most comfortable?

I actually just had lunch with a straight couple. I thought I might be nervous and have nothing to say. I thought they might be self-conscious dining downtown with a butchy dyke. Instead, it felt very natural. The woman is a major liberal who once, on the subject of gay marriage, angrily sputtered, "It's none of their business, who marries who!" She and her husband raised four children, with whom they are very close. Their lives are a world away from mine—or are they? We are neighbors, Democrats, work all the time, complain of high gas prices and town planning and medical costs. We are there for one another in emergencies, in political despair, in lending a helping hand. Although they've lived here almost thirty years, we're all transplants from back East. We hate war. They loved my girl.

What's straight got to do with it?

FUTURE DYKE (2006)

She was the most endearing baby butch I'd come across in a very long time. Slight, fine-boned, with country-cut light hair just short of a pudding-bowl do, a walk that was half-strut, and a face that was all eager bashfulness. She was like sunshine breaking through a cloud of straights.

I saw her in the old fishing town where I live now. The town is filled with hills and old buildings and fishing vessels to spare. The old bay front is crammed with tourist shops, but they have to share space with fish processing plants. There are crowds of sightseers, but there are also lazing, lolling, barking, panhandling harbor seals out on the docks.

Sometimes I feel a little guilty about living in such a place. Surely the Plains dwellers love their flat, dry spaces, and East Coast residents don't mind the cold and urban sprawl. In DC, legislators apparently don't mind the drought of reason either. The Supreme Court is about to seesaw to the right. Isn't there some way to find a balance before the guys in robes make or affirm laws that will take the starch out of that baby dyke when she tries to get a job or marry her girl or adopt a baby?

Here, it's been raining a lot, sometimes for days on end. The wind rattles and whistles past the cozy home I rent like it's trying to break in at the sliding glass doors or lift off the roof. Yet the next day, or even the same day, the town will go all balmy, the storm having swept in negative ions and ozonated the air. I can't help thinking that here I am basking in the beauty of it all while people who lost so much in the hurricanes may not even have homes.

This town that's rich with nature's bounty—the ocean, the bay, the river, the hills, the storms and the sunshine and rainbows—is an economically poor town. How do the people on the fish processing lines make it? How do the crabbers get any medical care when the buyers won't pay as much as last year and less still than the year before? There's a memorial walk along the bay front with tiles commemorating fishermen lost at sea. They do this for a dollar thirty-five a pound.

It's always relatively cool here. We complain if it gets much over seventy. Locals know shorts are a bad idea any time of year. The shady forests are dense with ferns and mushrooms, trees dripping even after the rain. It's beyond me how American troops survive in a climate like Iraq's or how the powerful can sit in air-conditioned rooms deciding to send kids like the baby dyke into a place with some of the highest temperatures anywhere in the world. Bad enough the soldiers risk injury—they're also felled by heatstroke. I feel spoiled because I wouldn't last an hour in that climate.

By night, here on the Pacific coast, I can see the lights of the marinas, the white masts of boats bobbing on the water, the fishing vessels gliding out under the bridge to the open sea. The Coast Guard station is all lit up, its ships glowing white and every light set like a jewel in a rich blackness that gives the night a feeling of adventure.

By day, I can walk along the beach, though it is sometimes strewn with birds dead of toxins we put in the sea. Twice a year there are beach cleanups, with hundreds of volunteers picking up tons of litter, from dumped refrigerators to miles of tangled fishing line, from rafts of Styrofoam to flotillas of plastic pop bottles. Now and then oil slicks or entire ships must be cleared from the innocent shores.

Did the baby butch grow up walking the beaches? Is she from a fisherman's family? Does she know how lucky she is to live in this beautiful place, or does she only feel her isolation? Will she go away, find a girl, bring her back? Will they help to take care of the beaches, fight to elect people who'll spend our tax money at home instead of squandering it in hot lands?

I can picture them, not all that long from now, walking the bay front at night, refreshed from the rain, holding hands. I want them to have that future.

HAVE THINGS GOTTEN BETTER? (2006)

The Pianist and the Handydyke cooked while the Butch Nurse, visiting for the weekend, and I hung out and got in the way. Things were better than they used to be, the three of them insisted, while I stuck to my position that improvements had done nothing to change the essentially vulnerable condition of gay people.

The Handydyke went to set the table but kept bopping back in to add to her list of things we could do now: hold hands in public, be with our partners in the hospital, buy property together, keep jobs, make love legally, live together without being hassled, adopt kids, get nondiscrimination laws passed—watch *The Ellen Show*!

Oppression has never been a problem for the Butch Nurse. A seminal moment occurred for her while vacationing in Hawaii. A nongay couple was walking in front of them, holding hands. She took the hand of her partner, the Femme Nurse, and resolved always to live openly. Since then, "We just live our lives," she explained, "worrying like everyone else about whether we can pay the mortgage."

It was a photograph of the Butch Nurse and the Femme Nurse that had started the discussion weeks before. They posed together in identical sparkly vests the Femme Nurse had sewn for them. Their small church was having a dance, and this was how they'd dressed up for it. They are the only gay couple in a congregation that not only accepts them, but whose minister, unbidden by the couple, has offered to marry them should they ever want to take that step.

"That would never have happened thirty years ago," declared the Pianist. She told us about a young woman and man who double-dated at their prom with a lesbian couple.

The Handydyke popped back in to recall a tale of a teacher who announced to her principal that she was a lesbian, in effect daring the principal to fire her. She kept her job—the principal, it turned out, was a lesbian too.

Both couples swapped stories about lesbian policewomen, how one lives a severely closeted life with her partner, never going anywhere because she's afraid of losing her job. The Handydyke, on the other hand, talked about a totally out lesbian cop who has an active community life with her partner.

Could it be our perceptions that drive some of us into the closet while others see no reason to hide? asked the Butch Nurse. "Do gay people hear about something like Matthew Shepard's killing and get too scared to be themselves in public?"

"By the time we left where we used to live," the Butch Nurse went on, "the parents in our cul-de-sac were telling their kids they wanted them to be just like us when they grew up, because we were the most normal people there, even though we were the only gay ones. Now our next-door neighbors are Mormon. The wife is having her eighth child. They're our closest friends in the neighborhood."

The Pianist remembered how she and the Handydyke lived before they retired from teaching high school in a large Western city. "We were scared all the time. We wouldn't even have a lesbian book in our home." When they moved to the Northwest they opened a bookstore and sold both children's and lesbian books. They have a friend who now leads a gay kids' group in a high school.

"We're not a threat to straights when we live normal lives," insisted the Butch Nurse.

"They didn't even have a word for us a hundred and fifty years ago," declared the Pianist as final proof of progress.

I think of the February murders of two gay men at a New Bedford, Massachusetts bar. That same month, despite the fact that sexual orientation is a protected status in South Africa and last year same-gender couples won the right to marry there, nineteen-year-old lesbian Zoliswa Nkonyana was attacked by a group of men and killed in Khayelitsha township. And I think, with all the outward signs of progress, the universal fear and aversion to gay people runs so deep, that as long as one gay man in Saudi Arabia—where homosexuality is a crime punishable by death—or one old gay woman shunned by the staff at in a nursing home in the US, is vulnerable, not much has changed at all.

AT HOME WITH THE EAGLES (2007)

As I just complained to a wise friend, it's darned difficult to concentrate with bald eagles cooing and whistling and squealing in the trees outside. I keep popping up to gape at them in wonder, and today, for the first time, I was able to watch two come in for slo-mo landings on their customary high branches, feathered pantaloons and feet first. It's a little disconcerting to find out that this powerful raptor, our national bird, sounds like a giant squeaky toy and appears to be wearing Elizabethan bloomers. And why did our forefathers choose a bird of prey to represent the United States anyway? It's just too accurate a portrayal right now.

Thanks to the Pianist and the Handydyke, I work on the second floor of their rental, close to the eagles, and I feed smaller birds on the deck. Right now an Oregon junco, aka snowbird, (because juncos, like RVers, return in the winter and are just as ubiquitous) is sharing the black oil sunflower seed feeder with a white-crowned sparrow and a female house finch, all decked out in her stripes. Bald eagles at the coast prefer to feed on fish, but if hungry, they will snatch smaller birds. As much of a thrill as it is to live with eagles, I worry about these little guys.

And the cats next door. I periodically call the neighbors to make sure their very small cats are not out when I see the red-tailed hawks, turkey vultures, and bald eagles hover over their front yard. The neighbors also have handsome dark cat statues on the edge of their deck. Even when the real kitties are inside, the vultures get so bold that the neighbors have to hide the statues.

This bird feeding business all started when the Pianist and the Handydyke mentioned that they enjoyed seeing the stellar jays—elegant black-crested, midnight-blue birds—drinking from the copper birdbath the Handydyke attached to my deck rail. Having become inundated with bird feeding duties at a former residence, I was opting for keeping it simple here, but the Pianist and the Handydyke brought over sacks of peanuts in the shell. Once a day, then twice, now three or four times, I fill my old wooden feeder with peanuts and the stellar jays put on their shows. When their town crier notices the refilled feeder, he perches on a tree limb, squawking with all his might that the grub has been served. They particularly like to stuff one or two peanuts, shell and all, down their maws and hold yet another in their beaks. Despite their constant appetites and raucous complaints when not fed on demand (the jays sound more dignified than the eagles), some of these peanut-ovores are fussy. I have watched a bird pick up and set down a dozen nuts before the other jays lose patience and rush the feeder, driving the fussbudget off with a fiercely held treat I always hope is the right one.

Our stellar jays have been reproducing plentifully. You can always tell the babies because they're a mess, with cowlicks and loose feathers and bewildered looks. "How," one can imagine a newly fledged bird saying, "am I supposed to get these peanuts out of the shell?" This summer I had the privilege of seeing Junior, then a second baby, Pigpen, grow up.

And these are just the winter and year-round birds. I also get to feed black-headed grosbeaks, red crossbills, golden-crowned sparrows, American goldfinches, black-capped and chestnut-backed chickadees, among others, as well as a mob of psychedelic house finches whose strange oranges and yellows are produced by a pox that affects them when they winter in Southern California. Some would say it also affects the Southern Californians who move to Oregon and start campaigns against gay rights. That, as a matter of fact, is how I got into feeding the birds originally. During the ballot-measure wars in the nineties, I found a social sanctuary with the local Audubon Society. They didn't fuss about my lavender color any more than they did about the birds' plumage.

To add to the distractions, the carpenter across the street has chosen today to repair his roof, its sheets of shingling having blown around the neighborhood when 125 mph winds came through two weeks ago. My sweetheart and I laughed about tomorrow's predicted tempest: only 65 mph. A bird's life is not easy on the stormy West Coast.

In the Southeast with my sweetheart last week, I spent perhaps five minutes in her backyard before I spotted an unidentified raptor and two kinds of woodpeckers, along with smaller breeds. The next day I photographed a snowy egret posing atop an SUV. Hanging out at a second-story window, I watched as an alligator in a small pond stalked some surprisingly agile red-nosed moorhens, while a little green heron flew overhead.

Back home, the gulls wheel over the bay to warn of the coming winds, the little guys are jostling one another at happy hour in the feeder. As my wise friend pointed out, there are worse distractions than eagles.

Lesbian Patriot (2007)

Once upon a time, a long time ago, I left the United States. It was only to travel to Montreal, and I was pretty excited that I'd be going through Customs and seeing an actual foreign country. From there, who knew? Maybe some day I'd get to France and Ireland to see the lands of my ancestors.

Almost immediately, I hated being outside the US. The traffic went too fast. There were so many bridges I was always lost at the wrong end of one. Camping was like being invited to a mosquito feast, and I was the main course. The city was just like a city in the States, only harder to navigate. I wanted to go home.

This was in the 1970s, when Nixon was president and we were still mired in Vietnam. It made no sense that I should be so attached to my native land. American citizens had been fleeing from it to Canada for years. It was even rumored that gay people were treated better north of the border.

I spent a miserable few days in Montreal with my lover. She wanted to show me the places she had lived and worked when she and her girlfriend ran away from home at sixteen, but the city was too changed to find her past. I wanted to see McGill, where I had considered going to college; seeing it, I realized college had been lonely enough for the only lesbian on campus without living in a strange, cold city too.

Crossing back into Vermont, I felt as if I'd barely escaped with my life. This was nonsense, of course, but I was so glad to be home. Forget the ancestral lands. I'd visit Mechanicville, New York where Grandma and Grandpa Lynch had met, and Petaluma, California, where Great-Grandpa Lynch bought a horse farm after a Gold Rush. The great-great-grandparents' inn by the sea in County Wexford, Ireland had probably fallen in by now anyway.

I relished the narrow country roads of Vermont after my great escape. What was wrong with being proud to be an American anyway?

What was wrong with being an outright American chauvinist? Just because we were (and still are) the overarmed bullies of the world, despised for our riches and polluting with no regard for our own or other populations, didn't mean I couldn't get all choked up when I raised and lowered the flag as a counselor at a Girl Scout camp.

It was on this trip that I learned lesbianism and patriotism are not incompatible. At the time, much of gay liberation seemed to refer to principles of Socialism, if not Communism. The most politically active gays were likely to be peace-loving tree huggers. There were a lot of anti-American feelings in the lesbian-feminist community, and who could blame us when multinational corporations were buying our government, and that government was more inclined to fund mass murder—of third-world citizens and our own military personnel—than antipoverty initiatives.

America was fixable, I thought, and worth fixing.

We camped in an elbow of the Vermont mountains. There were cabins, but we set up our old canvas tent in a meadow. These were to be some of the most peaceful days of my life. The paradox of loving my native country and hating its policies could not disturb my homecoming. I was moved to sing swift unmelodic passages of "This Land Is My Land" and "America the Beautiful" at odd moments. The shame of American actions in the world was still with me, the fact that the campground owners would have thrown us out had they known what went on inside our tent was no less real, but the pond outside our door flap was blue and untroubled, and the temperature at night was chilly enough to discourage mosquitoes.

I wanted to stay forever there, at my Walden Pond, like so many of my generation who retreated to Vermont and its equivalents all over the country. That is my point, of course: all Americans had rural Missouri towns where we could disappear or we could make sanctuaries of brownstones in Brooklyn or Victorian Painted Ladies in San Francisco.

I'm not quite sure what a patriot is anymore, after the word has been used for centuries as a bludgeon by angry politicians and as a recruiting slogan for the military. So many Americans think gay people are somehow un-American, and of course, we're not exactly welcome in the armed forces, those bastions of patriotism. I do know that this lesbian is as American as they come and glad of it. I believe in what the Statue of Liberty stands for and that we can be a peaceful force for good in the world. I'm not willing to give the word patriot to the nongay hawks. A patriot can also defend her country by protecting it from itself.

My Big Butch Gay Aunt (2008)

L ast fall, I brought my sweetheart to meet my family. In the course of an evening spent looking through old pictures and documents, my brother said something about a Great-Aunt Jo.

I knew the family on both sides had been riddled with women named Josephine. I knew nothing at all about this one. My brother added, "She never married. She had a friend from work named Vera who used to stay over."

During the 1930s and 1940s my father was mostly at sea. My brother, who is fifteen years older than me, grew up with my mother's family in a big old Boston three-decker, surrounded by aunts. By the time I came along my parents had moved to New York, so I never knew the great-aunts and -uncles.

I asked if he remembered anything else about Great-Aunt Jo. It turned out that she and Vera worked in a laundry. My brother said Great-Aunt Jo was big and strong and worked at the wringer. Wringers were large wooden rolls, operated with manual cranks. Smaller versions were used in homes, often built in to or set on top of washing machines. They were used to wring laundry dry by compressing clothing or linens and squeezing moisture out. It took enormous stamina and well-developed muscles to operate one of those things eight to twelve hours a day, five or six days a week.

I gleefully concluded that Jo Murphy was my big butch gay aunt. Finally, I had identified another gay gene in the family.

There were other possibilities. When my mother told me that a younger third cousin had divorced his wife, become a vegetarian, and moved in with another boy, I said to myself, "Yes!" But we are of the same generation. I wanted queer ancestors.

There was another longer-lived great-aunt, who kept house for her two single brothers. I have wondered what the brothers got up to when they went out with the boyos. None of that was conclusive though. Where had I come from? Did the lavender stork bring me?

I can imagine what a difference it would have made to have grown up knowing, or at least knowing about, Aunt Jo…My mother, Aunt Jo's niece, probably had no inkling. Lesbianism just wasn't in her frame of reference. As a Catholic, it's possible my great-aunt never came out at all and her relationship with Vera might never have crossed into sin. Since I wasn't out to them, no one in my family would ever have thought to tell me about her if Aunt Jo had marched in the gay contingent of the Patriot's Day parade. Even today, how many families announce to their offspring that there's a queer in the gene pool?

Aunt Jo herself might not have been very helpful. Say Vera stayed over now and then. Say they felt romantic about each other. Say they were both willing to physically express how they felt timidly, passionately, with great shame or with the glow of multiple orgasms making them fearlessly affectionate in front of their bemused—or amused—families. It still would have been verboten to come out to a kid, no matter how clear that I was headed for no-man's land.

So I went though the severe depressions, the suicidal thoughts, the misery of being bullied, and the isolation of secrecy just like my Great-Aunt Jo may have. Instead of offering intergenerational support, my family suffered from a common disease. I don't even want to call it homophobia. Most people are so uneducated about homosexuality they never think of it as an option for their kids, even though they may have lived and interacted with lesbian or gay male people all their lives.

Like any kind of abuse—and I consider the withholding of information about sex education and lifestyle options to be abusive—the cycle must be broken. Thanks to the courage of 1960s liberationists and would-be revolutionaries, thanks to the societal tectonics that altered the gay landscape way back during World War II, I was able, a number of years ago, to get past my fears enough to come out to my brother. As a consequence, his kids, neither of whom seems to have been fortunate enough to inherit a gay gene, know and embrace their gay aunt.

I hope Great-Aunt Jo and her Vera had some happiness together. I love the idea that they may somehow be blessing us when my sweetheart and I have our wedding. Maybe, someday, I'll be a gay great-aunt myself and can help some kid feel part of the family.

You Will Be My Wife, Will I Be Yours? (2009)

I spent way too much of my childhood learning not to be my mother. She was a wife and a housewife; I didn't want to be either. Every time I hear one lesbian call another *wife*, it sends shock waves through my system. I have the same problem when lesbians use the term *husband*, although it sounds perfectly natural to me when gay men say it to each other.

In the lesbian feminist movement of the 1970s, lesbian couples were sometimes accused of imitating heterosexuals. What was then called copping out is now a gay movement. I'm having a little problem segueing from the old revolutionary highway to the new, but my sweetheart and I hope to marry next year so I'd better get with the times.

Heck, the desire to formally, legally, spiritually, and officially marry is pretty much a surprise to me too. My best friend recently went down to a city hall in Connecticut and tied the knot with her partner of many years. She seemed a little squeamish about it, but her sweetheart and mine are both some years younger than us, and maybe part of the reason we found them appealing was this new mindset that doesn't reject tradition and does expect legitimacy. Yet at Provincetown's Women's Week this year, we lunched with a gay activist couple close to my age who skipped the American war on gays altogether and years ago married quietly in Canada. Our yearning for society's traditional blessings is stronger than our rebellion against the society itself.

Why must the terms for intimate partners, like everything else, be gender based? Our earlier appellations—lover, partner, companion— were gender neutral. Spouse is an option, but not a pretty one. I have no problem calling my sweetheart fiancée, although it evokes the concept of marriage as surely as that wife word, or worse, the questionable honorific Mrs. And as surely as *mate* conjures the barnyard, the pirate ship, and one's best British friends. *Significant other* became popular for a while but seems to have lost ground, on the forms I fill out, to *domestic partner*, and both imply shacking up rather than a legal arrangement.

It's not only that I don't want to be a wife, I don't want to burden my beloved with the baggage that I associate with wiving someone. Wasn't a wife originally owned by a husband? Mere chattel (the little woman) with no right to possessions or property for herself?

The idea of being pronounced bride and bride, in the tradition of bride and groom, equally unbalances me. It's just semantics, I tell myself, but the visuals those words create—matching white wedding dresses, bouquets, and equally abhorrent churches—are unsettling, maybe because I'm butch.

Despite my somewhat radical roots, which seemed moderate at the time, marriage to my sweetheart is vastly appealing to me. The fact that she wants to enter into a permanent and public agreement to be by my side and have me by hers for the rest of our lives astonishes me, and yes, that's what I want too. I'd also love to give her the kind of wedding I think many women have dreamed of since childhood. I'm no groom, though. I'm not taller, stronger, or a better provider than she is. I'm just a dyke with romantic notions dancing in my head who wants to honor my beloved with the rituals and titles respected by the society that produced us.

We're not reinventing the wheel here, simply claiming it as our own. The words we use may be as borrowed as is the token of good luck traditionally carried by a bride. The words we need may have to trail down the aisle after our brave actions. Meanwhile, I will boldly go where most everyone has gone before and claim that itchy garment *wife* for both myself and the woman I love. Centuries from now its connotations will have evolved. With more and more of us able to marry, and marrying, the word wife won't be the same at all. No, not at all.

THE NICE LESBIAN NEIGHBORS (2010)

I do get cranky sometimes when the doorbell rings. It's a learned response to solicitors. Got religion? I have my own beliefs thank-you-very-much. Buy chocolate bars? I'd love to, but the budget's too tight. Vote for who? Are you out of your freakin' tree? And yes, you can come in our yard to retrieve your whiffle ball, Frisbee, SpongeBob kite, little brother, and pet snake. But, once a year, Halloween makes me a complete curmudgeon.

My sweetheart is a nice person. She likes to support the local elementary school's baseball team. She'll buy those chocolate bars and give them away at work. She gives neighbor kids blanket permission to retrieve their whiffle balls, Frisbees, SpongeBob kites, little brothers, and pet snakes. She enjoys giving out candy to excited, costumed munchkins.

And she's right. It's good to be pleasant to the neighbors. Good for them, good for the neighborhood, good for the soul. It's especially important for us, because we want to be the nice lesbian neighbors. I can sign every online petition for ENDA, DADT, and NO ON DOMA that comes my way, but if I scowl at little kids congregating in our driveway or turn off the lights and don't answer the door at Halloween, I'm not only condemning myself to everlasting Grinchhood, I'm teaching nongays, who outnumber us in our development hundreds to two, that lesbians are unhappy grouches too different to be trusted or tolerated.

So I'm getting with the program, though in so many ways I don't know how. Take the tomboy across the street. Just because she acts like a daredevil on her bicycle, rides a skateboard with élan, has her own basketball hoop in her driveway, and walks like a seasoned butch doesn't mean she's going to breeze into holy dykedom at puberty. She's only about a half-a-step away from puberty now. Any day she's going to wake up and see her future living across the street from her.

While she comes to terms with her own sexuality, will she feel the need to make trouble for us: Call us names? Out us to young mischief-makers? Vandalize our home? Or will she come to our door seeking a way into the gay world? What if she flings herself out of her closet and brings attention to us? It won't be an easy journey for her as she has a passel of ragtail nongay relatives. The men drive diesel pickups with oversized tires. The women drive minivans with church stickers. There's also a tattletale girly little sister and lots of cousins: hard-staring little kids, very unlike the tomboy, who always averts her eyes.

I keep my distance. The last thing I want is to be the nice lesbian neighbor she decides to hang around. Or for her to swoon at my sweetheart's feet. I know what I was like when I first came out, crushed out on a teacher, too excited to hide who I was, longing for entry to the gay life, yet too shy and too scared and too outlawed to knock on any doors.

That was a long time ago. These days, any tomboy can look us up on the Internet. At the same time, the ancient taboos have not disappeared. She may ignore her instincts, go to her prom with a guy, and add her kids to the passel of relatives. Or she may ring our doorbell. What will she need to know? What can I give her? If she shows up on our doorstep, what's the right thing for a nice lesbian neighbor to do? Invite the kid in for a cup of tea and honest talk? Jolly her along with smirks and winks?

We keep our lawn green and neat, plant flowers, trim the shrubs, pick up after our dog. Our public displays of affection are minor, and only one neighbor knows we're married. We have no piles of loud dykes at parties. We smile and say hello, go to the community picnics, and admire the kids' accomplishments. We're the perfect neighbors except we're—you know—lesbians.

Maybe this is the best message we can send our tomboy neighbor, that she can expect to live happily ever after any way and anywhere she wants. That we are neither seducers nor threats. But, oh, what if she needs more than that? What if we can save her life?

What if I don't answer the door?

WE ARE LIVING HISTORY (2010)

Up on the podium is a short, wide dyke in a cowboy hat. Next to her is a shirtless gay guy in leather pants, suspenders, and cap. They take turns at the mic, exhorting the crowd. Down in the audience a slight balding man in a pink tutu periodically does demi-pliés as he applauds the speakers. Back a few rows two white-haired women, one in a wheelchair, are so moved they are crying.

Millions of gay people have now witnessed scenes like this. They've been happening for at least forty years now. It's an ongoing story with the makings of history even as we live it, even as gay historians document it.

When my first few books were published, readers thanked me for depicting our history. I'd explain at readings that I wasn't writing history, that I was writing reality as it is experienced by many gays who aren't on the ramparts. The stomping diesel dykes who wear high heels to work and effeminate male hairdressers who are still married to women, for example, are not anachronisms. They are alive and well and always would be with us in some form or other.

History happens in daily life. The first time a teacher came out to her school principal, she made history. Teachers continue coming out today. History is an accumulation of these acts.

When I meet young readers, I can see that nothing but the present is real to them. The way they see it, a book I wrote twenty-five years ago depicts history, while to me it's my reality. My fictional characters dress with a style that could seem a bit stale to kids with piercings and tattoos but is true to the dykes I see.

The irony is that I have always been bored silly by history. I would never purposely write an historical romance. At the library today I was perusing a two-volume edition of Herman Wouk's *War and Remembrance*. In his introduction, he called those towering novels historical romances even though all the events happened in his lifetime. Maybe I have been writing history all along.

I really hated world civ in college. This weird teacher would climb on the long table at the front of the auditorium and pace, gesticulating wildly with his mic. It was hard to concentrate on Roman emperors and Visigoths while waiting for him to fall off. In section classes he'd have us, college students, color in maps. He provided the crayons. I learned best from teachers who were passionate about their subjects. Guys like him bled passion out of history.

What if the schools had taught gay history, would I have liked the subject then? Well, they couldn't. It wasn't documented back then. We had no pictures of gay heroes, no Gayttysberg Address to memorize, no significant dates about which to write reports. Gay history was left to the novelists: Gale Wilhelm, James Baldwin, Radclyffe Hall, Gore Vidal, Mary Renault.

Today, because our history has become visible, it has also started to look more like our present. The tattooed baby gays are keyboarding us: churning out stories of the here and now that reflect this new world. They're doing love scenes between characters who can legally marry and mysteries featuring party boys unabashedly mobbing the streets of NOLA.

The tableau of the gay guy and the gay woman at the podium is a sign of both early and later post-Stonewall years; they couldn't get more current, yet they're making history. The lesbian pushing her lover's wheelchair and the gay boy dancing for joy in a pink tutu are living history. Their acts become bedrock we stand on. Every book a gay person writes about a gay life, every time we come out to a boss—or every time we hide while the bigots win elections—we may think we're just living our lives, but we're actually determining our history.

SOCIAL INSECURITY (2011)

Wow! I just got my first Social Security check!
Darn, I must be really, really old.

Not as old as Washington is planning for its kids and grandkids to be. As often as I hear that Social Security is about to go bust, I hear that it's fine. Hey, you guys in DC, like they say in 12-step programs, if it works, don't fix it!

I imagine visiting the Capitol and buttonholing a congressperson. Look, Representative Womanizer, I'd say, try this for a hypothetical. Your once-favored child grows up. He becomes an artisan, a tile setter, a job he's great at, but there's no pension. He saves the best he can, but one of his kids has a chronic disease and you voted to disembowel universal health care, so he's broke from medical bills. His partner dies, but your son doesn't benefit from his pension because you voted to outlaw gay marriage. Sonny boy's job does in his knees and back, and he develops an allergy to the glue he uses. In constant pain, asthmatic, he manages to keep setting tiles until age sixty-five. But, wait, you voted to increase the retirement age to seventy! You'd help him, but you're dead or in prison for skimming or scamming or conspiring. Is this the life you wanted for daddy's little boy?

The word security is pretty misleading these days. My father had a secure job with the federal government. When he died, my mother received a pension and health care for life. Which was good, since she'd light out of the house every day, well into her nineties, get on a bus or subway, and go shopping somewhere, anywhere. She was thrifty as only someone who survived the American Great Depression can be, so she only spent at sales.

Security died with my mother and father. The very concept of security gets more obsolete every year.

All my life I'd planned to retire at age sixty-five. Then congress changed the rules. So, okay, I can wait till sixty-six. Only I didn't. The

Republicans won some elections this November and are yammering about fixing Social Security. While I didn't lie awake worrying, exactly, I did panic.

Okay, I thought. If I retire in November 2010, how soon will I break even with the amount Social Security would have paid me if I'd waited another twelve months? I got as far as stating the problem in words and then I spaced out, escaping into a daydream of winning the lottery, enabling my sweetheart to retire and me to write full-time.

A month or so later, I took up the problem again. This time I mentioned it to my sweetheart. She's the math-head in this marriage. A minute later, or less, she'd calculated my answer. We had a decision to make. I could apply for Social Security immediately and start working at my job only three days a week. That sounded wonderful! I could take my first checks and buy the MacBook Air I'd been drooling over. Tempting, but kind of splurgy for a semiretiree. I could stash the whole year's payments—down to eleven months by now—in the bank and have it as a cushion. Or I could quit my job altogether and maybe finish my new book by the promised deadline. Wow. This was exciting. Thirty years earlier I would have gone for finishing the book.

But I don't have a pension. Or a 401(k) or company stock. I let all that go to finish the last dozen books. What I have is Social Security and you politicians are messing with it. What are you thinking? That no one you care about will ever actually need to live on the rather paltry stipend Americans are awarded for working all our lives? Well, I say, stop it, Representative Womanizer!

Stop kicking aging Americans' futures around in your power plays. Be fiscally conservative at the expense of someone who can afford it, like the beneficiaries of boondoggles from Boston to Bagdad.

Ah, Representative Womanizer, does it rile you to think entitlement programs feed and clothe Democrats and gays? Are you afraid seniors are going to use birth control and get abortions?

Wait! Social Security isn't an entitlement program! It's completely funded by employers and employees. We pay for it with chunks of our wages. We gave it to our government to hold until we needed it. Now, when more of us than ever do need it, you want to treat our contributions to our own futures as taxes so you can make government look lean? And keep your congressional seat? I don't think so.

I don't trust you, Representative Womanizer. I've decided: I'm going to keep working at my job, continue writing my subversive lesbian books. Then I'm going to vote you out of office.

QUEEN OF THE ROAD (2011)

Mrs. Bundt is our outdated, refurbished, very basic 3.5" Garmin Nuvi GPS. We named her after a heart-shaped bundt pan which was our first purchase as a couple. I can only say, by way of explanation, that the GPS voice sounds like a Mrs. Bundt.

One day, my sweetheart was imagining Mrs. Bundt's potential in more weighty endeavors than her role as navigator. She told me, "The first time Mrs. Bundt yelled, 'Turn right! Turn right!'—that confused me. Then I realized she was talking about your house and not criticizing my political leanings." I laughed with her, but I've heard Mrs. Bundt's voice drip with disapproval as she announced, "Arrival at destination—on left."

"Our country needs direction," my sweetheart said. "Wouldn't it be great if the politicians had a Mrs. Bundt to tell them which way to turn?"

What a fine idea. When the pols do something heartless and illogical like extend tax credits for the rich or undo a necessary health plan, Mrs. Bundt would cry, "Recalculating! Recalculating!" When the electorate chooses to install wacked-out crazies in office, Mrs. Bundt would screech, "Turn left! Turn left!" or, depending on the extremists' direction, "Turn right! Turn right!"

Ah, the Bunster, our little Bunster, all grown up and ready to run the government.

I hope she's less abused as a policy wonk. I know I've uttered a passel of bad words trying to get Mrs. Bundt to talk to me sooner, or more, or less, or at all. Or trying to get her to shut up. She gets so overwrought.

Sometimes I think it's because we're gay. Not that we've come out to Mrs. Bundt, but, well, the kisses at traffic lights, the affectionate hands, the hot little murmurs. She took us to our wedding, after all.

So call me paranoid, but does she get this snippy with everyone, or is it just us? Her insistence that we call her Mrs.—is that a hetero-chauvinist statement?

We would never call her the Bunster to her face—ah—to her screen. She's humorless and, I hate to say it, cold.

I've shared with Mrs. Bundt my feelings about Big Roads. But will she acknowledge alternatives to superhighways? No, not the Bunster. If it's got a federal or state highway sign on it, that's the road she wants. Never mind that we're in Florida and the highways are in continual rush-hour condition. Never mind that there's been a forty-three car pileup or a bridge has collapsed.

"Turn in point three miles." Her diction is perfect, her sentences clipped and to the point. She'll pause, then say, more insistently, "Turn in Point. Two. Miles." Another pause, heavy with impatient patience, and she commands, "Turn in point one mile." More quickly now, not caring if she sounds like a manipulative femme, "Turn in five hundred feet." Her voice is shrill with restrained panic. She shoots her white arrow around a corner, showing us the turnpike ramp. "One hundred feet!" she cries in desperation. "Turn right! Turn right!"

In the long pause that follows, I imagine her closing her eyes in exasperation, reminding herself not to take it personally, trying to think of us as errant kids because, given the chance, she'd say, "Effing dykes! Stuck on this dinky road behind a thresher going two mph. Why didn't you listen to me!"

Fortunately, the Bunster has no hair to pull out, or there'd be a continual mess on the dash. She gets control of herself eventually. Through obviously gritted teeth, she announces that she will, in her vast wisdom and with her generous forgiving spirit, recalculate our route: "Recalculating!"

I can hear the vindictive smile in her voice as Mrs. Bundt directs us to turn right and the screen shows some complex maneuvers that are the equivalent of a U-turn.

Queen of the road is our Mrs. Bundt. My sweetheart will give me a conniving look. I'll silence the sputtering queen. But before I can, Mrs. Bundt, as if by her efforts alone, crows with triumphant finality, "Arriving at destination!"

GAY GUMPTION (2011)

I thought it was all about the wedding, but boy, was I wrong. As they say, a wedding is tying the knot. You sign papers, make public vows, and accept the support of friends and family. You also tell your spouse that this is forever. And ever. And ever.

Once upon a time, there was nothing to signify a gay joining but a bedroom and an overstuffed VW hauling furniture, the stereo, and a cat in a carrier. All too often, a few months or years went by and the VW would head off in another direction, plus or minus a cat. But that didn't always happen. You just didn't hear much about the knots that stayed tied.

Recently, my sweetheart and I were invited to help celebrate the twenty-fifth anniversary of a couple who didn't have the advantage of a formal knot-tying ceremony. They fell in love in high school and had nothing but their love to keep them together. It couldn't have been easy. Certainly my early relationships succumbed to the wrath of the closet, which could scar one with a habit of easy dishonesty, especially within oneself. If you're not honest with yourself, how can you be with your partner? You end up stumbling around inside a house with no foundation, in a maze of lies and denial that make it impossible to sustain a relationship.

These days, I know of so many couples who stayed together till death did them part, and I know more who have hit the twenty-five mark, the thirty-five mark, forty years and beyond. By the time I was forty, I'd learned how to stay, but back in my twenties and thirties, I only knew how to unravel the rope, never mind tie a lasting knot. And even at forty, I didn't know enough to make good choices. That took another twenty years. How did these long-lasting couples who've come out since Stonewall know who to choose and how to make it work?

Our twenty-fifth anniversary friends had no guides. Those of us who came before sure didn't set a good example. I think this couple must have had gumption, hardheaded determination, and respect for themselves, for each other, and for their non-anointed marriage.

Not that we didn't have gumption before 1969. We had it all right, but most of us used it all up fighting the wrong fights. We fought ourselves because we'd been told we were demons. We had trouble respecting our unions. How could I think well of my partner if she chose a demon like me? How could I trust a relationship between demons? How could I even want it, much less confidently promise forever? It was always easier to get in the weighted-down VW and move on than to face my own demons.

Then, suddenly, the Stonewall riots, which scared me because I believed that shining a light on gay people was dangerous. Those rioters flipped on the whole circuit breaker. Closets melted in the heat of the lights. A glimmer of self-respect shone into our souls. At the same time, teenagers in small town America were falling in love and looking at the marching gay people on TV and understanding they were not the only ones, that they were not demons, that they were people of great value.

It still wasn't easy for our friends, because they loved in a world that continued to demonize people like them. It was dangerous outside each other's arms, but they didn't drown their fears in liquor, or sabotage their tie by moving away. They never found gay books until 2003, but they played sports and got good jobs and stayed together and saved money and bought a home with a good foundation. For their first dozen years they were so closeted they had no gay friends. Finally, a friend at work came out to them, and they had another couple who could share the special moments in their lives. They announced at the celebration that they made it this long partly because of that friendship.

My sweetheart and I drove twenty-five hours round-trip to witness their accomplishment. Relatively new ourselves, it was important. In the large convivial room there was a glow of accomplishment. The couples' two families were there as were work friends and team buddies. I imagined, afterward, the heartrending moments of rejection and eventual acceptance that made this day possible. This couple, whose gumption surely must have wavered now and then, gifted all of us by bringing us together to toast their example and their achievement.

See, their smiles seemed to say, there's no demons in this room. Not in us, not in you. They can't untie this knot.

THE BROOK (2012)

Many of us have had a favorite gay bar. The Brook was not mine. Nevertheless, when I heard that it was closing, I felt a tug at my heartstrings.

The most unique feature of the Cedar Brook Café in Westport, Connecticut, back in the mid to late 1960s, was its location. At the time, the state police barracks was right across the Boston Post Road. I always wondered whether that made the bar more of a target or offered it a tacit protection based on proximity. Of course, staying in business for seventy-one years also attests to the civility of Westport, one of the richest towns in what has sometimes held the title of the richest region in America, Fairfield County, Connecticut.

Before the Brook, I'd only gone to gay bars in New York City. Compared to their tight spaces and tiny dance floors, the Brook was a barn. The bar side of the building was long and deep. The dance floor was wide. Out back was a patio. The concept of gay people getting together outdoors right there on the Post Road was startling to me in those pre-Stonewall days. I wondered what the neighbors behind the Brook thought.

As college kids, we used to joke about the aged pickup trucks in the parking lot. I don't know if this was true or if we made up stories about gay men and women, fresh off the farm, hopping from the backs of pickups and brushing hay off their pants. Queers came from the farms, the housing projects, fancy houses, and probably a few state troopers found their way across the street over the years.

I had a fever for gay bars in those days. Not that I ever talked to anyone but whoever I arrived with. Maybe we'd do a little verboten making out. Gay bars were for being with our own kind, for holding hands and dancing among other dykes and gay men. They were for looking at one another and looking for someone to love, for drowning our sorrows and celebrating our special times: graduations, birthdays, one-week anniversaries. As pitiful as gay bars could be then—with their crooked money, their straight voyeurs, a culture of all-alcohol-all-the-time, their social imperatives like smoking and unsafe sex—I doubt that my Great-Aunt Jo had anyplace remotely like the Brook to take her "best friend."

The Brook wasn't just for young white men either. It drew anyone who could get a ride. We might have made fun of the hicks, but they were just part of the mix. This was gay territory and our bars were true melting pots. The democracy at the Brook might have sometimes been uneasy, but as far as I know, anyone with the price of the cover was welcome, and the cover wasn't very pricey. It was also pretty easy to get in with fake ID if you happened to be under twenty-one. It was almost as if, in moneyed, educated Westport, there was a kind of respect shown to the Brook and its clientele. As if the majority straight population deemed it appropriate for us to have a teeny bit of space in their world. They left us alone and, as a consequence, we had somewhere to go.

I had just about bought my first car, which would have allowed me more access to the Brook, when American gays and feminists found our voices. Like mushrooms in fertile soil, we pierced through the silence and hiding. There were women's dances and gay meetings and protests and collectives and food co-ops and concerts and festivals and conferences. Who had time to go to the Brook? Who wanted to spend an evening with a girlfriend in a smoky fortress with dirty toilets when you could spend the night on a bus headed to a march on Washington? Meet your friends at a feminist-vegetarian restaurant? Go to a reading of lesbian poetry at a newly out dyke's apartment?

Well, me for one. Yesterday, my friend Tex was telling me stories of her bar days in San Antonio, Houston, and wild Galveston. There was a pride in her voice about flouting the rules, about defying het society, and about risking everything to be with our people. She said she felt daring and invincible. There was a unique camaraderie in those dreary bars. You didn't have to talk, or drink much, or ask women to dance. You just had to be there. Every chance you got.

THE GIFT OF BEING OUT (2012)

I always fear bad consequences when I come out to other people. How will they react, will there be more pain than gain for them, for me? Coming out may be easier for some in 2012 than it was fifty years, twenty years, a dozen years ago, but for most it's still tough. I'm thinking of all the gay people who found coming out to be fatal, all the teen suicides, all the societies that treat their gay citizens as outcasts.

One recent Sunday, my sweetheart's aunt and uncle were passing through town and took us to lunch. This same couple had also traveled some distance to attend our wedding. In the course of lunch the subject of marches on Washington came up. My sweetheart's aunt mentioned having been at Martin Luther King, Jr.'s "I Have a Dream" speech. I've only known one other person in my whole life who attended that world-changing event. If I hadn't already known, I would have realized at that moment that I married into exactly the right family for me.

The conversation continued along those lines, and I mentioned having last marched on Washington in 1993. My new aunt asked if that was when the Quilt was there. She was referring, of course, to The Names Project AIDS Memorial Quilt, which has been at the National Mall many times and was there, in part, during the 1993 March on Washington for Lesbian, Gay, and Bi Equal Rights and Liberation. Were we at the same quilt exhibit? It doesn't matter at all. The fact that we were comparing notes on the subject was a gift of being openly gay.

Since I officially came out to my brother's family, my sister-in-law has spared me the angst that still goes with sharing who I am. She's eased my way through the world in an altogether unexpected role, sort of a guardian angel opening paths through family that were previously blocked by brambles of fear. In the past few years she got in touch with one of my birth family's first cousins, who happens to live in Florida, where I reside at the moment. My sister-in-law tested the waters for me so that when I actually got together with my cousin there was no awkwardness and we could just enjoy each other—and our respective spouses. Her spouse happened to be male. What a sense of freedom came with the privilege of being nothing other than queer old me.

Most recently, my sister-in-law and my brother got together with another first cousin. This cousin and his wife are staunch Catholics, yet my sister-in-law came out to them for me. They have no problem with my gayness. I always loved this cousin—love all of them, as a matter of fact—and being out to him gives me a sense of wholeness I never experienced before. Acceptance is nourishing. Rejection is a kind of starvation.

My youngest cousin never batted an eye. She made a point, each time we got together over many years, to let me know she knew. This quasi-communication we had was a way to connect with each other in the presence of my unenlightened mother. My young cousin simply told me that a childhood friend, who I knew when they were both little kids, lived with another woman and their children. The first time she told me, I wasn't certain she was saying she knew and accepted that I am gay. By the third time, I was convinced and consequently invited her to our wedding. How astonishing: these cousins that I'd grown up with and hidden from all my adult life now knew I'd married another woman—and the world didn't end!

On our most recent visit to New England to see my side of the family, both my brother and sister-in-law said they wished our visit could have been longer. As we ate at the local breakfast hangout that last morning, our sister-in-law introduced us to her whole middle-aged aerobics group, with the apparent delight of someone bringing friends and family together.

At our memorable Sunday lunch, my sweetheart's uncle also had a story about the 1993 march. He worked for a federal agency at the time and, as it happened, a gentleman in his field arrived from Cape Town, SA for a meeting just as a million or more queers marched through the city. The visitor later told my uncle-in-law that he saw all these high-spirited gay people and he simply joined the march. "This," he declared to my new uncle, "is democracy!"

That story never fails to make me smile. It was a story I would never have heard, a gift I would never have received, if my sweetheart wasn't out to her family and if we marchers hadn't left our closets and come out to the whole world.

FIRST WEEKS OF COLLEGE, TYLER CLEMENTI (2012)

I always thought I'd suffered my first few weeks of college. It was horrible, I was completely unprepared, but I survived. Instead of getting on a train and taking Tyler Clementi's long jump, I got on a train and went to my big brother's office to announce that I was quitting school.

What was I thinking? What did I expect my brother to do? *Was* I thinking? No; I was just feeling, and what I felt must have been similar to what drove Tyler off his bridge: despair, fear, hopelessness, humiliation, shame, blinding desire, loneliness, desperation. You can't think when you're a seething vat of emotions and hormones. You can't make a good decision. You just want to end the pain.

Like Tyler, I was assigned a straight roommate my first semester. Like Tyler's roommate, mine lived in a world so extremely foreign to me we could have been different species. She wanted to become a fashion designer, marry a nice boy, move back to Pennsylvania, and raise a family. I wanted to become a writer, fall in love with a thousand girls, move back to New York City, and drink like Dylan Thomas.

Instead of webcams back then, we had gossip. I dressed like someone out of the Beebo Brinker stories, in Bermuda shorts, kneesocks, and Oxford cloth shirts. I was the only student, female or male, to bring my bicycle to campus, and listened to FM radio jazz, not rock and roll. Like Tyler, I was just plain different. I learned later that the other students shunned me, made fun of me, whispered about me. There were three of us weirdos on my dorm floor. I was the queer one, although in 1963 nice girls barely knew what that meant.

The first night in our new lives, my roommate and I went to a freshman mixer together. It was packed, loud, filled with that foreign gender, boys. I backed off, lost the roommate, left immediately. Outside, on the strange campus that still appears in my nightmares, I was as alone as any being on this planet had ever been. I was as alone as Tyler Clementi. Thank goodness the romance of the bridge—Hart Crane's Brooklyn Bridge, Walt Whitman's "Till the bridge you will need be form'd, till the ductile anchor hold, Till the gossamer thread you fling catch somewhere, O my soul"—was not a romance that drew me. I simply knew I would get nothing but confusion and misery from four years in the alien land of hetero-college and that I would do better on my own.

On the other hand, I suspected those years were not the worst thing that could happen to a young gay. College was a privilege. The relative cloistering might have been a cosseted cushion between childhood and the demands of adulthood. It was not. Maturity gives us an anonymity and freedom to crash and burn that's hard to achieve in the microworld of school. Tyler knew he couldn't stay at Rutgers and escape the condemnation and ridicule his roommate's boorish video assault would bring. Maybe he hadn't been through and hardened by castigation and bullying before. Clearly, he had fewer defenses than I had.

Already, I'd toughed out the schoolyard hounding. Already, I knew there was a community out there, if I could just get to it. Already, I was on medications to still my fears. And I reached out to my semisensible brother who reached out to my sensible father. I said nothing about being a pariah. How can you tell your family a thing like that? I only told them I wanted to get a job and live in the city, that college was a waste for me. At my father's urging, I gave school one more try.

My poor innocent roommate avoided me. Complained about my drunken late nights. Never came back after that first semester. An artist down the hall invited me to room with her and we're still fast friends. I found a sort of girlfriend and spent many weekends in the city, feeling like an outsider in the gay bars, but the gossamer thread of my soul at least could anchor there.

Oh, Tyler, how I wish I, or someone, could have been your guardian angel through those hellish weeks. Mine was a straight male upperclassman named Jonathan who liked my writing, hung out with me, and impressed my tormentors with his motorcycle, marijuana, and getting kicked out of Columbia University. The other weirdo girls left school, but I made it through. I was lucky: Jonathan and his antiestablishment literary friends, all my elders, took me under their wings and kept my victimization from going viral. They became my lifesaving, not lethal, bridge.

Butch Stag Party (2013)

The Pianist and the Handydyke got married a couple of weeks ago in Seattle. I couldn't go because I had the honor of officiating at the wedding of the Lady and the Kid in New York at the same time. Therefore, it was very important to me to have a stag party for the Handydyke.

But what would such an event consist of? Sitting around talking about femmes who would probably be in the next room? Throwing a blowout party at the local brewery when neither I nor the Handydyke drink? There would be too many designated drivers. A lesbian strip club? Do those even still exist? To tell the truth, I never understood the attraction and we certainly don't have one in our little town.

How about pizza with the softball team? Thank goodness we're beyond softball field age. Did I mention that the Pianist and the Handydyke have been together forty-two years? The Handydyke is eighty-two.

We do, amazingly, have a Starbucks. Maybe we could stage a butch invasion and have a java jamboree, except we don't drink coffee either. A whale-watching wingding—but we did that for her seventieth birthday. I was beginning to think we'd have to do a boring old restaurant dinner.

The Handydyke was so excited about getting married; she deserved all the fringe benefits. She went all out on her wedding garb. She found a vendor in the United Kingdom that makes rainbow cummerbunds and bow ties. Then she found a supplier of rainbow cufflinks. She bought a pair for her best butch and another for me to wear at my New York ceremony. Her best butch gave her a ruffled white shirt located at a kitchen supply store. The Handydyke was all spiffed up! With her black tux and gray hair she was one handsome… groom? bride/groom? broome?

I did get to see the couple in their finery. They hosted a marriage equality fundraiser once back home and wore their wedding clothes, the Pianist in a gorgeous flowing blue patterned dress. The best butch wore her wedding gear too, matching the Handydyke's, and I wore the clothes from the day I married my sweetheart. The only change was the shirt: I had to find one with French cuffs for my new rainbow cufflinks. As it happened, I stumbled across a Brooks Brothers shirt in an upscale consignment shop that filled the bill. The Handydyke is an inspiration.

But what to do for a stag party? I should have asked the Kid if she had one. There are lots of ways to gay-party in New York. The Kid wedded in a silver tux with silver sneakers while the Lady wore an elegant yet simple cream gown. I'd guess hunting down those silver sneakers would make a hilarious stag party in itself.

I had no stag party. Unless you call spending every second with my sweetheart partying, but that's a pretty chronic state. Being married, these days, is a party in itself. Gay folks are celebrating their love at the same time we're celebrating an unexpected freedom. What gets me most is the family stuff. Writer Lori Lake sent me a beautiful video of a proposal in a Home Depot. It was all bouncy fun, and then the family joined the dancing gay friends. Watching it turned me into a blubbering mess.

As it turned out, the Handydyke came up with her own stag party idea. She invited the Quiet Butch and me to attend the disaster preparation event at our local armory. The disaster was not, of course, getting married. It was about living on the edge of the earthquake- and tsunami-prone Pacific Ocean.

The Handydyke and I have been gathering emergency paraphernalia for years. Our spouses may be glad, but I suspect it's really a way we can amass butch toys. Things like combination searchlights with built-in sirens, red warning lights, and weather radios which require eight D batteries that must be replaced frequently as the lights are stashed in our sea-air soggy cars. We have backpacks full of heavy socks, compasses, bug spray, jackknives, foil blankets, hats, flares, Sterno stoves, propane for camp stoves, survival water, ropes, multi-tools, toilet paper, canned foods. We have backpacks and duffel bags and army blankets and crumbling chocolate bars and first-aid kits.

What a stag party! We learned about (and bought) waterBOBs for bathtub storage and purifying sipping straws and museum wax for protecting our treasures. They gave out escape-route maps. We had a free lunch with a Red Cross guy just primed to educate us. It was great! Better than drinking or any of those traditional prewedding celebrations. I'd recommend it to any butch who ever longed to rescue her girl or, as we can now, at last, say, bride.

AFTERWORD

Not long after I moved from New Haven, Connecticut to Sunny Valley, Oregon, in 1984, my partner at the time, the late Tee Corinne, suggested that I start writing a monthly column about lesbian life. I didn't think I had much to say outside of fiction, but I agreed to give it a try. Renee LaChance, editor and publisher at *Just Out*, the highly respected Portland, Oregon gay paper, agreed to run it—and pay me for it. A group of Tee's friends and I sat around the dinner table trying to come up with a title. One of them said that the local dykes called the I-5 corridor from Southern California to Canada the Amazon Trail because of the mobility of West Coast women up and down the freeway.

The second paper to pick up "The Amazon Trail" was *Lesbian News*, in Southern Cal, and then the Trail took off. At one time or another papers in Florida, Ohio, New York, Illinois, Arizona, Texas, Louisiana, Virginia, Pennsylvania, Georgia, Connecticut, New Hampshire, and more ran the column. As our publications made the move to the cyber world, the column followed. Now it's sometimes called a blog and it's been snapped up by smaller communities that never had newspapers and at sites like lgbtSr.org and Epochalips. com. Links to "The Amazon Trail" on Twitter and Facebook bounce around the world.

What an amazing almost-forty-year ride. That's something like five hundred Amazon Trails. I hazard a guess that it's the longest-running lesbian, and maybe gay, column in the United States, if not the world. I have missed sending it out only twice, when I had major surgery. I am so grateful to whatever keeps my brain churning out words people like to read. I am so grateful to the readers. I am so grateful to the editors and publishers. I am so grateful to partners who never complained when I've typed away on a weekend and who, not infrequently, gave me ideas, proofread, or helped me wrangle a pesky computer. I have to thank, especially, the innumerable readers and editors through the years who have written or posted or told me at conferences and on the street that words in these columns have in some way touched them.

I admit there have been some months when the column has seemed a chore that, along with my job, kept me from writing fiction or playing with partners or friends. Other times, such as losing relationships or being ill, "The Amazon Trail" kept me in one piece, moving forward, surviving.

Who knew these monthly missives to the world would one day prove to have value as cultural and historical documents? Naiad Press collected the first couple of years' worth in a book titled *The Amazon Trail* (1988). The response was heartening: my columns had meaning for gay people.

Fortunately for us all, readers and writers alike, Ruth Sternglantz is an editor at Bold Strokes Books. Ruth is an ardent advocate of our literature. She proposed this new collection of Amazon Trails. Len Barot, President of Bold Strokes Books, a passionate and stalwart believer in LGBTQ authors (and my champion for the last ten years), believed that a second collection of "The Amazon Trail" would be a positive contribution to our community. She gave Ruth the green light. With intense care and professionalism, Ruth read the hundreds of columns, selected, organized, copyedited, and performed all the other difficult and expert work an editor must do to make any book a reality.

I am not much of a traveler, so this is not a travelogue in the true sense of the word. It is about traveling our culture, or the parts of it I have been lucky enough to experience. Have I reached the end of the Amazon Trail? Heck no. There's still lots happening in our world and lots to talk about. There are still gays in closets and gays in need. There are people coming out every day and night, at every age, who want to know what to expect. More and more often we're realistically portrayed on TV, in film and books, online. We are certainly making headlines. I like to think this common, ordinary, shy dyke, who came out over fifty years ago, still has something to give and can keep making a difference to some gay lives.

Lee Lynch
Oregon, 2014

A partial list of the publications in which "The Amazon Trail" has appeared since its debut in 1985:

Au Courant, Philadelphia, PA
Bay Area Women's News, Oakland, CA
Bold Strokes Books Authors' Blog (http://www.boldstrokesbooks
    authors.wordpress.com/)
Capitol Forum, Salem, OR
Chicago Outlines, Chicago, IL
Creative Loafing, Tampa, FL
Dallas Voice, Dallas, TX
Diversity Rules, Oneonta, NY
Erie Gay News (http://eriegaynews.com)
Epochalips, (http://www.epochalips.com)
Equality Herald, Nashville, TN
Etc. Magazine, Atlanta, GA
Express Gay News, Ft. Lauderdale, FL
Gay Community News, Salem, OR
Gay Life Newsletter, PA
Gaybeat, Columbus, OH
Gay RVA, Richmond, VA
Gazebo Connection, Richmond, BC
Gazette, Tampa Bay, FL
Golden Threads
Identity North View, Anchorage, AK
In the Life, Wappingers Falls, NY
Just About Write
Just Out, Portland OR
Keystone Alliance/GayLife Newsletter, PA
Lesbian Pride Nation, Denver, CO
Lesbian Pride Monthly, Tehachapi, CA
Lavender Womyn, Salem, OR
Lesbian Fun World (http://lesbianfunworld.com/)
Lesbian Community Project, Portland OR
Lesbian Connection
Lesbian News, Los Angeles, CA
Letters From Camp Rehoboth, Rehoboth, DE
LGBTQ Nation (http://www.lgbtqnation.com)
LGBT Sr. (http://www.lgbtsr.org)

Long Island Connection, NY
Mama Bears News and Notes, Oakland, CA
Metroline, Hartford, CT
Nebraska Gay Pride, Omaha, NE
New York Blade, NYC, NY
Open Arms, Indiana
Out In Maui, Hawaii
Out In the Mountains, Vermont
Philadelphia Gay News, Philadelphia, PA
Phoenix Resource, Phoenix, AZ
Pro Suzy, Tampa Bay, FL
Southern Voice, Atlanta, GA
Texas Triangle, Austin, TX
The Rooster, New Orleans, LA
The Standard Palm Springs, Palm Springs, CA
The Tucson Observer, Tucson, AZ
Washington Blade, Washington, D.C.
Womansource Rising, Ashland, OR
Womanspace, San Antonio, TX
Women's Community Connection, Tempe, AZ

About the Author

Lee Lynch wrote the classic novels *The Swashbuckler* and *Toothpick House*. Her most recent books, *The Raid*, *Beggar of Love*, and *Sweet Creek*, are available from Bold Strokes Books.

Most recently, she was the namesake and first recipient of The Lee Lynch Classic Award from The Golden Crown Literary Society. She lives with her wife, Elaine Mulligan Lynch, in the Pacific Northwest.

Books Available from Bold Strokes Books

Because of You by Julie Cannon. What would you do for the woman you were forced to leave behind? (978-1-62639-199-4)

The Job by Jove Belle. Sera always dreamed that she would one day reunite with Tor. She just didn't think it would involve terrorists, firearms, and hostages. (978-1-62639-200-7)

Making Time by C.J. Harte. Two women going in different directions meet after fifteen years and struggle to reconnect in spite of the past that separated them. (978-1-62639-201-4)

Once The Clouds Have Gone by KE Payne. Overwhelmed by the dark clouds of her past, Tag Grainger is lost until the intriguing and spirited Freddie Metcalfe unexpectedly forces her to reevaluate her life. (978-1-62639-202-1)

The Acquittal by Anne Laughlin. Chicago private investigator Josie Harper searches for the real killer of a woman whose lover has been acquitted of the crime. (978-1-62639-203-8)

An American Queer: The Amazon Trail by Lee Lynch. Lee Lynch's heartening and heart-rending history of gay life from the turbulence of the late 1900s to the triumphs of the early 2000s are recorded in this selection of her columns. (978-1-62639-204-5)

Stick McLaughlin: The Prohibition Years by CF Frizzell. Corruption in 1918 cost Stick her lover, her freedom, and her identity, but a very special flapper and the family bond of her own gang could help win them back—even if it means outwitting the Boston Mob. (978-1-62639-205-2)

Edge of Awareness by C.A. Popovich. When Maria, a woman in the middle of her third divorce, meets Dana, an out lesbian, awareness of her feelings bring up reservations about the teachings of her church. (978-1-62639-188-8)

Taken by Storm by Kim Baldwin. Lives depend on two women when a train derails high in the remote Alps, but an unforgiving mountain, avalanches, crevasses, and other perils stand between them and safety. (978-1-62639-189-5)

The Common Thread by Jaime Maddox. Dr. Nicole Coussart's life is falling apart, but fortunately, DEA Attorney Rae Rhodes is there to pick up the pieces and help Nic put them back together. (978-1-62639-190-1)

Jolt by Kris Bryant. Mystery writer Bethany Lange wasn't prepared for the twisting emotions that left her breathless the moment she laid eyes on folk singer sensation Ali Hart. (978-1-62639-191-8)

Searching For Forever by Emily Smith. Dr. Natalie Jenner's life has always been about saving others, until young paramedic Charlie Thompson comes along and shows her maybe she's the one who needs saving. (978-1-62639-186-4)

A Queer Sort of Justice: Prison Tales Across Time by Rebecca S. Buck. When liberty is only a memory, and all seems lost, what freedoms and hopes can be found within us? (978-1-62639-195-6E)

Blue Water Dreams by Dena Hankins. Lania Marchiol keeps her wary sailor's gaze trained on the horizon until Oly Rassmussen, a wickedly handsome trans man, sends her trusty compass spinning off course. (978-1-62639-192-5)

Rest Home Runaways by Clifford Henderson. Baby boomer Morgan Ronzio's troubled marriage is the least of her worries when she gets the call that her addled, eighty-six-year-old, half-blind dad has escaped the rest home. (978-1-62639-169-7)

Charm City by Mason Dixon. Raq Overstreet's loyalty to her drug kingpin boss is put to the test when she begins to fall for Bathsheba Morris, the undercover cop assigned to bring him down. (978-1-62639-198-7)

Let the Lover Be by Sheree Greer. Kiana Lewis, a functional alcoholic on the verge of destruction, finally faces the demons of her past while finding love and earning redemption in New Orleans. (978-1-62639-077-5)

Blindsided by Karis Walsh. Blindsided by love, guide dog trainer Lenae McIntyre and media personality Cara Bradley learn to trust what they see with their hearts. (978-1-62639-078-2)

About Face by VK Powell. Forensic artist Macy Sheridan and Detective Leigh Monroe work on a case that has troubled them both for years, but they're hampered by the past and their unlikely yet undeniable attraction. (978-1-62639-079-9)

Blackstone by Shea Godfrey. For Darry and Jessa, their chance at a life of freedom is stolen by the arrival of war and an ancient prophecy that just might destroy their love. (978-1-62639-080-5)

Out of This World by Maggie Morton. Iris decided to cross an ocean to get over her ex. But instead, she ends up traveling much farther, all the way to another world. Once there, only a mysterious, sexy, and magical woman can help her return home. (978-1-62639-083-6)

Kiss The Girl by Melissa Brayden. Sleeping with the enemy has never been so complicated. Brooklyn Campbell and Jessica Lennox face off in love and advertising in fast-paced New York City. (978-1-62639-071-3)

Taking Fire: A First Responders Novel by Radclyffe. Hunted by extremists and under siege by nature's most virulent weapons, Navy medic Max de Milles and Red Cross worker Rachel Winslow join forces to survive and discover something far more lasting. (978-1-62639-072-0)

First Tango in Paris by Shelley Thrasher. When French law student Eva Laroche meets American call girl Brigitte Green in 1970s Paris, they have no idea how their pasts and futures will intersect. (978-1-62639-073-7)

The War Within by Yolanda Wallace. Army nurse Meredith Moser went to Vietnam in 1967 looking to help those in need; she didn't expect to meet the love of her life along the way. (978-1-62639-074-4)

Escapades by MJ Williamz. Two women, afraid to love again, must overcome their fears to find the happiness that awaits them. (978-1-62639-182-6)

Desire at Dawn by Fiona Zedde. For Kylie, love had always come armed with sharp teeth and claws. But with the human, Olivia, she bares her vampire heart for the very first time, sharing passion, lust, and a tenderness she'd never dared dream of before. (978-1-62639-064-5)

Visions by Larkin Rose. Sometimes the mysteries of love reveal themselves when you least expect it. Other times they hide behind a black satin mask. Can Paige unveil her masked stranger this time? (978-1-62639-065-2)

All In by Nell Stark. Internet poker champion Annie Navarro loses everything when the Feds shut down online gambling, and she turns to experienced casino host Vesper Blake for advice—but can Nova convince Vesper to take a gamble on romance? (978-1-62639-066-9)

Vermilion Justice by Sheri Lewis Wohl. What's a vampire to do when Dracula is no longer just a character in a novel? (978-1-62639-067-6)

Switchblade by Carsen Taite. Lines were meant to be crossed. Third in the Luca Bennett Bounty Hunter Series. (978-1-62639-058-4)

Nightingale by Andrea Bramhall. Culture, faith, and duty conspire to tear two young lovers apart, yet fate seems to have different plans for them both. (978-1-62639-059-1)

No Boundaries by Donna K. Ford. A chance meeting and a nightmare from the past threaten more than Andi Massey's solitude as she and Gwen Palmer struggle to understand the complexity of love without boundaries. (978-1-62639-060-7)

Timeless by Rachel Spangler. When Stevie Geller returns to her hometown, will she do things differently the second time around or will she be in such a hurry to leave her past that she misses out on a better future? (978-1-62639-050-8)

Second to None by L.T. Marie. Can a physical therapist and a custom motorcycle designer conquer their pasts and build a future with one another? (978-1-62639-051-5)

Seneca Falls by Jesse Thoma. Together, two women discover love truly can conquer all evil. (978-1-62639-052-2)

A Kingdom Lost by Barbara Ann Wright. Without knowing each other's fates, Princess Katya and her consort Starbride seek to reclaim their kingdom from the magic-wielding madman who seized the throne and is murdering their people. (978-1-62639-053-9)

Season of the Wolf by Robin Summers. Two women running from their pasts are thrust together by an unimaginable evil. Can they overcome the horrors that haunt them in time to save each other? (978-1-62639-043-0)

The Heat of Angels by Lisa Girolami. Fires burn in more than one place in Los Angeles. (978-1-62639-042-3)

Desperate Measures by P. J. Trebelhorn. Homicide detective Kay Griffith and contractor Brenda Jansen meet amidst turmoil neither of them is aware of until murder suspect Tommy Rayne makes his move to exact revenge on Kay. (978-1-62639-044-7)

The Magic Hunt by L.L. Raand. With her Pack being hunted by human extremists and beset by enemies masquerading as friends, can Sylvan protect them and her mate, or will she succumb to the feral rage that threatens to turn her rogue, destroying them all? A Midnight Hunters novel. (978-1-62639-045-4)